THE SLAYER

AND OTHER TALES FROM THE PULPS

THE SLAYER

AND OTHER TALES FROM THE PULPS

H. DE VERE STACPOOLE

WILDSIDE PRESS

THE SLAYER AND OTHER TALES FROM THE PULPS

CONTENTS

THE MIDDLE BEDROOM

ARE ALL living creatures represented in the human race, so that we find shark men — or, at least, men with the instincts of sharks — sloth men, cat men, tiger men, and so on? Le Brun started the idea, I believe, and I take it up as bearing on the case of Sir Michael Carey, of Carey House, near Innis Town, on the west coast of Ireland.

I would ask another question before starting on my story: If a man were to give way to his natural instincts and retire from the world would he develop, or, rather, degenerate, along the line of his main instinct? Who can say? I only know that Sir Michael, the builder of the house that took his name, was known a hundred years ago amongst the illiterate peasantry as " the spider," that so dubbed on account of his mentality and general make-up, he lived alone in his house like a spider in a gloomy corner, that, according to legend, the devil came and took him one dark night, leaving neither rag nor bone of him and that his ghost was reputed to haunt Carey House and the country round, ever after.

The next of kin, Mr. Massy Pope, tried to live in the house. He left suddenly on account of the "loneliness" of the situation and succeeded in letting the place, with the shooting and fishing rights, to a hard-headed Englishman named Doubleday.

Doubleday didn't believe in ghosts nor care about them, snipe was his game and cock; he was a two-bottle man — it was in 1863 — and if he had met with a ghost any time after ten o'clock he would scarcely have seen it, or seeing it, would not have cared. But his servants were the trouble. They left one day in a body, being softheaded folk and unfortified and having a very good reason of their own. Then some years elapsed and the story of the next let, as told to me by Micky Feelan one day, out shooting, was as follows:

"When Mr. Doubleday had gone, sor, the house laid empty, spilin' the country for miles round, not a man would go into the groun's to trap a rabbit nor a woman enter its doors to lift a window, and Mr. Pope squanderin' his money to advertise it. That's the man he was, he wouldn't be bet by it, rowlin' in riches what did it matter to him whether it lay let or empty, not a brass farthin', but he wouldn't be bet by it, it was like a horse that wouldn't rise at a ditch and he'd canther it back and try it again and lather it over the head, squanderin' his money in the advertisin' till all of a sudden he got a rise out of a family be name of Leftwidge.

"Dublin people they were, with a grocer's shop in old Fishamble Street. There was a dozen of them, mostly childer and one red-headed strip of a girl to do the cookin'. Twenty pound a year was the rent, I've heard tell, and they lived mostly be trappin' rabbits, the boys doin' a bit of fishin' and the groceries comin' from the shop where the ould father stuck at work in his shirt sleeves while the rest of the lot was airin' themselves in the counthry.

"Be jabers, they were a crowd, ghosts! Little they cared about ghosts shamblin' about widout shoes or stockin's and the boys wid their sticks and catapults killin' hens be the sly and maltreatin' the country boys like Red Injuns, the shame of the county.

"Norah Driscol was the name of the redheaded slip and many a time me mother has seen her wid her apron over her head rockin' and cryin' wid the treatment of them boys and the botheration of the rest of them, for there was a matter of a dozen or more, rangin' like the pipes of an organ from Micky the eldest son six fut and as thin as a gas pipe, to Pat the youngest not the height of your knee.

"Well, sor, the ghost lay aisy at the sight of the lot of them and didn't let a word out of it for a full month. Then one day, Norah Driscoll was goin' along the top flure passage whin the band begin to play. The bedrooms was mostly on that passage and the house agent had warned them against havin' anythin' to do with the middle most bedroom, for, says he, there's rats there that can't be got rid of and that's the cause of all the trouble in the lettin' of the house, says he. It would be a hundred and twenty a year rent, only for them rats, says he, so they're worth a hundred a year to you if you just keep the door shut and don't bother about the noises they do be makin' at odd times — sometimes it's like as if they was sneezin' and blowin' their noses and sometimes it's like as if they was walkin' about with their brogues on and sometimes it's like as if they was cursin' and swearin'. Don't you mind them, he says, but keep sayin' over and over to yourself they're worth a hundred a year to me. That's what he tould Mrs. Leftwidge.

"Well, sor, Norah was moonin' along the passage, sent to fetch a duster or somethin' when she opened the dure of the middle bedroom be mistake. There was no furniture in it, not as much as a three-legged stool and the blind was down, but a shaft of the sun struck through be the side of the blind and there in the middle of the flure was sittin' a little old man dressed as they was dressed a hundred years ago in an ould brown coat wid brass buttons and all and the face of him under his hat topped the sight of him, for Norah said it wasn't a face, but more like one of those masks the childer make out of a bit of paper with holes in it.

"The screech she let out of her as she banged the dure to, brought the family runnin' from downstairs, and the boys slammed open the door to get at the chap but there wasn't a speck of him.

"'It's a rat she saw,' says Mrs. Leftwidge, 'Downstairs wid the lot of you or I'll give you the linth of me slipper — and open that dure again if you dare.'

"Down they went, Norah bawlin' and the old woman pushin' her and nothin' more happened that day till the night. Half a dozen of the little ones slep' in the same room with their mother to save the light and be under control and gettin' on for twelve o'clock the old woman, snorin' wid her mouth wide, was woke from her slape be one of the childer.

"'Mummy,' says he, 'listen to the bagpipes.' She lifted herself on her elbow, but, faith, she could have heard it with her head under the clothes, for the dhrone of the pipes filled the house comin' from the middle bedroom.

"Next minit the whole lither of them was in the passage, the old woman with a gutherin' candle in her hand, and as they stood there keepin' time with their teeth to the tune of the pipes, the noise of it suddenly let off and the handle of the middle bedroom dure began to turn.

"They didn't wait to see what was comin' out; no, your honor, you may bet your life they didn't, they was half of them under their beds the linth of that night and next mornin' they began to pack to go back to Dublin, gettin' their old traps together and strippin' the garden to take back wid them in hampers. Micky, the second boy, was sent runnin' to hire two cars to take them to the station, for the railway in those days had just come to Drumboyne, twelve miles away, and whilst he was gone they tore up the potatoes and cut the cabbages and faith they'd have taken the flurin' away if they'd had manes to shift it.

"Well, there they were strapped and ready to go when Mrs. Leftwidge, sittin' in her bonnet on the boxes and atin' a sandwidge, suddenly stops her chewin' and looks about her like a hen countin' her chickens:

"'Where's Pat?' says she.

"Pat was the youngest, as I've tould you, sor, a bit of a chap in petticoats, no size at all and always gettin' astray.

"'I don't know,' says one of the boys, 'but faith, I hear him shoutin' somewhere upstairs.'

"Upstairs they all rushed led be the woman and they hadn't no sooner reached the top passage than they seen Pat bein' whisked through the open dure of the middle bedroom, dragged along be somebody's hand, and when they reached the dure, there was Pat bein' dragged up the chimney.

"It was one of them big ould chimneys a man could go up, and the heels of the child was disappearin' when Mrs. Leftwidge lays hold of a fut and pulls, bawlin' murder Irish, till the thing in the chimney let go its holt and Pat comes into the grate, kickin' like a pup in the shtrangles and liftin' the roof off with the hullabaloo of him.

"She tuck him be one fut like a turkey and down she runs with him and into the garden and there when they'd soothed him he gives his story, how he'd been playin' in the passage when a little ould man, the funniest ould man he'd ever seen pokes his head out of the bedroom dure. Pat, poor divil, bein' sated at his play couldn't get his legs under him wid the fright, he could only sit and shout whilst the head of the little ould man pops in and out of the dureway like the head of a tortoise from its shell.

"Then out he comes the whole of him and grabs the child be the hand and whisks him off into the bedroom and goes up the chimney heels and first haulin' Pat after him. Goes up like a spider.

"Well, they was sittin' about on the boxes they'd hauled out of the house waitin' for the cars and tryin' to squeeze more of the news out of Pat, when up comes the cars wid Sergeant Rafferty and Constable O'Halloran on wan of them, to see they weren't takin' the house away wid them — they'd got that bad name in the county.

"And when the sergeant heard the story, up he went to the bedroom and down he comes again.

"'Here,' says he to O'Halloran, 'take this lot off to the train and go to the barracks and fetch me two carbines wid buck shot ca'tridges — the same ould Forster used to shoot the boys with, bad luck to him — and look slippy,' says he, 'for I'm a brave man, but I don't want to be no longer here be myself than's needful.'

"Off the cars went wid the family packed like flies on them an' in a matter of a couple of hours back comes the constable wid the guns. Up they go to the bedroom.

"'Stick your head up the chimney,' says the sergeant.

"'I'll be — if do,' says the other.

"'Well, then, shut it,' says the sergeant, 'and keep still.'

"They listened but they didn't hear nothing at all. Then the sergeant begins talkin' in a loud voice, winkin' at the other.

"'There's nothin' there,' says he, 'it was a ghost they saw and it's gettin' oneasy I am meself. Let's get off back to Drumboyne and have a glass and lave the ould house to look afther itself.'

"'I'm wid you,' says the constable and downstairs they tramped, makin' as much noise wid their big boots as a rigiment of soldiers. Then in the hall they sits down and begins takin' off their boots.

"'All the same,' says the constable as he pulled the laces, 'I'd be just as aisy in me mind if I was three miles off trampin' on the road to

Drumboyne.'

"'So would I,' says the sergeant, 'and it's there I'd be only I'm thinkin' of promotion.'

"'I'm thinkin' of ghosts,' says the constable wid the boot-lace in his hand.

"'Go on unlacin' your boots,' says the other, 'and don't be a keyoward, this is no ghost. Ghosts can't pull childer up chimneys.'

"'Faith, you seem to know a lot about them,' says the constable, 'but it's I that am thinkin' it's holy water and Father Mooney ought to be on this job instead of you and me and guns.'

"'And how would you get holy water up the chimney?' axes the sergeant.

"'Wit a squirt,' replies him, 'and how else?"

"'Squirt yourself out of them boots,' says the sergeant, 'or it's me ramrod I'll take to you, and now follow me,' he says, 'and walk soft.'

"Wid the loaded guns in their hands up they wint makin' no more sound than shaddas in a wall, and when they got to the room down they squats one on each side of the chimney.

"They hears nothin' for a while, but the tickin' of the sergeant's watch and the sounds of their own hearts goin' lub-a-dub. Then comes a cough. It wasn't a right sort of cough, for, let alone that it was comin' down a chimney, it sounded to be the cough of a chap that had died for want of water and lain in a brick kiln afther.

"The constable said next day he'd have been up and off only the sound cut the legs from under him, the sergeant wasn't much better and there they sat sayin' their prayers and listenin' for more.

"They waited near an hour hearin' nothin', and then all at once began a noise, a scratchin' and a scrabblin' like a cat comin' down a drain pipe.

"'It's comin' down,' shouts the constable.

"'Begob it's not,' says the sergeant and wid that he shoves the muzzle of his gun up the flue and fires.

"He fired from fright to keep it up, so he said at the inquest, but, he jabers, he brought it down like a cock pheasant, tumblin' and clawin' and when they stretched it out on the flure it was a man right enough. A bit of an ould man as brown as a spider, and there he lay dead as a grouse wid the buckshot holes in him and not a drop of blood no more than if he'd been made of cardboard.

"'Cover the face of him,' says the constable, for that was the sort of face he had, better than I can tell you, and havin' nothin' to cover it they turned him face down, and made off runnin' to Drumboyne for the residint magistrit.

"Well, sor, when they took that chimney down they found a room off it, all littered with bones and birds' feathers and rats' tails. It wouldn't do to be tellin' you of that room, more than it had no winda to it and had been built on purpose be Sir Michael Carey when he put the house up. He'd took to live in it, for that was the way his heart was, and at long last he took to live nowhere else, and that was how the sergeant brought him down and he must have been a matter of a hundred and tin years of age, they reckoned.

"FHe had his bagpipes to cheer him and frighten away tinints and he'd be out be nights scavengin' for food — they say they found the bones of childer in the room, but may be that was a lie got be him tryin' to drag Pat Leftwidge up the flue — but faith I wouldn't put it beyond him. For that chap was a spider, sor, they said his face was the face of a spider, and his arms and legs no better.

"He'd begun in the shape of a man, maybe, but the spider in him got the bether of him. Look, there's all there's left of the house, sor, thim walls beyond the trees. They set a light to it to get shut of that room and if you knew the truth of it all you wouldn' blame them."

MAGIC

IN TILAFEAA there lived, many years ago, two young men, Tauti and Uliami by name, and brothers in all things but birth. Tilafeaa is a high island, very large, and many ships come there for copra and turtle and beche de mer, and at night you can see the reef alight with the torches of the fish spearers, and there is a club where the white captains and the mates from the ships meet with the traders to drink and talk.

The town is larger than the town here at Malaffii, but more spread, with trees everywhere, and between the houses, artus and palms and bread fruit, so that at night the lights of the town show like fireflies in the thick bush.

Tauti's house lay near the middle of the great street, near to the church, while the house of Uliami was the last in all that street but one, a pleasant house under the shadow of the true woods and close to the mountain track that goes over the shoulder of Paulii and beyond.

It was at the house of Uliami that these two chiefly met, for Uliami was the richer man and his house was the pleasanter house and he himself was the stronger of the two — not in power of limb but in person. You will have noticed that, of two men equal in the strength of the body, one will be greater than the other, so that men and women will come to him first, and he will be able to get the better price for his copra, and in any public place he will find more consideration shown to him.

It was so with Uliami. He was first of these two as he might have been the elder brother, and, though first, always put himself last, so great was his spirit and love for Tauti. When they went fishing together, though he caught more, it was always Tauti that brought home the heaviest basket. The ripest fruit was always for Tauti, and once, at the risk of his own, he had saved Tauti's life.

As for Tauti, he was equally fine in spirit. Though Uliami might fill his basket the fullest, he always tried to contrive that in the end Uliami had the better fish and fruit, and once he, too, had risked his life to save a man — and that man was Uliami.

Now since these two were inseparable and had given in spirit the life of the one for the life of the other, nothing, you will say, could separate them but Death which separates all things.

II.

One day Tauti, coming up alone from the fishing and taking a byway through the trees, came across a girl crouched beneath the shelter of a bread fruit whose leaves were so great that one of them could have covered her little body.

It was Kinei, the daughter of Sikra the basket maker, and she was stringing flowers which she had plucked to make a chaplet. He knew her well, and he had often passed her; she was fourteen, or a little more, and had for nickname the "Laughing One," for she was as pleasant to look at as the sunshine through leaves on a shadowed brook. She was so young that he had scarcely thought of her as being different from a man, and she had always, on meeting him, had a smile for him, given openly as a child may give a pretty shell in the palm of its hand.

But today, as she looked up, she had no smile for him. He drew near and sat down close to her and handed her the flowers for her to string. Then, as he looked into her eyes, he saw that they were deep as the deepest sea, and full of trouble.

He made inquiry as to the cause of the trouble and Kinei, without answering him, looked down. He raised her chin and, looking at him full, her eyes filled with tears. Then he knew. He had found Love, suddenly, like a treasure, or like a flower just opened and filled with dew.

On leaving her that day he could have run through the woods like a man distracted and filled with joy, but instead he sought his own house, and there he sat down to contemplate this new thing that had befallen him.

Now, in the past, when any good had come to Tauti, no sooner was it in his hand than he carried it to Uliami to show; and his eyes now turned that way. But, look hard as he would, he could not see Uliami, for there was now no one else in the world for him but Kinei.

He could not tell his news, but hid it up, and when Uliami met him and asked him what was on his mind, he replied "Nothing." And so things went on, till one day Uliami, walking in the woods, came upon Kinei with Tauti in her arms.

He would sooner have come upon his own death, for he, too, had learned to love the girl, but his love for her had made him as weak as a maiden and as fearful as a child in the dark of the high woods, when there is no moon. Love is like that, making some men bold as the frigate bird in its flight, and some timorous as the dove, and the strongest are often the weakest when taken in the snare.

Uliami, having gazed for two heartbeats, passed away like a shadow among the trees and sought his own house and sat down to consider this new thing that had come to him, Any bad fortune of the past he had always carried to Tauti to share it with him, and his eyes turned toward Tauti now, but not with that intent.

At first, and for some time covering many days, he felt no ill will — no more than a man feels toward the matagi that blows suddenly out of a clear sky, driving him off shore to be drowned.

Then came the marriage of Tauti to Kinei, and a year that passed, and a son that was born to them.

And then slowly, as the great storms rise, the storm that had been gathering in the heart of Uliami rose and darkened, and what caused that storm was the fact that Tauti, in his happiness, had forgotten their old-time bond of brotherhood, and was so happy in his wife and his little affairs that Uliami might as well not have been on that island.

Tauti had robbed him not only of Kinei but of himself; Kinei had robbed him not only of herself but of Tauti — and they were happy. But the storm might never have burst, for Uliami was no evil man, had he not one day discovered that Kinei was no longer faithful to Tauti. She was of that sort, and the devil, who knows all things, did not leave the matter long to rest, but took Uliami by the ear and showed him the truth.

Now what the devil does to a man that man does often to another. Uliami showed Tauti the truth, and in such a manner that Tauti struck him on the mouth.

"So be it," said Uliami, wiping his mouth. "All is ended between us, and now I will kill you — not today, but tomorrow, and as sure as the sun will rise."

Tauti laughed.

"There are two to that game," said he, "As you say, all is ended between us, and tomorrow I will kill you as sure as the sun will set."

Then they each went their ways, not knowing that their words had been overheard by Sikra, the father of Kinei, who had been hiding in the bushes by the path where they had met.

III.

This Sikra was only a basket maker and knew only one trade, but for all that he was the wisest man on that island, and the most cunning, and the most evil. And Sikra said to himself, "If these two men kill one another over Kinei and her conduct, all may be discovered openly which is now known only secretly and to a few."

He went to the lagoon edge, and there, in the shelter of the canoe houses, he sat down, and, with his hands before him, began contemplating the matter, twisting the facts, this way and that, with the fingers of his mind, just as the fingers of his body had been accustomed to twist the plaited grass, this way and that, into the form of his baskets.

He knew that this thing was a death feud, and that by the morrow's sunset one of the two men would be no longer alive, unless they were separated and one taken clean away from that island. But more than that, he said to himself, "Of what use is there in taking one away, for if Tauti is left he will maltreat my daughter and search more deeply into this matter and bring more confusion upon us. And if I were to kill Uliami tonight in his sleep, as has just occurred to me, would not the deed be put down to Tauti, who, in trying to free himself, might in some way bring the deed home to me? And if I were to kill Tauti, might not the same thing happen?"

Thinking so, his wandering mind crossed the lagoon to the two ships there at anchor — a schooner and a brig — and both due to leave by the flood of the morrow's dawn. It was then, with the suddenness of the closing of a buckle, that a great thought came to Sikra, making him laugh out loud so that the echoes of the canoe house made answer.

He rose up and, leaving the beach, made through the trees in the direction of Tauti's house. There, when he reached it, was Kinei, seated at the doorway. He knew, by this, that Tauti was not at home, and so, nodding to his daughter, he withdrew, making along that street toward the sea end where presently he met his man leaving the forge of Tomassu, the smith, who makes and mends in iron things and sharpens fish spears and knives. Tauti had a knife in his girdle, and, noting it, Sikra drew him aside into the lane that goes through the bushes of mammee apple, past the chief trader's house to the far end of the beach.

Here he stopped, when they had passed beyond earshot of the trader's house, and, placing his finger on the breast of the other, says he:

"Tauti, what about that knife you were having sharpened just now at the forge of Tomassu?"

"Tomorrow," said Tauti, "I have to kill a pig."

"You are right," said Sikra. "He is a pig, I heard you both when you were talking on the path, and I heard the name he gave my daughter, and I saw you strike him. But you will not kill him tomorrow."

"But why?" asked Tauti.

"Because," said Sikra, "he has left the island."

Tauti laughed, disbelieving the other.

"Since when," asked he, "has Uliami taken wings?"

"An hour ago," replied Sikra. "I rowed him over to the schooner that lies there in the lagoon; most of the crew were ashore getting fruit, and the rest were asleep, and the captain and his mate were at the club drinking, and the hatch was open and Uliami crept on board and hid himself among the cargo. His lips were white with fear."

"But Uliami is no coward," said the other.

"Did he return your blow?" asked the cunning Sikra.

"That is true," replied Tauti, "but hiding will not save him. I have sworn his death and my hatred is as deep as the sea. I will go on board the schooner now and tell the captain what sort of cockroach lies hidden in his ship; and when they bring him out I will kill him."

"And then the white men will hang you," said Sikra. "Child that you are, will you listen to me?"

"I listen," said Tauti.

"Well," said Sikra, "you go aboard the schooner now and become one of the crew. They are in need of hands, as, indeed, is also that brig that lies by her. Then in a day or less, when Uliami knocks to be let out, you will be on board and on some dark night, or peradventure at the next port the schooner reaches, you can do the business you have set your heart to."

Now this counsel fell in not only with Tauti's desire for blood, but also with his wish to be shut of that island for a while and the wife who had betrayed him.

He thought for a moment on the matter, and then he fell in with the idea of Sikra, and, not even returning to his house, just as he was, let himself be led to the far end of the beach, where Sikra, borrowing a canoe, rowed him to the schooner, whose captain was right glad to have him, being, as Sikra had stated truly enough, short of hands.

IV.

Sikra, having got rid of one of his men, paddled back ashore, and, waiting till dark had nearly fallen, took himself to Uliami's house. Here he found Uliami seated with a fish spear across his knees and a whetstone in his hands; a knife that had just been sharpened lay beside him.

"You are busy?" said Sikra, "but your labor is useless, for the man you would kill has flown. Hiding in the bushes I heard all that passed between you and Tauti. He has left the island for fear of you and has crept on board the brig that lies at anchor in the lagoon. With the help of a friend who is one of the crew, he has hidden himself in the hold with the cargo.

"Then," said the other, and almost in the words Tauti had used, "I will row off to the brig and tell the captain what sort of reptile has hidden in his hold, and when they drag him forth I will kill him."

"And the white men will hang you," said Sikra. "Child, listen to the words of Sikra, who is old enough to be your father. Go on board the brig pretending nothing, become one of the crew, and then, when Tauti knocks to be let out; you can have your way with him some dark night, or peradventure, at the first port the ship touches at. I wish to be shut of him as a son-in-law for many reasons, but I do not want him killed on this island."

Uliami brooded for a moment on this. Then he rose, and, taking only the knife, followed the other to the beach.

It was now dark. When they reached the side of the brig the captain was called, and glad enough he was to get a new hand and willing to pay three dollars a month, which is better pay by a dollar than what they were giving on the plantations — and paid in dollars, not trade goods.

Uliami climbed on board, and then Sikra put back ashore, where he sat on the beach for a while, looking at the lights of the two ships and holding his stomach with laughter. Then he made for the house of Tauti and beat Kinei, and took possession of all the belongings of her husband. Next day he went to the house of Uliami and took the best of the things there, assured in his mind that neither Tauti nor Uliami would ever get back to that island again.

V.

Now when a man finds himself in his grave he may like it or not, but he cannot get out; and so it is with a ship.

Uliami presently found himself in the fo'c's'le of that ship where the hands were having their supper by the light of a stinking lamp, and so far from eating, it was all he could do to breathe.

Neither did the men please him, being different from the men he had always met with. There were men from the Solomons, with slit ears and nose rings; and there were men from the low islands, whose language he could scarcely understand; and he would have been the unhappiest man in the world, just then, had it not been for the thought of Tauti so close to him hidden among the cargo and fancying himself safe.

At the same time, on board the schooner, Tauti was in the same way, wishing himself in any other place, but upheld by the thought of Uliami hiding from him, yet so close.

Then, with an empty belly, but a full mind, Uliami turned in, to be aroused just before break of day by the mate. On deck he was put to haul on ropes to raise the sails, and on the deck of the schooner, lying close by, he might have seen, had there been light, Tauti hauling likewise.

Then he was put to the windlass which pulls in the chain that raises the anchor, and as the sun laid his first finger upon Paulii the anchor came in and the brig, with the tide and the first of the land wind, drew toward the reef opening and passed it. Uliami, looking back, saw Tilageaa standing bold from the sea and the reef and the opening with the schooner passing through it, and he wished himself back for a moment, till the remembrance of Tauti came to him and the picture of him hidden there among the cargo.

He reckoned that he would knock to be let out as soon as the ship told him by her movement that she was well on her voyage, and, being on the morning watch, he managed to keep close to the cargo hatch with his ears well open to any sound. At first the straining and creaking of the masts and timbers confused him, but he got used to these, but he heard no sound. An hour might have gone by when a new thought came to Uliami. He would lay no longer waiting for the other to make a move, but go straight to the captain and tell him that a man was hidden there under the hatch, for he was more hungry for the sight of Tauti's face and the surprise on it at their meeting than a young maiden is for the sight of her lover.

At that moment the captain himself came on deck and began to look at the sun, holding to his face a thing so strangely formed that Uliami would have laughed, only that laughter and all gay thoughts were now as far from him as Tilafeaa.

The captain was a big man with a red face, and when he had done looking at the sun, and when he heard what Uliami had to say, he swore a great oath, and, calling to the mate, he ordered the tarpaulins to be taken off the hatch and the locking bars undone, and then the hatch was opened, but there was no man there.

Then the captain kicked Uliami, and the mate kicked him, and at that very time, or near it, they were kicking Tauti on board the schooner for also giving them word that a man was hidden in the cargo.

Of a truth these two, who had set out so gayly to kill one another, were receiving payment through the hands of Sikra; each of these men had seized the devil by the tail and they could not let go, and here he was galloping over the world with them, from wave to wave, like a horse over hurdles, for the brig and the schooner, though separated by many leagues, were going in the same direction.

VI.

They passed islands, and there was not an island they passed that did not make Uliami feel as though he had swallowed Paulii and it had risen in his throat.

At first, and for many days, he noticed in his ears a sound which was yet not a sound. Then he knew it was the sound of the reef that had been in his ears since childhood, but had now drawn away and gone from him, leaving only its memory. The food displeased him, and the work and the faces of his companions, and he would have given his pay and all he possessed for a sniff of the winds blowing from the high woods, or a sight of the surf on the shores of Tilafeaa.

He had only one companion — his anger against Tauti. He saw now that he had been served a trick, and put the whole matter down to the wiles of the other, little thinking that it was Sikra who had played this game against them both.

VII.

One day the brig, always butting like a ram against the blue sky and empty sea, gave them view of a mountain and land, stretching in the distance from north to south as though all the islands of the ocean had been drawn and joined together making one solid piece.

Then presently, as they drew in, Uliami saw a break in the land near the mountain. They told him it was the Golden Gate and the city of San Francisco where all the rich men in the world lived, but he had little time to listen to their tales. For they were now on the bar, and the brig was tumbling this way and that, and the mate and captain cursing and kicking those in the way, and giving orders to haul now on this rope, now on that.

Uliami had been used to swearing and cursing on board that brig, but, when they got to the wharf, what he heard overpassed all he had heard in that way, as though all the curses in the world, like all the men, and all the houses, and all the ships, had come to roost at that spot.

But Uliami did not mind. He was filled with one great desire — to go ashore to see for himself the great houses and the rich men and the new things to be seen. Next morning when the crew were paid and he had received five dollars as his pay, he joined up with Sru, a man from the low islands, who had been friendly to him on the voyage, and the pair, crossing the plank, set their feet on the wharf, and Sru, landing, made for the first tavern. That was the sort of man Sru was, old in the ways of harbors and ports, and with a liking for rum. But Uliami had no stomach for drink and, presently, he left the other and found himself in the streets round the dockside.

It was very windy here and his thin coat and trousers flapped around him as a flag flaps on its staff, and the dust blew with the wind in great clouds. And, just as things touched by a wizard change and alter, so the mind of Uliami began to wither in him, for here there were no rich men to be seen, only dirty children playing their games, and there was not a child that did not see in him a man new to the place. They called after him, ridiculing him, and the houses were not proper houses set in gardens, but all of a piece and evil-looking beyond words. Then pursuing his way he found himself in a broader street where cars ran without horses and where there were so many people that no one noticed him.

And that was the most curious thing that had happened to him yet, for at Tilafeaa every one had a nod or a smile or a word for every one else, but here the people all passed along in two streams, rapidly, like driven fish, with not a word for each other, nor a look nor a smile, so that, in all that crowd, Uliami felt more alone than in the woods yet not alone — for here were men and women, almost in touch, by the hundred and the thousand.

Then the shops took him where the traders exposed their goods, not in the open but behind windows of glass, each ten hundred times bigger than the window of glass in the church at Raupee. But the goods exposed were things, many of them, which he had never seen before, and they caused no desire in his mind, only distress and more loneliness, till he came to a shop where great bunches of bananas hung just as though they had been new cut down from the trees at Tilafeaa.

Here he hung, disregarding the other fruit exposed, and with tears filling his eyes, till the man of the shop spoke to him roughly, asking him what he wanted and bidding him be gone.

VIII.

Now at Tilafeaa the day was always cut out in pieces, with things to do in each piece, and on board the brig it was the same, but here the day was all one, with nothing to do but walk from street to street, among people blind to one another and always hurrying like leaves blown by a wind.

Uliami stood a while at a corner and watched these people, and it seemed to him, now, that they were each, like the cars that went without horses, or the boats in the bay that went without stern or side wheels, driven by some purpose that no man could see.

He felt that it was no good purpose that made men disregard one another and push one another aside and be blind to a stranger as though he were a ghost they could not see. He felt sick at heart, for even the sun had changed and here its light fell on nothing good. The great buildings and the little, it was all the same, they were equally hard with the hardness that lay in the faces of the people.

It was on noon when, wandering like a lost dog, he found himself in a most dismal place passing along by a great wall. Beyond the wall lay a building reaching the skies with chimneys that smoked and fumed, and here in the lane lay refuse and old empty tins and such truck with the sun shining on them and the light of it turned to mournfulness and desolation. Turning a corner of this lane he came face to face with Tauti, whose ship had come in to the bay only the morning before, and who, like Uliami, had been wandering hither and thither, like a lost dog.

Each man had still his knife in his girdle, and thus they stood facing one another, as they had stood when they parted last, in the woods of Tilafeaa. And surely, for a killing, no place was better suited than this, where there was no one to watch or take notice or care except the devil of desolation lurking in that lane, which of all places in the city seemed his truest home.

For a moment, as they stood, all things were shattered around them; everything wiped away but themselves, and their minds sprang back to the point of anger as a bow springs back to the straight, and who knows what might have happened between these two, but at that moment from the great building there came a howl like the voice of the whole city howling out in pain because of its own desolation.

It was the voice of the horn that is blown at midday for the work people, and as Tauti and Uliami looked round them in fear and wonder it seemed to them the voice of the dust, and the high walls and the streets, and the rubbish on the ground, and the hard-faced people on the foot walks. When it ceased, and they faced one another again, they were no longer alone, for that voice had reached Tilafeaa, and the high woods had come trooping to its call right across the sea, and they were standing as they had stood when they parted last in the company of the trees and amid the beauty of the flowers, and all anger had passed from their hearts where there was nothing now but the grief of exile and love.

Surely that was magic greater than the magic of the pictures that move, or the machines that speak, and surely places are the true gods that rule over man, for the voice of the city had brought an island from a thousand leagues away, and the island had brought love to Tauti and Uliami.

No man could have reconciled these two. But Tauti died. Before ever he could get back to Tilafeaa a fever took him. It was many years ago.

I am Uliami.

KADJAMAN

KRAY'S LITTLE son was playing with the big Siberian pup in the doorway. From where I sat I could see the child and the dog, and beyond them and framed by the door opening the pine-clad mountains cutting the blue sky of summer, and beyond these Omstjall, the snow peak and grandfather of the glacier that takes its name.

Kray has given up hunting these five years and is now manager of the Sellagman Salmon Canning Company, at least he looks after the fishing and the canning and gets two thousand dollars a year for the job, while I expect the real manager, the man who looks after the New York office and the prospectuses and so forth, gets ten — maybe more. I don't know, neither does Kray, neither does he care. He says he has hunted everything in his time but the dollar, and that a free life in the open air is all he wants now that he has done with hunting and got married. He was sixty-seven years old when he married and didn't look more than fifty, so he says; he doesn't look more than fifty today, at a little distance.

He has hunted everywhere and shot everything and he started his business at twenty so that when he married he had been at the job nearly fifty years. That is a long time, for a year in the wilds is longer than a year in a city and the risks are greater.

Said Kray, looking at the child and the pup: "Olaff takes after his mother, don't he? Same flax-colored hair coming. First I thought he was going to be darker, but it's coming true enough. Scandinavian flax, there's no other color like it. Gets on with the pup, don't he? I saw the old dog lickin' them both yesterday same as if Olaff was hers, too. I've sent her off to the Skagga *fjord* till the autumn."

"The big Siberian dog I saw here last?"

"Yes, the mother of that pup. I've sent her off till the autumn, Olaff will be bigger then."

"But why did you send her off — because she was treating Olaff as if he were her pup?"

27

"Well, not exactly," said Kray, "and yet maybe that was a bit of the reason. But mainly I expect it was something that happened years ago that rattled me; thirty years ago it was when I was with Becconi in Borneo on the exploring job. He was after minerals and if he'd stuck to them in his drinks as well as his prospectin' he'd have pulled through; but the whisky did him. I'd been out East with a chap called Milner hunting, and we struck Sarawak coast. Milner was going home from there, and I was paid off with a bonus. I could have gone back with him to England, and maybe would only for this chap Becconi who happened along while we were waiting at Bintulu for a boat.

"Boats in those days weren't plentiful along the coast, and you didn't often know where they were going when they came, but as long as they took you somewhere else it didn't much matter. That's how we were placed at Bintulu when out of the sea haze one day a little paddle-wheel boat came snortin' and tied up to the rotten old wharf where the Sea Dyak children used to sit fishing when they weren't playing head-hunting with wooden *parangs*.

"The *Tanjong Data* was the name of the boat, and she was bound for Rejang and Kuching and ports beyond with a mixed cargo and a big monkey for the Dutch government that had been caught somewheres to the north of the Tubao River. The *Tanjong* had blown a cylinder cover off or something, and she lay at Bintulu a week for repairs and while she was repairing and taking more cargo I was often on board talking to the captain and Becconi, who had come by her and was sticking on board till the last minute, seeing that his cabin was a sight more comfortable than shore quarters. The monkey interested me a lot, for in all my shooting I'd never come across the big monkeys much, and this chap was big. He must have weighed all of two hundred pounds, and he was turning gray with age. He was what the Dyaks call a Mayas Kassa, which means an orangutan, with a face like a full moon. I'm not joking. There are three kinds of orangutans; the Mayas Kassa, the Mayas Rabei, and the Mayas Tjaping, but the Kassa takes the bun for beauty. I never did see such a face. It was like nothing so much as a full moon broadened out, same as you see it when the moon's rising through a bank of mist and in the middle of it two eyes and a nose, to say nothing of the mouth. That was what the monkey was like, and they had him in a cage close to the engine-room hatch, and he'd sit there the day long, scratching himself and talking to himself, his eyes traveling about round the decks as if he was watching something passing, and sometimes he'd look up at you, but he'd never meet your eye square, at least not for longer than the flick of a snapshot shutter.

"Taking him altogether he was near five feet in height and his chest looked as thick as a tree as he sat there scratching the fur on it, his hands were as big as hams; and I reckon he could have taken two ordinary men and knocked their heads together same as if they'd been two rag dolls.

"Becconi took a lot of interest in the chap, too, and we'd sit under the double awning they'd rigged aft of the funnel and have our drinks and watch Kadjaman, for that was his name, given him because he was caught at Kadjaman, which is north of Fort Bellaja near the Tubao River. Becconi, when he had the whisky in him, would stand up for Kadjaman having a soul of his own, same as a man; but if the whisky was out, and maybe a touch of liver on him, he'd be the other way about. I used to use the monkey on him for fun, or to see the state of his health, and then Kadjaman would sit watching us and pretending not to.

"We didn't know that he'd been at work of nights, when the whole of Bintulu and the chaps on board were snoring. He'd worked on the cage bars, loosening them by degrees and little by little, so that the time might come when one big pluck could rip them out.

"No, sir, we didn't know that or we couldn't have sat there sucking our cheroots and bug juice and talking about monkeys having souls.

II.

"Now I must tell you that Milner had a servant, Tuan Marop by name, and Tuan had his child with him, a little chap of six or so, named Ting. Mrs. Tuan had been dead over a year, and he'd brought Ting down to Bintulu to leave him there while he accompanied Milner on his expedition. Ting and Kadjaman had struck up a friendship of sorts. The child would talk to the brute in the Dyak lingo and Kadjaman would scratch himself and talk back in orangutan. I tell you it was talking.

"You've seen a child talking to a dog — you've heard Olaff talking to that pup; well that was the sort of thing, only Ting wasn't a soft little chap like Olaff. Ting was a Dyak, Sarabas Dyak, with a hundred generations of head hunters behind him, and what he was saying to Kadjaman didn't seem popsy-wopsy talk from what I could gather, though I didn't know a word of his lingo.

"I asked Becconi to ask Tuan to listen and report, and Tuan said Ting wasn't talking Dyak, but the monkey language. Seemed to think it a joke, but he was in dead earnest all the same. There is a monkey language as sure as there's anything else in this world, and what they say to each other, Lord only knows, but they say a lot, and Ting seemed to have picked it up same as children do with foreign languages. Tuan said that the Dyak children, now and again and once in a hundred years, so to speak, could pick out what the monkeys were saying when they held their jamborees in the forest, but he'd never seen or heard of a child talking to a monkey before like Ting did, for the reason that the Dyaks didn't keep monkeys in cages and so the children hadn't a chance. He seemed proud of the fact, same as if Ting had taken a prize at college.

"So things went on like that till the *Tanjong Data* had done tinkering at her cylinder covers, and the day before leaving came, with the docks all of a clatter with fruit cases for down coast and rolls of matting and boxes of tobacco and Lord knows what else and the niggers all bug house with being driven and getting in each other's way.

"Then, coming along four o'clock in the evening, when things had settled down and the breeze was rising, Becconi and I were sitting in deck chairs talking and saying good-by to Milner and the captain. Tuan had brought us up some tea which the steward had made for us, and Ting was playing near the gangway by himself. All of a sudden, swish! the bars of the cage went, and Kadjaman was out.

"I was sitting with my back to the cage, and when I turned I saw Kadjaman on the deck, a cage bar in his fist, and the bar was in the act of dashing a nigger's brains out. It was all as sudden as that. I didn't wait to see more. It was every man for himself, and I had no charter to clear the decks of the *Tanjong Data* of orangutans armed with five-foot iron bars; besides I hadn't my gun with me. I guess if I'd had a popgun even, I wouldn't have taken a nosedive into the Bintulu River like I did. A man's courage lies in his gun often enough — unless he's fronting a moral duty, which I wasn't. I just dived and got to the other bank and watched.

"Everyone had skipped from that deck either overboard or through the saloon hatch and there was Kadjaman with his bar in his fist, a free man, so to say, soul or no soul. He was pretty busy, too. He wanted more blood, it seemed, but he was afraid of going below for it, afraid of traps, so he smashed away at the saloon skylight cover, beating the brass rods of it to knots. Then he beat the starboard rail; in fact, he gave that steamer the biggest thrashing of her life. Maybe it was his having been kept in a cage six months that was coming out, or maybe it was just his own nature; but he did take it out of that old hooker. He near beat the cockroaches out of her, and you can fancy that the chaps hidden in the cabin had a lively time expecting him down the saloon companionway.

"However, all of a sudden, he let up. I could see him standing sniffing the air as if he smelt danger. He stood like that for half a tick and then he stooped down and picked up something from the deck and threw it over his arm like a sack. Same moment he made a jump for the gangway and next he was on the bank.

"I saw now what he was carrying — and heard it, too — it was Ting. The child had been playing on the deck as I told you and hadn't got below with the others. Maybe he'd sat admiring the ways of his friend, but that's as may be; the fact was he was now shouting murder or what sounded like it in Dyak and Tuan was responding.

"Tuan had found a creese down below, and, before the monkey had made twenty yards, he was on deck and after him to recover his property. Becconi and Milner, who'd armed themselves, were after Tuan to lend a hand, and there was I stuck on the opposite bank only able to look on.

"On the flat Kadjaman was nowhere, but once he'd got among the trees he was the whole of the circus and the elephant.

"Just by the river there, the undergrowth's so thick you can't go more than a yard in a precious long minute. You should see it; wait-a-bit thorns three inches long, python lianas that twine about and knot themselves just like snakes, ground tangle that gets you just by the ankle. That's what the goin's like, and Kadjaman was up in the branches. I don't know how he got along with Ting, swinging himself from branch to branch. I expect Ting clung to him for safety and so saved trouble and gave him the free use of both arms.

"Anyhow he got away — got clear away, leaving Tuan lamenting and the rest of them pretty well spent. Then they came back, and I met them, having swum the river, and we went back on board, and you should have seen that deck — the rail bent and skylight hashed and lashed so's to look like nothing, and a dead nigger on the planks with a hundred thousand flies on his head like a buzzing turban.

"Tuan had come back with us. He'd altered in color a bit, but otherwise he seemed same as ordinary. He knew quite well there was no use chasing any more after Kadjaman, yet all the same he got his discharge from Milner that night, and he went off with a blowgun. That was all the weapons he wanted, so he said, but he didn't catch Kadjaman.

III.

"Next morning the *Tanjong Data* started with Milner on board, leaving us in that God-forsaken place face to face with the mosquitoes. Havana mosquitoes are bad, but these chaps laid over them, striped brutes like tigers. Then there were the Sanut *tingal pala* ants; these chaps bite you and hang on with their teeth like bulldogs; if you pull them off they leave their heads behind. A cheerful place, with nothing to listen to but the rainy noise of the palm leaves, shaken by the wind and the howling of Dyak songs from the village, and nothing to see but the Bintulu coming down to the sea between banks of trees that seemed crowding one another into the river.

"There are parts of the Bintulu where no man could make a landing on the banks, by reason of the tangle of growth, vines and whatnots; but at Bintulu it's been cleared, though in those days it was bad enough within half a mile of the town.

"Becconi wasn't going to start for three days, so I had my work cut out killing time and mosquitoes. I'd sit sometimes by the river watching the gunfish by the hour. You'd see them prospecting along the bank, and then when they'd marked down an insect sitting on a leaf, they'd take aim and spit, letting fly a jet of water aimed sure as a rifle bullet. Then I'd sometimes watch the Dyak girls going about, the rummiest sight, in their brass arm rings and leg wear, and sometimes I'd sit and talk to Tuan, for Becconi had taken him on as a servant.

"He didn't talk English bad, and at first I tried to comfort him about Ting, till I found out he wasn't needing any. It wasn't that, he hadn't been fond of the child, but it was just that he seemed to reckon Ting dead. Not corpsed, but dead to him and his tribe. I had some talks with Tuan on the business then and afterward, and he told me that the big monkeys took off Dyak children now and then and sometimes the children were got back after they'd been living a year or two with the monks, and that they weren't any use; they weren't humans any more. Tuan, though he didn't know anything much more than the difference between the two ends of a blowgun, said all men had been monkeys once, but so long ago that man had forgotten, and if a child was to go and live in the trees with the monkeys he'd revert to the old times in a year or two, and not twenty or fifty years would fetch him back.

"I thought he was talking through his hat, but out in India, since then, I've seen the truth of what he said. You've heard of wolf children? Wolves are always carrying off children; some they eat and some they don't, and the ones they don't they bring up as wolves, and the children take to it and go on all fours and, after a year or less they're fixed, can't ever get back to be men. Why, they had a wolf child in the Secundra Missionary Asylum and kept it there till it grew up to a man over thirty. It died somewhere about '95, and it never learned to speak, couldn't do more than run about on all fours and snarl. Rum, isn't it?

"Meanwhile Becconi was getting the lads together for his expedition, and he wasn't finding it an easy matter, for in those days Sea Dyaks weren't anxious for payment much except in human heads, and even heads were sometimes pretty much at a discount. The head-hunting chaps have got a bad name, but they weren't so black as they were painted. They weren't always rushing about, either, hunting for heads. It was mostly when they were in love and wanted to give a girl a present that they went hunting, or when they had a down on a chap and wanted to do him in. Becconi's crowd that he managed to collect at last were head-hunters to a man, but I'd sooner trust myself alone with any one of them than with a New York tough — a long sight.

"We started on a Saturday at dawn, crossing the Bintulu and striking toward the Tatan River. I've said Becconi was after minerals and so he was, but his main proposition was gold. Down along south of the eastern ports he'd heard stories of a gold river somewhere in Sarawak north of the Rejang, and he carried the idea in his head, and I suppose that was what made him strike south from the Bintulu.

"We had with us Tuan and half a dozen of the Sea Dyaks and provisions for a month, and we hadn't more than crossed the river and gone a few yards when the trees closed behind us, shutting out the sound of the village and cutting us off from the morning sun as a closed door might. I've never got used to the jungle, that's to say the real thing, and it's my opinion it is not the place for a man. It's a kind of old glass house where the beginnings of life come from, and it's my opinion it has outlived its uses and would be as well done away with. Maybe I'm prejudiced, having done near all my hunting in the open. Anyhow, that Saturday morning I wasn't in any too high spirits. If I could have broke my contract and turned back I wouldn't, though, bad as I wanted to, because I'd taken a liking to Becconi, and I had my misgivings as to his pulling through without a white man's help.

"I've hinted he drank. We took a good stock of liquor with us, but it went under my eye. That was one of my conditions, and I knew if he was left alone with it the jungle would soon have done with him.

"We struck a big stretch of soggy ground where Nipah palms grew and nothing else. I'm just going to give you a sniff of that hell place they call the jungle in Borneo, and I can't begin it better than by saying we hadn't gone more than five hundred yards from the river when we struck this swamp. It wasn't a true swamp, either. It was solid enough in bits, and you'd be going along saying, 'It's all right now,' when your foot would go, sucked down, and you'd pull it out with a pound of black mud like treacle sticking to your boot. We went along mostly clinging to the palms that grew along the solid tracts and gave us a lead. Then, when we'd passed the swamp we found ourselves before the Big Thorn. That's what the Dyaks called it, a big patch of wait-a-bit thorn we had to cut our way through, and it took us the whole day to do that.

"Then when we camped on a bit of high ground the black ants raised objections, and the black ants of Borneo sting like wasps.

"I give you that as a sample of twenty-four hours in the jungle. You didn't get swamp all the time nor wait-a-bit thorn all the time, but you got lots of other things not much better, and it was always that infernal glass-house damp heat and smell. It's the smell that gets you, not a bad smell, mind you, but just the smell of a glass house — only more so.

"Then at the end of a week we struck a rival prospector. It was the rummiest meeting. He was a chap by name of Havenmouth. He'd shoved east with an expedition from Maka, crossing the Balinean River, and he'd found the gold. But he was dying. I never did see such a skeleton. The jungle fever or something like that had done for him, and he said he'd been living on quinine and whisky, but that he didn't care as he'd found the gold. It was in a little stream to the nor'east. He said there was dead loads of it, even though the stream was so small.

"He said that little stream must have been washing its gold for ages to make us rich. There he lay with his hands like a skeleton's and his face like a skull painted with fever, handing us out all that talk; and then he showed us a sample of gold grains he'd taken from the stream.

"Sure enough some of them were as big as split bullets. Then he died with a whoop, and we buried him. But the bother was, he died before he could give us the exact location by compass. He hadn't got it written down, for we searched him and his effects; he'd been carrying it in his head. He'd given us the gold grains, though.

"Well, that was the worst present a man ever got. Havenmouth had said: 'It isn't more than twenty miles way back there,' and that was the string that tied us to the circle, for we went wandering round like the Egyptians in the wilderness, round and round, hunting for that darned stream for months and months. You wouldn't believe it, unless you'd been there, how that thing held us. I'm not overset on money, but it held me, same as when you draw a chalk line round a hen and put her nose to it, she's held.

"We struck streams, all sorts of little tributaries of the Rejang and the Tatan, and we struck mud turtles and spitting fish and water lizards and snakes, but we struck no gold. Becconi was so full of the business that he forgot his wanting to drink. And so it went on for more than three months, till one day the madness lifted from us, and we saw that we were done. We'd got to get back to Bintulu and get back prompt, for we were near done for grub.

"I'd managed to shoot a good deal, and we had the remains of Havenmouth's store. Still, all the same, we'd got to get back; and over the fire that night, when we'd come to the decision to clear out, Becconi had his first drink for a long time. We were sitting there smoking and talking when all of a sudden from the dark outside the firelight comes a whistle and Tuan gives a jump where he sat. Then he whistles between his fingers as if in answer and out of the dark comes a chap crawling along with his hair over his eyes. He creeps up to Tuan, and they begin to talk. Then Tuan comes to us and tells us the news. One of the Dyaks, a fish trapper that had done a journey up the Tatan on some business of his own, had come on Kadjaman's house.

"That's what Tuan told us with a straight face, but we didn't laugh, for we knew what he meant. The orangs build houses of sorts away up in the trees. They haven't walls or roofs or lavatory accommodation; they're just platforms built between two branches and furnished with bundles of brushwood and leaves. This fishing Dyak was a blood relation of Tuan's. He knew Ting, and he knew of the carrying off, and a month before, going along through the forest by the river and chancing to look up, he saw Kadjaman's platform away up in a tree.

"He wouldn't have took any more notice, monkey houses being common, only for a face looking down at him out of the leaves. He saw at once it was Ting's face, and he called out, thinking the child might come down. Instead of that Ting went up the remainder of the tree like a flash and hid on the platform.

"He marked the place and then he'd set out to hunt for Tuan and us. He'd seen us start from Bintulu and he knew the direction we'd gone; but how he found us after a month's hunt — well, search me! But find us he did.

"Tuan having got the yarn, said it was necessary for him, now that he had the indication, to drop everything else and get his child back. He said he couldn't lead us any longer till he had that matter settled, and Becconi agreed that it was only right and proper to get the child back and said he'd wait there with the whisky while Tuan and myself made the journey and fetched the goods. The place was only a day's Journey from where we were. I agreed. I judged he couldn't kill himself with the whisky in two days and that if he did it'd maybe be a mercy for him, and taking my gun I followed Tuan and the fisher Dyak, striking in the direction of the Tatan.

"It was less than a day's journey, and when we got there it wasn't above ten o'clock in the morning, and there, like as if a chap had hoisted a mattress and stuck it between two of the branches away up in a big tree, we saw Kadjaman's house; but there wasn't a sign of the owner nor of Ting. We didn't go to knock at the door. We all sat down in the undergrowth which hid us while giving us a view of the premises above and there we waited. I didn't know what Tuan proposed to do to get the child back, but I did know one thing, he was going to get it back now he'd found the address. I reckoned he'd kill Kadjaman and then climb for the child; but I was wrong as it turned out.

"I nodded off to sleep, for I was bone tired with the journey, and I'd been dozing maybe an hour when Tuan joggled me awake. I looked up and there was Ting crawling along a branch twenty foot up, following in the track of a big monk that was Kadjaman's twin brother if it wasn't himself. You could see at a glance that the child had joined up with the monkey folk in the three months he'd been with them.

"But I wasn't bothering about that, I was watching Tuan. Tuan had his blowgun with him. It was a better weapon and twice as deadly as a Colt's automatic. It was death itself, for the dart was poisoned. Tuan was standing up and leaning back with the gun to his lips. Up above against the sprinkling light through the leaves, Kadjaman made a target as big as a barn door and not more than twenty-five feet off and Tuan with that infernal gun could hit the middle of a sixpence somewhere about the same distance. So there didn't seem much chance for the monkey, did there?

"Well, all of a sudden I heard the 'phut' of the blowgun, and right on it Ting, up in the branches, let a squeal out of him and I saw he'd been hit, hit right in the neck where the big vein is and where the poison of the dart would act quickest.

"Then he came tumbling, kicking, and catching at twigs, bang into the bushes, dead as Pharaoh's aunt. Tuan gave the body a stir with his foot to see if it was dead all right, and finding it so was satisfied. He didn't bother about Kadjaman, though he could have killed him easy enough. He'd got his son back, anyhow, and stopped him from going lower than he'd gone, You see he wasn't a chap to believe in *Tarzan of the Apes* or *Mowgli*, seeing that he knew what the jungle is and what monkeys are, and what men can become.

"Tuan wasn't a popsy-wopsy father by no means, but I've often thought it's chaps like Tuan, stuck by nature in the door in old days, that's stopped humans from backsliding into beasts — but maybe I'm wrong."

ME AND SLANE

"I'VE TOLD you," said Brent, "that Slane had an old uncle in San Francisco, Pat O'Brien, worth over two million dollars they said he was and I don't doubt them. Pat had landed in New York somewhere in the fifties or sixties without a jitney, then he'd come along to Frisco; he hadn't struck gold, he hadn't struck oil, nor luck in any special way as far as we could make out, he'd just become a millionaire and one day when we were on the trip back to Frisco with a full cargo, I said to Buck, 'Look here, Buck' I says 'you and me has been trading together the last ten years. We're up to every game on the Pacific Coast, we aren't simple sailors no more than a mule is all an ass. Well, we've got sixty thousand dollars between us put by, but four years ago we had forty thousand. We make our money hard and earn it slow, seems to me. Look at Pat, he's none of our natural advantages, the chap can't more than read and write his name, he's only one brain and we've got two, but look at him, rolling in dollars. How's it done?'

"'Search me,' says Buck. 'It's the way they all do it. Seems to me it's the start. If you're American born you start selling newspapers, if you're only a blistered alien you land without a cent in your pocket, whereas, we'd got a few dollars; but there's no going back.'

"We left it at that and got into Frisco next day and went to the lodgings we had in Tallis Street. We'd always lived small considering that we could have cut a bigger dash if we'd chosen, but the fact of the matter is, living big for the likes of us would have meant soaking in bars and all the trimmings that go with that. It's God's truth that a plain sailorman who isn't what the darn fools who run the world call a 'gentleman' is clean out of it in the big towns — unless he's a millionaire. So, not being able to sit on the top of the pyramid we just sat on the sand waiting for some big strike and stuck to our rooms in Tallis Street in a house kept by a Mrs. Murphy.

"Well, as I was saying, we went to our lodgings and a couple of days after, old Pat O'Brien hearing we were back, called on us. Pat, though he was near eighty, was an early bird, and though he was worth two millions he always footed it about the town. He was the spit and image of *Mr. Jiggs* in the comic papers and as we were sitting at breakfast in he came with a cigar butt stuck in the corner of his mouth.

"'Lord love me,' says Pat, 'nine o'clock and you at breakfast. No,' he says, 'I won't have no coffee. A glass of hot water is all I take till one o'clock in the day and then I have a porterhouse steak and a pint of claret and that's why I have all my teeth though I'm close on eighty — and how's the old *Greyhound* been doing this trip?'

"I've told you before how Buck got the *Greyhound* out of Pat at our first go off and he made it a habit always to call on us when we were in from a trip to ask after her. He didn't care a dump about her, he just wanted to pick up island news that might be useful to him in his business — but we never pretended we knew that.

"'Doing fine,' says Buck.

"Then Pat sits down and borrows a match to light his cigar stump and in half an hour he'd got to know all he wanted. Then, when we'd given him a cigar to get rid of him, off he goes stumping down the stairs and a minute after, the window being open owing to the hot weather, we heard him talking to Micky Murphy, the landlady's little boy, who was playing in the street. Couldn't hear what he was saying at first till a bit of a breeze came in and we heard him say to the child, 'So, Micky is your name,' he says. 'Well, come along and bring your play toy with you and I'll buy you some candy.'

"I stuck my head out of the window and there was the old chap and the child hand in hand going off down the street toward the candy shop at the corner.

"'Well,' I says, 'Buck, we've misjudged him, he's got a heart somewhere and he's not as mean as he advertises himself.'

"Buck was as much taken aback as myself. You see, we'd had a lot of dealings with the old man and he'd always forgot his purse if a tram fare was to be paid and I've seen him pick up a match in the street to light his cigar which he was always letting go out to save tobacco — and there he was going off to buy a child candy.

"But that was only the beginning of things, for two days later we had a note from him asking us to dinner.

"He had only asked us to dinner once before, years ago, and that was when he was shook out of himself by a deal we'd done over pearls, and it was at a restaurant. This time he was asking us to his house.

"'What's he after?' says Buck, turning the letter over. 'Day before yesterday he was giving Micky Murphy candy, and now he's asking us to dinner. He'll bust himself with generosity if he doesn't mind out. Will you go?'

"'Sure,' said I, and we went.

"Pat was married, as perhaps I haven't told you, and when the colored man let us in there was Mrs. Pat waiting to receive us in the big room hung with pictures opening from the hall, and a minute after in come Pat's daughter Sadie with her hair frizzed out and when Pat toddled in after, if it wasn't McManus' *Jiggs Family* to the life, call me a liar.

"We didn't feel comfortable by no means, not being used to female society done up in diamonds, but they were anxious to please, though I could see plain enough that behind everything those two women looked on us as plated goods. But Pat kept the ball rolling, chatting away, and at dinner after the champagne had gone round the girl suddenly turns to Buck, and, 'Tell us about your last voyage, Mr. Slane?' says she.

"'Oh,' says Buck, 'there's nothing much to tell. We went to Levua. We've been there three trips, there's several German traders we're in with and they give us a lot of business. We're off there again in a month.'

"'Is it a long way?' she questions.

"'Yes, it's a good bit of a way,' he answers, and it would be longer only the *Greyhound* is no tortoise.'

"'How interesting,' she says. 'And I suppose you see plenty of other islands on the way there and back. Are they as pretty as people say?'

"'Well,' says Buck, 'as a matter of fact we stop nowhere but a place we call Palm Island. We put in there for water and fruit. It's not on the charts and there's no trade to be done there, but it's pretty enough.'

"He describes the place and then she tackles him on Levua again, and the manners of the natives, and then Mrs. Pat cuts in and talks of the opera and the theaters and such.

"Dinner over we go to the drawing-room where the women squall at the piano for a bit and then we go to Pat's den for cigars.

"I remember Buck, who was livened up a bit with the champagne, asking Pat how to become a millionaire.

"'Why,' says Pat cocking his eye at the other, 'you just pick a million up and stick to it. It's not the picking it up that's the bother, it's the sticking to it,' he says. Then we went home thinking that Pat had been joking with us. But he hadn't.

II.

"Levenstein was the name of the chief German trader at Levua. We had big dealings with him amounting to a share in his business and we were going out this time with a cargo of trade goods and with some agricultural stuff for a man by name of Marks who had started a plantation on the north of the island. Our hands were pretty full for we were our own stevedores, not trusting the long-shore johnnies over much, and one day as we were on deck, the both of us, who should come along the wharf but Pat. Pat looked down in the mouth and as if something was troubling him. He gave us good day and asked us how we were doing, and then he told us his bother. Sadie wasn't well, the doctors thought she was going into consumption.

"'There's nothing but trouble in this world,' said Pat. 'First I lost my partner six months ago, then I lost a cargo which wasn't full insured by a mistake of a darn clerk, and now Sadie is took bad. Well, good day to you, boys, and better luck than is attending me.'

"'Now I wonder why he came along the wharf to tell us that,' says Buck. 'Blessed if I can make the old man out. His compasses are wrong, he ain't sailing true, he's doing things he's never done before. Maybe he's breaking up with old age and that's what's the matter with him.'

"'He seems to have taken a fancy to us anyhow,' I says, 'and if he's breaking up let's hope he won't forget you in his will.'

"Then we went on with our work thinking no more about him till two days later up he turns again, comes down to the cabin of the *Greyhound*, pulls out a big handkerchief, blows his nose and wipes his eyes and starts his batteries.

"'Me child's going to die,' says he. 'Oh, it's the cruel disease as has caught hold of her. It's only trotting now but once it begins to gallop Doctor Hennessy says he won't give her a fortnight. Nothing will save her, he says, but a long sea voyage away from excitement with the good God's ozone round her. Steamships is no good and there's nothing in Frisco but Cape Horners and timber ships. Buck, you're me nephew, and by the same token you had the old *Greyhound* out of me for next to nothing, though I'm not worryin' about that. Take her for a trip and I'll pay the expenses; she can take the old Kanaka mammy with her, that brought her up, to look after her. If it's ten thousand dollars you can have it, but get her out into God's good ozone, away off to Honolulu and away round that way for a six months' trip. Fling your cargo in the harbor,' he says, 'and I'll pay, for it's me house is on fire and me child is burnin' and what do I care for money where her life is concerned?'

"'Sure,' said Buck, 'I'd take her jumping, but well you know I'm under contract, and as for throwing the cargo in the harbor, barring what the port authorities would say, it's not mine to throw."

"'Well,' says the old man, 'take her along with you, cargo and all. You've got an after cabin you don't use, with two bunks in it, that will do for them; you two bunk here in the main cabin, don't you? Well there you are, and I'll pay you a thousand dollars for the trip.'

"'Not a cent,' says Buck. 'I don't eat my relations when they're in trouble. If I take her she goes free — and, sure, how am I to refuse to take her seeing what you say?'

"'That's me brave boy,' says Pat, 'the true son of me sister Mary, God rest her soul.'

"Then when we'd done some more talk he goes off.

"'Well,' I says to Buck, 'here's a nice cargo.'

"I've told you Buck was married to a woman who had run away

from him. He'd never bothered to get divorced from her, fearing if he got among lawyers he'd be sure to be robbed and feeling that as he didn't ever want to get married again buying a divorce would be like a chap with no heart for music buying a concertina.

"'Well,' I says, rubbing it into him, 'here's a nice cargo. I'm no marrying man and you're hitched, so what's the good of her; a thousand dollars won't pay us for freightage and if there's a scratch on her when we get back, there'll be the devil to pay with Pat. S'pose she dies on us?' I says.

"'And what would she die of?' asks he.

"'Why, what but consumption?' says I.

"Buck laughed.

"'Consumption of victuals is all that's wrong with her,' he says, and then he says no more, but goes on deck leaving me harpooned.

"I'd taken in this consumption business as honest coin and now, by Buck's manner and words, I saw that Pat had been lying to us.

"The skylight was open and seeing Buck's shadow across it, I called him down and, 'For the love of Heaven,' I says, 'don't tell me that the old man has been stuffing us. What's his meaning?'

"'It's a family affair,' says Buck, 'and I'd sooner leave it at that till we get to the end of it. But if you ask his meaning, why I'll tell you straight that Pat has only one meaning in everything he does and that's robbery. He's making to best me. I can't see his game yet or what he is playing for, I can only say the stake's big or he wouldn't be pulling the girl into it.'

"'But where's the meaning of it?' I says, 'unless he's sending the girl to queer our pitch with Levenstein and that wouldn't be worth his trouble. There's not enough business doing at Levua to make it worth his while considering the big deals he's always after,'

"'Well,' says Buck, 'I don't know what's his game, but I'm going to find out.'

III.

"Day before we sailed, down came two trunks and a hatbox and the next day down came the girl herself with the old Kanaka mammy and Pat.

"He stood on the wharf-side and waved to us as we were tugged out, and Sadie stood and waved back to him. She had a lot of good points, that girl, though straight dealing wasn't one of them, and she didn't seem to mind, no more than if she was going on a picnic. She took the tumble at the bar as if she was used to it, and she settled to the life of the ship same as a man might have done.

"She was always wanting to know things — names of the ropes and all such, and she hadn't been a week on board before she began to poke her nose into the navigating and charts. She used to cough sometimes at first, but after a while she dropped all that, saying the sea air had taken her cough away.

"Now you wouldn't believe unless you'd been there, the down we took on that piece before a week had gone.

"It wasn't anything she said or anything she did, it was just the way she carried on. She was civil and she gave no more trouble than another might have done, but we weren't her style, and she made us feel it. Only a woman can make a strong and straight man feel like a worm. It wasn't even that she despised us for being below her class — she didn't. She never thought of us and she made us feel we weren't men but just things — get me?

"'Buck,' I says to him one day, 'if you could hollow that piece out, stick her on a pivot and put a lid on her, she'd make an A-1 freezing machine.'

"'She would,' said Buck, 'and if you were to plate her with gold and set her with diamonds you couldn't make a lady out of her.'

"'That's so,' said I, 'but all the same she'll be an A-1 navigator before she's done with us.'

"One evening somewhere north of Palmyra — we'd been blown a bit south of our course — I was on deck. Buck was below and a Kanaka was at the wheel and a moon like a frying pan was rising up and lighting the deck so's you could count the dowels. I'd turned to have a look over the after rail and when I turned again there was Buck just come on deck and an hour before his time.

"He came up and took me by the arm and walked me forward a bit.

"'I've found it out.' he says.

"'What?' I asks.

"'Why Pat O'Brien took Mrs. Murphy's child off to buy it candy,' he says.

"I thought he'd gone off his head for the moment.

"'I've been thinking and thinking ever since we left Frisco,' he goes on, 'thinking and thinking and there it was under my nose all the time.'

"'What?' I questions.

"'The reason of the whole of this business,' says he. 'Why Pat O'Brien, the brother of my mother Mary — God rest her soul — parted with five cents to buy a kid candy, why he asked us to dinner, why he pretended that freezing mixture down below had consumption, why he shipped her on board the *Greyhound* and what it is she's after. It's all as plain as day and there's more to it than that. Brent, we're millionaires.'

"'Look here,' I says, 'like a good chap. Will you take your mind off the business and pull yourself together — you've been thinking too much over this business. Forget it.'

"Buck was a queer devil. You never knew how he'd take things. Seeing I thought his head had gone wrong, instead of explaining like a sensible chap he cut the thing off short.

"'Maybe you're right,' he says. 'Maybe I'm crazy, maybe I'm not. I'll say nothing more. We'll see.'

"I left it at that, not wanting to stir up trouble in his head and we didn't talk of the thing again — not for a long time, anyhow.

"But a change had come over Buck. He'd got to be as cheerful as a cricket and I'd see him sometimes at table sitting staring in front of himself as if he was looking at the New Jerusalem, instead of the bird's-eye paneling of the after bulkhead. Then, by his talk I could tell his head was traveling on the same old track; when a man talks of the building price of steam yachts you can tell how his mind is running same as when he talks of rents on Pacific Avenue and such places. But I said nothing, just kept my head shut and let him talk and glad I was the morning we raised Levua.

"It's a big island — if you've never been down that way — moun-tainous and with no proper reef only to the west, for east the sea comes smack up to the cliffs — but it's pretty, what with the trees and all and there's a big waterfall comes down on the south from the hills that's reckoned one of the sights of the island.

"Levinstein's house was on the beach to the west. A run of reef, broken here and there, kept the sea pretty smooth on the beach and there was ten fathoms close up to the sand. A lot of scouring goes on there with the tides and the fishings, the best I've seen anywhere, just in that bit of water.

"Old Pat O'Brien hadn't asked to see a photograph of Levenstein, else maybe he wouldn't have been so keen on shipping Sadie off on her travels. I'd forgot the fellow's good looks, but when he boarded us after we'd dropped the hook I remembered the fact and I saw he'd taken Sadie's eye.

"Levenstein wasn't unlike Kaiser Bill, only younger and better looking. He was the sort women like and he could coo like a darn turtle dove when he was in the mind, but he had the reputation of having whipped a Kanaka to death. I'd just as soon have given a girl's happi-ness to that chap as I'd have given a rump steak to a tiger cat trustin' in it to honor it. No, sir, that build don't make for happiness, not much, and if Sadie had been my girl, when I saw her setting her eyes on him like that, I'd have put the *Greyhound* to sea again even if I'd had to shove her over the reef to get out.

"But I wasn't bothering about Sadie's happiness. I reckoned a little unhappiness mightn't do her much harm. I reckon Buck felt the same. So, having business in the trade room and ashore enough to last us for days, we let things rip and didn't bother.

"Sadie and the old mammy were given the overseer's house on shore and the girl settled down to enjoy herself. She was awfully keen on exploring the island and seeing the natives and she and the old Kanaka woman would make excursions, taking their grub with them and having picnics all over the place and Levenstein would go with her sometimes and Marks, from the north of the island, would come over sometimes, and it made my blood fair boil to see her carrying on with those two Germans because she thought them gentlemen, and at the same time cold-shouldering us as if we weren't more than the dirt she walked on.

"I said the same to Buck and Buck he only says: 'Leave her to me,' he says. 'She's come out to get what she won't get, but she'll get what she little expects if she marries Uncle Lev,' says Buck. 'Leave her to me,' he says, 'I'll l'arn her before I've done with her,' he says. 'Damn her!' says he — which wasn't the language to use about a girl, but then Sadie wasn't so much a girl as a china figure all prickles, no use to hold or carry and not the ornament you'd care to stick on your chimney piece if you wanted to be happy in your home.

"One day Buck says to me, 'Come on over to the north of the island,' he says. 'I want to have a talk to Marks.'

"What about?' I asks.

"'The beauty of the scenery,' he replies.

"Off we started. Germans are some good, they can made roads — if I haven't told you Levua was a German island, I'll tell you now. I'm saying Germans can make roads and if you doubt me go and see the twelve-mile coral road they've made round Nauzu or what they've done in German New Guinea, and the road to Mark's plantation was as good as those.

"Coming along for late afternoon we hit the place and found Marks in. Marks was like one of those Dutchmen you see in the comic papers, long china pipe and all, but he was the most level-headed man in the islands, and I soon found that Buck had come to him for information and not to talk about the beauty of the scenery.

"We had drinks and cigars and presently Buck says to Marks, 'Look here,' he says, 'you're a man that knows everything about the West Pacific. S'pose I found an island that wasn't on the charts and didn't belong to anybody, which of the blessed nations would make a claim to it? Would it be the one whose territory was closest to it?'

"Marks leans back in his chair and lights his pipe again, then he says, 'If you find an unknown island it would belong to England or Germany. All depends on where it lies in the West Pacific.'

"'How's that?' says Buck. 'Why wouldn't the French or Dutch have a look in?'

"'It's this way,' says Marks. 'Germany in old days wasn't a sea-going nation much and so the English and French and Dutch took up nearly all the islands of the Pacific, leaving Germany in the cold till 1865 when she began to want things and show that she could get them. She took a big bite of New Guinea, then she come to an arrangement with England that she and England would take all the lands and islands in the West Pacific no one else had seized and divide them between them. Get me?'

"'Yes,' says Buck.

"'The line starts from New Guinea,' says Marks, 'then goes east, then north to fifteen degrees north latitude, and one hundred and seventy-three degrees thirty seconds east longitude. Anything new found west of that would be German, anything to the east, British.'

"'Show us the line on a map,' says Buck, and Marks gets up and fetches down a map and draws the line with a pencil.

"Buck gives a great sigh and thanks him and then we started off back home with the rising moon to show us our way and a three hours' tramp before us.

"On the way I tried to get out of him what his meaning was in asking those questions, but he wouldn't tell.

"'You thought I was mad when I tried to tell you first,' he said, 'and now you'll have to wait till I've landed the business. But I'll tell you one thing —'

"'What?' I asks.

"'Never mind,' he says. 'Shut heads are best where a word might spoil everything.'

IV.

"Three weeks at Levua got the cargo out and the cargo in, and the morning came when we were due to start. Sadie and Levenstein had been getting thicker and thicker. She was one of those girls that take the bit between the teeth and it didn't knock us down with surprise when, coming on board with her trunks, she said she'd been married that morning to Mr. Levenstein by the native parson and that Levenstein was going to follow her on to Frisco by the next boat he could catch.

"Did you ever hear of such a tomfool arrangement? She could just as well have waited till he got to Frisco and then she'd have had time to change her mind. That's what Buck told her as we put out, with Levenstein waving to us from the shore.

"Buck handed it to her proper, he being a relative and all that, but I doubt if he wasn't as glad as myself to think of the face Pat would pull when he found his daughter had married herself to a small, island trader and a German at that. She took his lip without saying a word and a day or two after she made inquiries as to when we should reach Palm Island.

"'Oh, in a day or two,' says Buck.

"Now we weren't due to touch at that place for fourteen days if the wind held good and when I got him alone a few minutes later I asked him why he had told her that lie.

"'And what would you have had me say?' he asked.

"'Why, that we wouldn't be there for a fortnight,' I answered.

"'Well,' said he, 'that would have been as big a lie for we aren't going to touch there at all. I've got extra water casks from that cooper chap at Levua and an extra supply of bananas.'

"'What's your reason?' I asks.

"'I'll tell you when this deal is through,' he answers, and knowing it was useless to ask any more, I didn't.

"A few days later Buck told us that we'd passed the location of the island and that it wasn't there, must have sunk in the sea, he said, same as these small islands sometimes do.

"When he sprung this on us you might have thought by the way Sadie went on she'd lost a relative. Said that she wanted to see it more than the New Jerusalem owing to Buck's description of it, and asked couldn't we poke round and make sure it was gone and that we weren't being deceived owing to some error of the compass.

"Buck says: 'All right,' and we spent the better part of two days fooling about pretending to look for that darn island and then we lit for Frisco.

"No sooner had we got there and landed the cargo, Sadie included, than Buck says to me one morning, 'Clutch on here,' he says, 'while I'm away. I'm going to London.'

"'London, Ontario?' I asks.

"'No, London, England,' he says.

"'And what are you going there for?' I questions.

"'To see the Tower,' says he.

"Off he goes and in two months he returns.

V.

"I was sitting at breakfast when he comes in, having arrived by the early-morning train.

"Down he sits and has a cup of coffee.

"'How's Pat?' says he.

"'You're even with Pat,' I says. 'Levenstein got here a week ago and Pat don't like his new son-in-law. There's been the devil to pay.'

" I'm better even with him than that,' says Buck. 'Brent, we're millionaires.'

"'Spit your meaning out,' I says.

"'Do you remember,' says he, 'my saying to you last time we touched at Palm Island that the place seemed built of a sort of rock I'd never seen before and my bringing a chunk of it away in my pocket? Well, what do you think that rock is but phosphate of lime.'

"'What's that?' I queries.

"'Seagull guano mixed with the lime of coral,' he says, 'the finest fertilizer in the world and worth thirteen to fourteen dollars a ton. How many tons would Palm Island weigh, do you think? — and it's most all phosphate of lime.'

"I begins to sweat in the palms of my hands but I says nothing and he goes on.

"'Palm Island being a British possession, since an Irishman has discovered it and it lies to eastward of the German-British line, I went to London and I've got not only the fishing rights but the mining rights for ninety-nine years. I didn't say nothing about the mining rights, said I wanted to start a cannery there since the fishing was so good and an old cockatoo in white whiskers did the rest and dropped the mining rights in gratis, like an extra strawberry. Then, coming through N'York I got a syndicate together that'll buy the proposition when they've inspected it. I'll take a million or nothing,' says he.

"'But, look here,' I says, 'how in tarnation did it all happen; how did you know?'

"'Well,' says he, 'it was this way. That chunk of rock I was telling you of, I stuck in my sea chest, and unpacking when I got back I gave it to little Micky Murphy who was in the room pretending to help me. He used it for a play toy.

"Now do you remember Pat O'Brien that morning he left us, talking to Micky outside, and taking him off to buy candy? Well, next day Mrs. Murphy said to me that the old gentleman was very free with his money but she didn't think he was quite right as he'd offered Micky a dollar for the stone he was playing with. I didn't think anything of it at the time, but later on — you remember that night on board ship — the thing hit me like a belt on the head.

"'Micky had told the old chap I'd given him the stone when I came back from that trip and Pat had recognized it for what it was. The only question that bothered him was where I'd picked it up. He knew I traded regular with Levua and when he found we stopped nowhere but Levua and Palm Island he knew it was at one of those two places. Phosphate of lime was to be found, enough maybe to double his fortune. He sent the girl to prospect, and she'd have done me in only that night I suddenly remembered a chap telling me about the phosphate business and saying the stuff was like rock, striped in places. I'd never thought of it till then and what made me think of it was that I'd been worrying a lot since I'd left Frisco over Pat and all his doings. Seems to me the mind does a lot of thinking we don't know of.'

"'Well,' I says, 'when he set the girl to prospect he didn't bargain she was going to prospect Levenstein.'

"'No,' says Buck, 'seems to me we've got the double bulge on him.'

"But we hadn't.

"Buck got a million for his phosphate rights and gave me a share, and, as much will have more, we flew high and lost every buck in the Eagle Consolidated Gold and Silver Mining Corporation, Inc.

"Pat met us the day after the bust and we asked him how the Levensteins were doing.

"'Fine,' says he. 'He asked me how to become a millionaire last night and I told him it was quite easy, you only had to pick up a million and stick to it.' 'But mind you,' I said, 'it's not the picking it up's the bother, but the sticking to it. Now look at that Eagle Consolidated business,' I says, 'many's the fine boy has put his money in tripe stock like that, tumbling balmy after working for years like a sensible man.'

"'You know the stock I mean,' he finishes. 'The Eagle Consolidated Gold and Silver Mining Corporation, Inc.'

"'Yes, I know,' says Buck.

"We didn't want to have no last words or let the old boy rub it in any more so we hiked off, Buck and me, resuming our way to the wharf and the same old life we'd always been living but for the three months we'd been million-dollar men.

"Pat seemed to have the joke on us," added Brent, "but looking back on those three months and the worries and dyspepsias and late hours that make a millionaire's life, I'm not so sure we hadn't the bulge on him over the whole transaction, 'specially considering that Levenstein went bust, forged checks and let him in for forty thousand or so to save the name of the family.

"That's the last transaction we ever had with Pat," finished Brent. "He dropped calling on us to tell us how to become millionaires, seeing we'd given instructions to Mrs. Murphy always to tell him we were out."

BLIGHT

TOWNLEY is an insignificant-looking little man till you look at his face; then you forget his size and all the things that at a first glance make for insignificance, for his face is lit by a spirit, patient and indomitable, kindly, genial, and full of genius.

He is a doctor and his patients live in all sorts of places. He has been called to consultations in the forests of India, in the forests of the Amazon, in the plantations of English dukes and American million-aires, always in places where trees grow, for his patients are trees. He is a tree doctor. He will attend vines and bushes and flowers, but trees are his specialty, or, rather, sick trees, and if you can get Townley to talk on the subject he will tell you that trees and plants and flowers are just like men and women and children, subject to cancer, subject to tumors, par-asitic diseases and all sorts of maladies, some known, some partly known, some unknown. That they can show like and dislike, that they can fret and pine. He will tell you that flowers and plants and trees require love as well as attention, that Luther Burbank is a lover as well as a magician and that the roses of Dean Hole drew their perfection from the heart of the gardener no less than from the soil of the garden. And so he will go on till you fancy yourself talking to a mystic and a poet, and you will be right, he is both, but he is also one of the most practical men on earth. He was born and educated in England; and his genius came to him perhaps through his father who was a gardener at Kew. But England could not hold him, her ideas were too small, her trees too few. In America where tree doctoring is a profession and pa-tients to be reckoned in hundreds of millions, he found his soil. A book on transplantation published when he was twenty-five gave him fame right off, and he never looked back.

However, I am not setting out to write a biography of William Townley, but a story he told me and which has more to do with men than trees. This is his story.

* * *

"I thought I knew something about rubber at that time. I had studied it, vine and tree — under glass. I thought I knew something about men, too, I had studied them, man and boy — but under glass, as you may say. I hadn't then come on to the fact that all man's experience contained in mind and books is a small thing compared to what he doesn't know of man and nature. Men run in a herd in a big groove of their own cutting, the country around is pretty much unknown. Even Shakespeare ran in it else his works wouldn't be of universal appeal.

"I had not seen the Amazon then, either, and he who has not seen the Amazon has not really seen God.

"It was a book of mine on the parasitic diseases of trees that brought me the letter, and the letter was from Colonel Alonzo Perreira, of the Esperanza plantation on the right bank of the Amazon, one thousand seven hundred and fifty miles from the mouth. It was a strange letter, typewritten in faultless English, practical in a way, yet producing on my mind the feeling that the writer was under the dominion of an agitation and an urgency not entirely accountable for in the matter.

"The trees on the Esperanza estate had come under a blight of some sort, that was the gist of the business, he wanted me to come and see them, to come at once, without a moment's delay. Money was of no object, absolutely none, and after all this and the signature was the postscript in manuscript, 'Come, I pray you, at once.'

"He gave me the name of his agents in Philadelphia, Milligan & Forsyth. I wrote them and got the reply that Perreira was the richest rubber man on the Amazon, that he had cabled me a credit on them of twenty thousand dollars — ending with the perfectly superfluous advice that I would be well advised from a monetary point of view to take up the proposition.

"I was not thinking so much of the money. I wanted to see the Amazon, I wanted to see those sick trees, and I wanted to see Perreira, this multimillionaire who lived seventeen hundred miles from Para, which lies seventeen hundred miles from everywhere. It seemed to me that Perreira was as sick as his trees. My mind is like that. I sometimes imagine things, and sometimes I am right.

"That letter was the call of a sick man, it seemed to me, not the hail of a planter only concerned about his pocket. The fancy came to me that Perreira loved his trees and then, somehow, my mind refused that idea for no special reason. I sometimes refuse ideas for no special reason, and sometimes I am right.

"But I was going. They have a cable up the Amazon, and I cabled that day, Saturday, it was, and on the Tuesday following I started.

"I had fixed my fee at ten thousand dollars and traveling expenses, I could have had twenty, but I wanted a holiday and I wanted to see the Amazon, and I am not a hog, anyway.

"I took passage up the Amazon in a big ocean-going steamer, the R. M. S. *Tamar*, and I was on deck most of the time I was not asleep or at meals. The Amazon is not a river, it is a moving sea, and all the trees in the world seem to have grouped themselves on the banks to watch it; palms and matamatas and sand boxes, embaubas and ferns, in leagues and millions, and the forests you drop at sunset you pick up at dawn with the blue toucans still yelping over them and the great butterflies coming out to see the ship, and the blazing parrots screeching at her, and the egrets drifting over her like puffs of snow, white as the egrets you dropped a thousand miles back, and the river just as broad and the trees just as many and as new and fresh and green as they were before the pyramids were built or Egypt thought of.

"Then one morning at breakfast the captain said to me, 'In an hour we will be at the Esperanza landing stage.'"

"Then as I stood on deck with my traps beside me I saw the plantation open beyond a cape of trees and the landing stage, big as a deep-sea wharf, and in another ten minutes I was shaking hands with Perreira. He had come down to meet me and he was something of the sort of man I had expected to meet; nervy, dried up and dark as a native, a Peruvian of the best sort and with all the manners of a Spanish grandee.

"I liked him, right off, but I did not like his house, nor the dinner he put before me that day. I was unused to houses with scarcely any furniture, to farina and black beans and coffee without sugar or milk, but one gets used to most things after a little while, and after a while I got used to Perreira's way of living; I had other things to think of besides comfort and food.

"Those trees — the second day I was there he took me off into the forest past a palm belt and into the true jungle where the giants stood festooned with climbing vines and bush ropes, then close to a pachuaba palm, standing on its exposed roots as if they were stilts, he showed me a rubber tree, the first we had come on. He showed me where it had been tapped.

"'You see,' said Perreira, 'it has given scarcely any milk, look at it, touch it, it is sick.'

"It was. I could see that at a glance. The bark had a leprous look, dry beyond ordinary, and scaling off in parts, though not much.

"'Let's look at another,' said I.

"'There is no use,' said Perreira, 'they are all the same, for hundreds of miles, wherever my estate reaches, they are the same. It began last year. It does not reach beyond my estate, the blight only touches me.'

"'That is strange,' said I.

"'Yes,' said he, 'it is strange.'

"He said no more but stood looking at me as I cut some of the bark off for microscopical examination, then we went back to the house and I set to work that day in the little laboratory he had rigged up for me. I worked for several days and with entirely negative results. I could discover no fungus or parasite to account for the condition of the bark. There was a thickening of the cellular tissue and the fistular cavities were reduced in size, empty, or blocked. That was all.

"On the night when I told Perreira of my results we were sitting in his office, which was the coolest and pleasantest room in the house, in cane rockers and with a table laden with rum, crushed ice, lime juice, and cigars between us.

"'You can arrive at no conclusion, then,' said he, 'except that my trees are dying from, shall we say, a general debility without appreciable cause?'

"'That is so,' I replied.

"'In your book,' said he, 'there is a chapter at the end which speaks of the likes and dislikes of trees, a strange chapter in a practical book, yet it was the mind revealed in that chapter that caused me to send for you; here, said I, is a man who sees beyond the surface and who is not afraid to say what he sees and to whom I can speak what I think. Now I am going to tell you what I think. I would not tell it to any other man but you. I think my trees are blighted by an act of mine; that they are dying because, out there in the forest, many days journey from here, my brother lies dead and unburied.'

"'Did you kill him?' said I.

"The words came from me almost without volition, our minds seemed for a moment absolutely in tune, and it was as though I had read his thoughts and repeated them like a gramophone.

"'In a way I did,' replied he, as though the question were quite an ordinary one. Then he rose up and began to mix some drinks at the little table where the tray stood. I watched him as he handled the sugar and the rum and the pounded ice, measuring everything carefully, but doing so, evidently, with his mind a thousand miles away.

"Then, when he had handed me my drink, he took his own and sat down again in the cane rocker.

"'I will tell you exactly what happened,' said he, 'and how it happened, but I must first tell you that we are an unlucky family — or were, for I am the last of them all. My grandfather was a trader of Lima and my father inheriting all his wealth began trade in rubber with Para and eventually took up this estate. He was a hard man to the natives, and he was killed one day by a blowgun man; walking in the garden here something flecked his cheek and stuck to it; he plucked it off thinking it was a flying insect and found that it was a blowgun dart. He knew that he must die in twenty minutes or so, and, coming into the house, he made his will leaving the estate to my eldest brother, Ramon. Juan, the second eldest, was appointed overseer under Ramon, with succession in the event of Ramon's death, while I, the youngest, was directed to study law so that I might be of assistance to my brothers in the management of the business. My father was a very clever man, and he knew the tricks of lawyers and how they prey on business men for the sake of their fees, I was to be the lawyer of the firm, with a share in the profits of the business and succession to the estate should I survive the others. Having made his will and smoked a cigarette, he died. I said we were an unlucky family, and three was our unlucky number. We were three, nine is a multiple of three, and nine years after the death of my father my eldest brother Ramon died a violent death. He was out crocodile shooting with Juan and the breech of his rifle burst, killing him.

"'I was at Para when the news reached me, and I came here by the first steamer and found Juan quite broken down with grief. Juan was a big, domineering, violent-tempered man, yet I found him on my arrival in tears, weak as a woman and the shadow of his old self, without volition and with only one desire — to get rid of the estate. All this surprised me, for I had loved Ramon far more than Juan had appeared to love him, yet I was myself, though, indeed, sad enough, as you may imagine.

"'I did not wish to part with the estate, and without my consent a sale would have been impossible. I argued with Juan, pointing out the folly of such a course with rubber increasing in value as it then was, offering at the same time to leave Para and come up and help him in the practical working of the business. He agreed with this, and after a while he began to recover and find his old interest in life, and in six months he was himself again, domineering, violent-tempered, a hog — as you say in America — for work and the terror of the malingerers and bad hands. A man difficult to get on with, yet with whom I never had a difference, for I knew his temper to a hair and managed to lead him by humoring him.

"'So it went on for three years — for three years, mark you — till, one day, Pedro, the chief of the workers on the estate, came back from the forests with a tale.

"'Pedro had been sent with half a dozen of the hands on an exploring expedition with a view to discovering new rubber tracts. You must know that this estate is so vast that for us, the owners, or, rather, for me the owner, it is beyond the river belt in large parts, unknown.

"'Pedro at a point six days' journey away had found a rich rubber tract, but he had found something else which in his flowery language he described as a river of gold. He had done gold mining in his young days and he was not wrong. He had found a river with large deposits of auriferous sand and from the specimens he brought back with him we determined that the thing was worth exploring. That was human nature. We were rich, richer than many an American millionaire, for our riches rested on the firm foundation of the forests, they and Para were our real gold mines, yet, such is the power of the yellow metal that we could not rest and we, who had gold a thousand times beyond our needs, dreamed of gold and talked of gold as though we were beggars. We set about making preparations for a great expedition. We arranged to take twenty men including Pedro and to build a hut or *tambo* at the end of each day's march so that, were the river to prove workable, we might establish a regular road to it through the jungle with resting places for the gold getters and their burdens.

"'All our men were native to the spot and used to the forests, with that instinct for direction which the forest breeds in men. We started on a Tuesday and the third of the month, and just as the sun was rising above the trees.

"'Pedro led the way with the hands and we followed on the beaten track left by them. We had bad luck from the first, one of the men injuring his foot against the thorny stem of a pachiuba palm. We had to lie up for a day at the first *tambo* we built. We built our second *tambo*, like fools, close to a great patch of embauba trees. These trees, you must know, are poisonous with malaria. Pedro said it did not matter, so far from the river, but he was wrong, for next morning Juan was in a fever. No one else was touched. I wished to delay the march or even return till he was better, but he would not listen to this. It was not in his nature to turn back or to lie up for a touch of fever, so we pushed on ever deeper into the forest and ever farther from help. He was worse that night, but the next morning he declared himself better, though his appearance had now begun to alarm me; his face was shrunk and his eyes were brilliant

as the eyes of a woman at a fête, and his hands shook as they held the
coffee cup, but his legs, under the dominion of his powerful will,
seemed unaffected. He would go forward, and forward we went.

"'That evening he seemed better. We had now reached the fringe
of the true wilderness, the rubber trees had ceased, and we had struck a
great belt of matamatas and fig which grow together finely. Mixed with
them were unknown trees, and everywhere the vine and the liantasse
and brush rope festooned the air; the trees seemed hung with drapery of
torn lace festooned with orchids, and the air shoots of the wild pine and
the tubes of the water vine rushed up through the gloom to be lost where
the parrots shrieked and the monkeys chattered.

"'The moon was near the full, and when she rose the noises of the
night began; you have heard the Mother of the Moon, that little owl
which fills the night here with its melancholy cry, but you have not
heard it out there in the forest, nor the roar of the howling monkeys
rocking themselves on the branches, nor the hundred sounds made by
unknown things that only speak at night when the moon turns all that
place into a great green cave like a cave of the sea where the vines and
the air shoots seem climbing up through green and waving water.

"'Next morning Juan declared himself still better, but it was the
declaration of a man on the verge of bankruptcy. He did not know it, nor
did I know that the fever, though suppressed, was still working in him,
so we pushed on making good progress day by day, each night building
a *tambo*, a work that only took the hands three hours, and each morning
leaving it behind us. So it went on till we had built our sixth resting
place by the bank of the little river that held the gold.

"'Pedro had spoken truth. The river is small, but it is there, and its
mud and sand are laden with gold deposited through the ages and
brought down from some source of gold far up to the west, but maybe,
indeed, not so far — who can tell?

"'We are rich,' said Juan as he sat that night when we had finished
washing and weighing a specimen of the sand taken at haphazard, 'we
are rich enough to command fleets and armies. We will be kings.'

"I had never heard him talk in an extravagant way before; it was the fever that he had been carrying for days like a demon in his bosom and which was now about to claim him.

"'At supper he talked like a man drunk. I thought it was the gold; it was the fever. Next morning I knew.

"'Ah, that was a bad time, six days' march from any help, with few drugs and the roughest food, without a woman for a nurse, for in sickness as in childhood what can we do without a woman's hand?

"'The *tambo* was given over to the sick man, and for three days he lay fighting the disease with what poor help we could give him, then on the evening of the third day he sent for me. I was asleep in a shack we had built among the trees when Pedro called me saying that Juan wished for me at once. I came, and there he was, lying on the bed of leaves we had made for him, his eyes half closed and his hands folded on his breast.

"'He opened his eyes when he heard my step and motioned me to sit down on the ground beside him. Then he closed his eyes for a moment. I thought he had fallen asleep, but he was not asleep. Suddenly in a clear, sane voice he began to speak to me.

""'When I sent for you from Para," said he, "I told you that Ramon had died from an accident, that his gun had burst while he was out shooting with me. Have you seen that gun?"

""'No," I replied, wondering what he meant. I thought for a moment that his mind was wandering, but I dismissed that idea, his manner and his tone spoke of perfect sanity.

""'No," he replied, "you took my word for it, you did not ask for evidence of his death, you did not imagine that I lied to you. Ramon did not die from an accident. I killed him."

""'You killed him!'

""'I killed him. Would you prefer the word murder? I murdered him. I am near death, and I wish to confess."

"'I sat with my hands folded. I knew he was speaking the truth, my tongue lay like a pebble in my mouth. Then I said:

"'You murdered Ramon!'

""'Call it that," he said.

""'But why — but why?' I asked, speaking as though to get out of a darkness that had suddenly surrounded me. 'Why — why?'

"'It was done in passion, about a girl," he replied. "She favored him; I loved her; he was the real master of Esperanza. I never cared for Ramon — you know my temper; I often held it in, often; he always managed to cross my wishes, yet I held my temper in. I hated him at times, for he was always right on business matters, and somehow I was always wrong, that touched my pride. Then I fell in love; she was the daughter of a *seringuero*, as low down as that, but she had eyes like the night; but Ramon had been before me with her, she would not look at me, the daughter of a *seringuero*.

""'Then Ramon and I had our quarrel, and I killed him in the woods not far from that spit where the alligators sun themselves. We had our guns with us. I wrapped his head in leaves and threw his gun in the river beyond the spit, where it lies six fathoms deep. I carried him home and told the hands it was an accident; there is no questioning of statements at Esperanza.

""'I killed him, and now that I am dying I tell you and ask your forgiveness."

"'I sat without speaking. Ramon was my favorite brother, this thing had stricken the life in me, Juan was dying, the whole world seemed suddenly to have come to an end.

"'He asked me to forgive him. I scarcely knew what he meant. I had no anger in my heart, only grief. Had he been strong and well all would have been different, then rage would have filled me, no doubt, and I would have avenged Ramon or handed the murderer to justice, but he was dying and he had confessed. Did I forgive him? Before God, I cannot say whether I did or not. I cannot read my mind as it was just then. It seemed, indeed, just then a blank, but I know that when he asked again, 'Do you forgive me?" I answered, "Yes."

""'Then," said he, "I die in peace." He closed his eyes and I left the *tambo*.

"'The sun was setting and the open space by the river was filled with the light of sunset, great moths flew in the golden, gauzy light and the smell of the forest was altering; few men seem to have noticed this change in the scents that fill the air of the forest when day begins to turn into night. I believe I myself had not noticed it till just then. My senses had suddenly become more acute as though the shock I had received had sharpened them, also my perception of things, as though my mind, ever so slightly joggled from its base, were seeing things from a fresh viewpoint.

"'Right before me between two branches a bird-eating spider had spread its huge web in which a little colored bird had become entangled. This thing which was common seemed to me new and monstrous and strange — strange as the new world which had suddenly surrounded me.

"'I walked a little way among the trees, and, taking my seat on a fallen log, I tried to pull my mind together, to think and to remember.

"'Pictures of Ramon came up before me and of our boyhood. I had always been his favorite. I was the youngest brother, rather delicate, the spoiled child of the family. Ramon had always stood between me and the rough things of life, he had been generous to me with money. Had I forgiven his murderer?

"'Had I betrayed Ramon? Looking into my heart I could find no anger against Juan. Death had intervened, destroying anger and the thoughts of vengeance, but I had not forgiven him. I had said the words, it is true, but I had spoken out of a mind rendered negative by contending forces and under dominion of the great power exercised by the dying.

"'That power was on me still.

"'I left the trees and returned toward the *tambo*. Pedro and the others had lit a fire some distance away. It was now dark, and the flicker of it showed against the night of the trees and strangely fierce against the still silver of the moonlight.

"'At the door of the *tambo* I paused. There was no sound. I entered and struck a match. Juan was still lying on his back with his hands folded, but he was not dead; he was sunk in a profound sleep, his face had changed, miraculously as though he had gained ten years of youth and his forehead was dewed by a gentle perspiration. Death had passed him by, the fever had left him, he would not die; he would recover and be well and strong again. He had been at the turning point when he had sent for me to make his confession, and that sudden ease coming to his mind had cast the die for life.

"'The match went out. I lit another and stood till it burned my fingers gazing on him.

"'Then I went out into the night and came to the fire where Pedro and the others were seated smoking, with the great white moths flitting about them and the great white moon shining above. I told them that I would look after Juan that night and then I went and lay down in my shack among the trees with all the noises of the forest around me and the great problem before me staring at me like a sphinx.

"'My forgiveness was withdrawn with the withdrawal of death. I was now the judge and also the guardian of the honor of our house and its good name.

"'Would you believe me that in that terrible position and freighted with that great trust, I slept? I slept as soundly as the man in the *tambo*, and with the first screaming of the parrots and yelping of the toucans I woke.

"'The dawn was strong, and, creeping toward the hut, I looked in. Juan was still asleep, lying, now, on his right side and breathing easily and lightly, I entered and, listening, I counted his respirations. They were normal. In an hour or so he would wake a new man, weak, very weak, but on the road to recovery. Yet he must never return to Esperanza. I did not say that, Justice said it, and the ghosts of my forefathers and the ghost of Ramon.

"'I left the place, and, going to where the men were still asleep, I woke Pedro.

"'"Pedro," said I, "Senhor Juan is dead, rouse the hands, collect the stores, and give the order to march. There is no need to dig a grave, the *tambo* will be his tomb, so he has willed it."

"'The men awoke yawning in the light that was now full, and without question, and like beasts of burden they shouldered their loads.

Pedro gave the order to march, and they wheeled back along the road we had come, I, following, leaving the golden river and the sleeping man, who was my brother, in the *tambo* that was to be his tomb.

"'You are the only man who knows this and now my heart seems lighter. You can understand, and also that the judge pays for his office a far larger sum than the salary he receives. That was three years ago, and now see in the third year my trees are telling me that my payment is due. I have got to die like them, but first I have got to bury what remains of Juan. It is all a fate working out intricately. I don't know how I will die, maybe the fever will take me as it took him when I make my journey into the forest to find his bones and to bury them.'

"I made that journey with him," finished Townley. "When he had told me that story it was as though a strong bond had been woven between us. I went with him. We found the old ruined *tambos*, one by one, but we did not reach the river, for in the fourth *tambo* from the start we found a skeleton. It was the skeleton of Juan. He had dragged himself back thus far, miraculously, despite the want of food and the weakness that must have been his. It was the knowledge of this fact that killed Perreira — with the help of a Mauser pistol.

"We buried the brothers beneath a great matamata tree.

"That is the Amazon, where the men are as strange as the trees, and the trees as the river, and where the great plantations turn rubber into gold that no man can spend in a climate that few men can live in — where the sure things are fever and fate and the shouting of the toucans by day and the roaring of the howling monkeys by night."

BRUTUS

IF YOU want to know the truth about things you must go among the men who make a practice of life. Only yesterday I met a perfectly luminous tramp on the Cambridge road who showed me an England quite different from the England I knew — or thought I knew — and, eleven years ago this June, Siebert, the big-game hunter told me a story that cast a new light for me on the human and the animal creations.

Siebert at that date ranked third, after Selous and Schillings, among the famous big-game hunters of the world. He is dead, so is Selous, and Schilling alone remains of that trio whose chief glory was their understanding of the beasts they hunted.

He was a big man, quick of action but slow of speech; I had met him years before in Africa and meeting him again in a German town, I went with him one day to the zoological gardens to see the beasts.

At that date the Berlin Zoo was far behind the London, and maybe still is. The German African colonies sent practically nothing and, as Schillings notes, Manges was the chief importer and his animals came chiefly from Somaliland. The other zoological gardens of Germany were no better, a fact that Siebert lamented as we passed along from cage to cage till we came to the rhinoceros.

He stood there in his enclosure, his broadside turned to us, a huge brute, five feet high at the shoulder and twelve, if an inch, from rump to snout; the anterior horn must have been four feet in length, a mighty weapon, but useless against the iron bars of his prison. Motionless, as though carved from granite, he seemed asleep or dreaming under the hot sunshine of the July day and the faint breeze blowing across the pen brought us his musky scent.

"Now, if we were to go to the other side and get to windward of him," said Siebert, "he would rouse up and come to us. He knows me and would pick me out by my smell. I was the man who brought him to Germany many years ago when he and I were younger than we are now. Brutus was the name I gave him and it sticks to him still with the keepers. If you go to the Berlin Zoo you will see Fatima, the rhinoceros presented by Schillings, a female and the first to be brought to Germany. These are the only two beasts of the sort in the country."

There was a shady seat near by and we sat down to rest while Siebert went on.

"A man said to me some time ago, 'When you die, Siebert, aren't you afraid that all the animals you have killed will haunt you, and hunt you in the spirit world?' I said, 'Not a bit, death is nothing in the wilderness, but sometimes I am doubtful of my reception by the animals and birds I have exported, giving them the bars of a prison and taking from them the one great gift — freedom.' Well, I don't know whether beasts have souls, but in captivity the wildest of them will show you a mind if you know where to look for it. I'm going to tell you a story about Brutus known only to myself, Kemplin, and a woman. I think it will interest you but anyhow it won't take long in the telling.

"Kemplin in those days was the rival of Manges. He had a place outside Hamburg and he supplied Hagenbeck, I believe, as well as the different German zoos. He was an extraordinary man, a trader pure and simple, hard, without pity. I was going to say heartless, but that would be wrong; he had what one might call an intellectual heart. Not only was he kind to his animals out of policy. He understood them. From what I have seen of the world more men have an understanding of Greek than of animals and the understanding is based on sympathy. With Kemplin its basis was logic.

"He commissioned me to supply him with a variety of specimens, offered me prices higher than I was likely to get elsewhere, and a week later, having settled up my affairs, I left Hamburg on my sixth African expedition. German East Africa was my hunting ground and at Tanga I got my expedition together, bearers and askaris, nearly a hundred and fifty men all told.

"This was quite a different business from the ordinary hunting expedition. I was out more to catch than to kill and I had five or six absolutely dependable men with me for the purpose of taking live specimens back to Tanga there to wait my return; all the same I did a good deal of hunting for the sake of hides and tusks and there was lots to be done in that way for it was after the rains and the whole country was out. The herds were on the move and by the Rufu River the buffaloes were coming down to drink, clouds of gazelles showed moving In the distance where today the gazelles may be reckoned by dozens and on that expedition I met with eight or ten roan antelope, yet today the roan antelope is all but extinct.

"Day after day the snows of Kilimangaro stood clearer and higher in the blue sky and day after day the country before us grew more vast.

"It is the attribute of a great mountain that it casts its size like a cloak on the country around it and on the soul of the observer.

"Day by day the storks flew overhead for it was the season of the migration of the storks, and day by day the game we met with showed less knowledge of man — that is to say, less fear.

"We met in with elephants at the big bend of the Rufu. I secured four pairs of tusks, the longest weighing some two hundred and fifty pounds, and then, leaving the Rufu, we struck for the hills surrounding Manyara Lake.

"I had sent back two lots of specimens to the coast and now I was so far from Tanga that I had to arrange a central depot, a halfway house, and I chose a native village midway betwccn the Rufu and Manyara. Here I put up for two days to rest and make arrangements which included the purchase of half a dozen cows. Exporters fail as a rule because they fail to assure a supply of milk for the young animals they catch, but I was used to the game and taught by experience, and so established my nursery, the first denizen of which was a young elephant. A little pinkish brute, not very much bigger than a big Newfoundland dog. I labeled him Carlo — it is one of my fads, I suppose, but an animal always names itself to me and once I have given it its name we always get on well together.

"One of my men happened the day after upon a lioness with one whelp. She was lying in the long grass, disabled. I had never seen a case like it before, both front paws were affected by jiggers, those beastly parasites that are the curse of Africa. They were inflamed to the size of boxing gloves. She could not walk or crawl and I shot her, taking the cub, which I named Ponto.

"Next day I met Brutus.

"I was pushing on for the lake when one of the askaris struck fresh rhino spoor. An hour after, getting along for sundown, I saw what looked like the stump of an old tree away to the east. Next moment I saw it was a rhino. Through the glasses I saw it was a female. I could only see the head and anterior horn and a foot of the shoulder but the horn was enough. The horn of the female is thinner and different from the horn of the male.

"I reckoned she might have young with her and that here was a chance of getting what Kemplin hungered for more than heaven — a young rhino.

"The wind had fallen dead. I lit a match and the flame stood up without a bend or quiver — it might have been carved from cairngorm.

"Then I spread my men to circle as much as possible the place where she was and that done, I began to creep toward her.

"She had sunk down again in the thick stuff. I could see nothing as I drew close to the great tuft of which she formed the unseen center and the rhinoceros birds, as one sometimes finds in the case of a female with young, were absent.

"I had not gone two yards when suddenly a coolness came to the nape of my neck and the long grasses of the tuft quivered. A breeze had suddenly risen. I remembered it was near sundown and cursed my luck.

"I knew that she would have beaten down the grass in the center of the tuft till it was like a great pie dish and I was reckoning on the chance of getting close enough to fire through the grass wall. That was all up. The breeze had scarcely stirred the cover when I heard her getting her legs under her, and then out she came.

"That chap there is half blind, all the rhinoceros folk are and his mother was no exception, but she had the scent of me and she was charging down it holding on to it as a half-blind man might hold on to a leading string.

"Every second it grew stronger and every second her fury increased. If you can imagine the engine of the Cologne express armed with purpose and a horn you can imagine what the mother of Brutus looked like to me as I stood there tied to the metals, you may say, and right in front of her as she came, Brutus after her.

"I fired twice. The first bullet made her swerve, the second got her through the heart and next moment my arms were round the neck of Brutus. He had charged me with his chunky head but I had managed to get my grip. Three of my men came up at the run and between us we managed to get him back to camp.

"I tied him to a tree and then he stood dazed and stupefied with no more fight in him, swinging his box-shaped head slowly from side to side. He seemed tamed all of a sudden but I would sooner have seen him in a fighting mood. I brought him a pan of milk and tried to feed him with a Heinz pickle bottle. I let him sniff the milk in the pan, knowing it would talk to him and tell him he wasn't among enemies, but he cared nothing for enemies or friends and wouldn't touch food. Ten o'clock that night it was just the same and I knew he was going to die. Well, next morning, when I came out of my tent I found he had chummed up with a goat.

"Bimbi, one of the goats that were with us had sniffed him out in the night and there they were close together and as thick as thieves, and a couple of hours later he took his first milk.

"Well, I got him to the coast and I got him across seas, to Hamburg, him and the goat, to say nothing of the other specimens, and Kemplin was pleased. To Kemplin it was not a baby rhinoceros so much as victory over Manges and the rest, to say nothing of the profit. He was so pleased that he asked me to stay at his place a fortnight for a rest, and I did.

"For the first day or two the telegrams were coming and going all the time negotiating for the sale of Brutus. Then, one morning Kemplin came into my room in his pajamas.

"Said he, 'The goat's dead!'

"It was; it had died in the night and the body had been removed.

Brutus was moving about here and there in his pen, fretful and restless, he had taken no food. Kemplin was at his wit's end. He had another goat brought and Brutus turned on it when he had got its scent and charged it like a battering ram. He had no horn, but he knocked it to the rails and we got it out half dead.

"At six o'clock that evening his mood changed to depression and next day at noon we knew it was all up with him. He had taken no milk for twenty-four hours.

"Kemplin had resigned himself to the loss and as we stood there watching the poor little beast, he explained that Bimbi had been what he called a 'mothering animal,' some animals being so tightly charged with mother love that they will expend it on anything young, no matter of what species. It was like an electric force, he said, and that was why Brutus after loving his mother had chummed up with Bimbi. He was talking like this when Neumann, one of his assistants, passed going to his cottage near by for dinner, and Kemplin, as if struck by a sudden idea, flung his cigar stump away and ran after him, spoke to him a moment, and came back.

"'There is still a chance!' said he.

"'What way?' I asked.

"'Wait,' he replied. He lit a new cigar and we stood, scarcely talking. Then along the path came a woman. A woman of the people without a hat just as she was when called from the kitchen where she had been preparing her husband's dinner. Yet her face had that refined look which suffering gives to the commonest countenance.

"'Ah, there you are, Gretchen,' said Kemplin. 'I want to see if you can make this beast take a little milk. Come into the pen. He won't hurt you, he's only a baby. There, put your hand on his head. The milk pail is over there in the corner in the shade. No, he won't take it yet, just make friends with him first. He's only a baby and he's lost his mother. That's what's wrong with him. He's lost his mother.'

"Kemplin didn't say another word, and Gretchen, saying she would do what she could, got down on her knees beside the little creature and began stroking and talking to it.

"Then Kemplin took my arm and walked me off to the house.

"'She's lost her baby,' said he.

"The day I left I saw Gretchen going about the grounds followed by Brutus. Neumann's cottage had a pigsty and the pig was ejected, new straw put in and Brutus installed. She'd be up half a dozen times in the night to look after him and her face had changed — it had lost that horrible, searching, far-away look. Brutus had changed too, frisky as a pup and impudent as a bagful of monkeys.

"'And the end?' I asked.

"Well, in a year or so, Kemplin told me, Gretchen had another baby and Brutus had a six-inch horn, and he tusked the pigsty down one night and went back to his pen. He was no longer a baby but just a rhinoceros — look at him now."

I did, and it was strange enough to think that, chief among the architectural forces that had gone to the building of that vast and monstrous figure, one had to reckon the love of a goat and the love of a woman, the same spiritual force, neither human nor animal, but universal and divine.

CASTLE INNIS

IRELAND is perhaps the most conservative country on earth. She clings to her past as she clings to her virtue, and she would exchange any day a new town hall or drainage system for an old misery or grievance to pet and dandle, supposing that such a thing could be unearthed.

Here one may still believe in haunted houses without discredit — and rent them without disappointment, sure of a banshee if nothing else, and here, a few years ago, the Reverend Arthur Ridgwell Dilnott, rector of Pebwell, Cambridgeshire, came for the hunting as a guest of Mr. Michael Blake, whose estate lies in the top horn of Tipperary, not a hundred miles from Loch Derg.

Dilnott did not believe in ghosts. He was a full-blooded parson of the old type, riding fourteen stone, fond of good port, a good dinner, a good cigar, and a hand at whist; beloved by his parishioners. Brother parsons called him pig-headed. He was, at all events, in his beliefs and disbeliefs. He did not believe in ghosts, but he believed in demons and evil spirits, holding, however, that these latter belonged to a past day, though capable, perhaps, still of earthly manifestations.

Riding to the meet this morning with Michael Blake, the Round House on the Arranakilty Road brought his mind in clash with the mind of his host, a man steadfast in opinion as himself.

"That's where old Micky Doolan was killed in '61," said Blake. "He was a piper, blind as a bat, and he used to sit there the day long on a stool under that wall, with his long pipes under his arm, playing away whether folks were passing or not. You'd hear the droning of the pipes at the turn of the road, and there he'd be sitting, not asking for a copper or minding you, just playing away to himself. My father gave him many a shilling, and the poor folk, specially on market days, weren't behind hand. They said he was rich and carried all his money in gold in his pocket and one evening, close on dusk, two fellows crept up on him from behind the wall and killed him for his money. That was on the fifth of December, and every fifth of December since then there he sits,

playing his pipes from dusk till dawn, so that not a soul from Arranakilty to Cloyne will use the road."

"You mean to say his ghost sits there?"

"And what else would be sitting there?"

"You don't believe that nonsense surely."

"Don't believe it?" said Blake. "And why shouldn't I believe it?
Half the countryside has heard him."

"But there are no such things as ghosts — the manifestations have
been proved over and over again to be fraudulent as far as apparitional
appearances, the result of mediumistic influence, are concerned, illu-
sory as to the rest. Rats and neurotic women and practical jokers; sub-
tract those factors and the whole theory of haunted houses falls to the
ground."

"I tell you there *are* ghosts," replied Blake, and then the argument
began getting so acute that as they rode into the main street of Arranakilty, Dilnott was saying:

"I don't wish to quarrel with you, my dear fellow; let us leave the
subject. It is simply repugnant to common sense."

That is the sort of man Dilnott was.

Blake laughed, but he said no more. The street was crowded with
all sorts and conditions of people drawn to the "meet of the houn's,"
several pink coats the worse for weather showed up in front of the Dog
and Badger Inn, and here, now, from the direction of Clogher, came
Hennessy, the master, the hounds, and the hunt servants, jigging along
against the dull gray background of the road, greeted and greeting all
and sundry.

Blake introduced Dilnott to the master, who declared his intention
of first drawing Boyles Wood, and presently, on the stroke of ten, the
hunt pressed back along the Clogher Road, passed through a gate, and
entered a stretch of waste land, where, across a rise of the ground, a
clump of firs and larches showed, cutting the sky line a quarter of a mile
away.

It was a dark, gray, luminous morning; weather that in England
would have indicated rain before noon. But there would be no rain, for

the hills were set away in the distance, hills across which the wind was blowing, warm and scented from leagues of heather and bog land.

There was a fox in Boyles Wood, and he broke cover to the west like a red streak among the bushes and broken land. Dilnott, who was mounted on Rat Trap, a fiddle-headed brute that carried him like a feather, brooked no interference with a straight line, and was wound up by nature to go all day, found himself at the end of the first five minutes facing a stone wall; then it was behind him, Rat Trap taking it as a cat takes a larder window sill, and before him a hillside, falling to a river in spate, shallow and broad by a mercy.

Across the river, a rise took him to a hog's back along which the hounds were streaming straight as if along a ruled line, over humps and dips in the teeth of the wind, and with a view of all Tipperary from Loch Derg to Kings County on either side. Then another valley set with pines and winter-stripped trees and echoing to the tune of hounds and horn gave them check for a moment, only to pass them on across a bridge and another spating river and by a village where cocks were crowing and chimneys smoking, but not a soul in sight; to a waste land, where the hounds, dumb and flowing like hounds in a dream, led them still in the teeth of the wind; killing at last, not a hundred yards from the covert, that in another hundred seconds would have swallowed the tail of the good red fox.

"Thirty minutes from the wood," said Hennessy, looking at his watch.

Dilnott, tipping forward, ran his hand over the neck of Rat Trap, unblown and fresh almost as at the start. Thirty minutes of real life had brought fresh blood to his cheeks and youthened him by a full ten years, and the blowing wind had so banked down his prejudices that had you said the word "ghosts" to him he might have resented it without snapping your head off.

But ghosts were as far from his mind at this moment as from the minds of Hennessy or Michael Blake. Hennessy, after a look round, determined to draw Barrington Scrub a mile away over the moorland. They drew it blank, passed on to a big spinny a couple of miles away in the direction of Silvermines, and here the hounds started a fox, running into him and killing him two miles away and right on the edge of a wood by the road to Silvermines.

It was now one o'clock, and along the road appeared Rafferty, Blake's groom, with two fresh horses. Dilnott creaked out of his saddle, devoured the sandwiches he had brought with him, and consumed half a flask of sherry; then mounted the Cat, half sister to Rat Trap, a strawberry roan with a fleering eye and uncertain manner.

"Go gentle with her, sir," said Rafferty. "Once she gets warm, you can handle her like butter, but till she's taken her first fence don't lay whip or spur to her or she'll have you off and rowl on you."

It was three o'clock, and Dilnott was handling her like butter across a country of fields and stone walls when, clapping spurs to her, the stone wall before him wheeled to the right, then came a sickening slither, and he was seeing stars, with the Cat trying to "rowl" on him.

He had managed to disengage himself, however, and when he had finished stargazing and feeling around for broken bones, he got on his feet, recaptured his mount, led her through a gate onto the road, and got into the saddle.

The hunt had vanished. The faint toot of horn through the dull gray weather came from away toward Silvermines, but without awakening any echo in his heart. He had done enough hunting for one day. When one is over forty-five a cropper toward the end of the day is a different thing from a cropper at the start. Dilnott found himself thinking of a hot bath, followed by a cigarette and a comfortable armchair and just forty winks before dinnertime.

Mounting the Cat, by a miracle unhurt and now subdued and in her right mind, he turned from the direction of Silvermines. A mile along the road, he met in with an old man driving a donkey cart. This individual was deaf, but after a while and by dint of shouting came to understand his questioner.

"Castle Blake, did you say, sor? It's right forenint you, a matter of twelve miles and a bit as the crow flies and eleven by the road. What's that you say, sir? I'm hard of hearin'. There ain't no cows. I was sayin' crows. Keep ahead sthrait as an arra, and you'll see the top of it poppin' up beyant the trees of Gallows Wood; you can't make no mistake."

Dilnott resumed his way. Five miles on, a lady feeding hens before a cabin gave him more information.

"D'you mane Mr. Michael Blake's, sor? Why, it's nigh into Kings County from here; it's maybe siventeen miles you'll have to go. When you get to the crossroads take the way to Castle Down; keep sthrait ahead till you fetch the crossroads; you can't make no mistake."

Dilnott resumed his way till he came to a place where the road forked. There were no signposts, and the two ways were equal in breadth. He uttered no pious ejaculation. Leaving the matter, with loose rein, to the instinct of the Cat, that animal selected the right-hand way, brought him to a crossroad with no signpost, and, being left again to instinct, began to browse on stray tufts of grass and snatch sustenance from the hedgerows.

Meanwhile dusk was falling and the wind was rising and the trees whispering to the wind. Half an hour later, in full dark, lit occasionally by a glimpse of moon peeping through the broken clouds, Dilnott was riding along a road that Gustave Doré would have loved, looking no longer for Castle Blake, but for anything with a roof on it that would give him a light, the sight of a human face, and even a boiled potato.

He was faint from hunger — faint, yet ravenous. Roast legs of mutton flanked by decanters of port rose before him as he rode. Boiled turkeys and celery sauce, hams, York hams, brown and crumbed over. Larks on toast. So, in the desert, men conjure up date palms and shadowy wells, and now, just as though his hunger had conjured it up, Dilnott, waking from his food musings, became aware of the lights of a big house through the trees on the left of the road, and, on the wind setting from there, a smell recalling roast pheasant hung just to the right moment. More, it recalled bread sauce and a salad of Pebworth tomatoes sliced in vinegar and oil.

The constructive imagination of the man was adding a dish of Arran Chief potatoes bursting in snow through their brown jackets when a wide-open gateway and a drive leading to the house took his eye lit by a glimpse of the moon. He turned the Cat into the drive, and rode up it, sure of the one thing a stranger may be sure of in Ireland — a warm reception and a real and concrete hospitality, including in its form the best bed and the biggest potato.

The door of the great house was open, casting lamplight on the drive and on a carriage that had just set down a gentleman in a cloak who was mounting the steps. Two grooms in half livery were cracking jokes with the driver of the carriage. One of these ran to take the newcomer's horse. Dilnott slipped from the saddle and gave him the reins.

"What house is this?" asked he.

"Castle Innis, sir, and you're only just in time, for they be just goin' in to dinner."

"Who's your master? I'm staying at Castle Blake and have lost my way."

"Sir Patrick Kinsella's the master here, sir, and glad he'll be to see you."

"Thanks," said Dilnott. He went up the steps and entered a big hall. The hall was paneled with oak, black as ebony with age, hung with suits of armor, and lit by a galaxy of candles extraordinarily beautiful in their number and effect amid that setting of gloom and armor and oak.

Down the broad staircase were coming the guests; a troop of men, led by a stout gentleman of fifty or so in a red coat, with a face to match, joking and laughing as he came with the fellows behind him, and evidently gone in liquor. Not far gone, but gone — joyous, exuberant, and, clapping eyes on Dilnott when he was almost up with him, almost embracive.

"I have lost my way," said Dilnott, "and though I do not wish to intrude —"

But the great Kinsella, not even listening, with his arm half round him, swept him along, still bandying gibes with the fellows behind, into a huge room where a table was set out that would have seated forty.

Hungry as Dilnott had been and was, he would have thought twice before entering that house, seeing the condition of its occupants. Fond enough of his half bottle of port, he had a very great horror of intoxication in any form, even the mildest, and, seated now at the left of his host, who occupied the head of the table, he could not but perceive the condition of the men about him. The noise was terrific, and now servants were flying in every direction, clapping down plates in front of the guests — plates that were empty.

Now, opposite Dilnott and on the right of the host, sat an evil-looking, long-visaged man with a patch covering half of his face. Behind the host and above the fireplace was hung a big mirror with a slight tilt forward. Dilnott, glancing by chance at this mirror, was astonished and horrified to see in it the reflection of a skull, looking in the surrounding gloom and glow like a picture by Holbein.

The candlelight lit it to perfection, and, moreover, demonstrated the monstrous fact that it was moving, tilting from side to side, rotating slightly, while the movements of the lower jawbone caught in profile could be plainly seen.

Suddenly, and corresponding to a burst of laughter from the man with the patch on his face, the thing tilted back and the lower jaw fell.

Then Dilnott knew that it was the true reflection of his vís-à-vís.

He sprang to his feet and made the sign of the cross.

The Cat stumbled, nearly unseating him, and he awoke. He had never dismounted; he had entered no house. Musing on York hams and roast pheasant Sleep had sandbagged him and Fantasy had introduced him into that most extraordinary society. It was a nightmare, arising from the home of nightmares — the stomach.

Horse hoofs and a voice behind made him turn. It was Blake, mud to the eyes, but happy.

Dilnott told of his cropper and how he had fallen out of the run, and as they rode on he began to tell of his further adventures.

"I must have fallen asleep for a moment," said he, "and I had a most extraordinary dream."

"And what was the dream?" asked Blake.

"Well, it was this way," began the other. Then he stopped. They had reached a gateway clearly shown by the moonlight through the thinning clouds. It was the gateway he had entered in his dream, and there lay the avenue up which he had ridden. He reined in.

"Where does that lead to?" asked he.

"Castle Innis," said Blake. "Look, you can see the ruins through the trees. It was burned out in the thirties, set fire to one night old Pat Kinsella was having one of his jamborees. The whole crowd were burned, and a good riddance. I've had the story often from my father. Kinsella and Billy Knox, who was his chief henchman in all sorts of wickedness, and Black French and Satan Moriarty — and a score of others — only three of the lot were sober enough to escape."

"What sort of man was Kinsella?"

"A huge, big chap riding fifteen stone. He was the master of the hounds — but he couldn't master the whisky bottle."

"And Knox?"

"Oh, Knox was a devil. My grandfather laid him out once for mal-treating a horse; half his face was afflicted with some disease or another, so he had to wear a patch to cover it, and he had a squint eye and an impediment in his speech, and with all that he was a great man after the girls — there's no knowing what girls will take to. Well, what was this dream you were telling me of?"

"I've clean forgot it," said Dilnott.

A good raconteur, tingling and burning to tell, his mouth was stopped by Micky Doolan, the blind piper of the Round House.

A year later, unburdening himself of the story to me, he began: "Now I'll tell you one of the strangest *coincidences* you ever heard of."

That is the sort of man Dilnott was.

COCKTAIL, SAR?

THERE ARE situations that may be best described as mixed. Patrick Michael O'Sheanus Cassidy was a professional gambler, a man of mark in two hemispheres and a man absolutely to be trusted. Like the great Sheedy, his word was as good as his bond; like the late lamented Mr. John Oakhurst, he had a heart as well as a purse; but he had no soft spots in his character. He knew men and he knew women, and he knew little good of them. He had absolutely no mercy for fools and knaves, and the weak of knee, but for an honest fellow mortal in distress, Cassidy was a sure standby, and truth was, for him, religion.

Cassidy's knowledge of art was almost equal to his knowledge of men. He was always traveling and picking up treasures, storing them to be used some day when the spirit moved him to drop the cards and dice and settle down. He was fond of music. He was fond of so many simple things that his character, coupled with his wealth, formed a problem. Why did he continue in a profession ranking in pious eyes only a little above the profession of a burglar?

Perhaps he knew that in private life his past would follow him. Had he been a gambler in wheat, in stocks, in land, or the lives of his fellow mortals, all would have been well, but he had chosen to be a gambler, pure and simple, and, though he had chosen a cleaner game than that which they often play in the Wheat Pit or Wall Street, convention was against him. Perhaps the game dominated him. Perhaps the study of men and of character conducted across the green board held him in its grip. Who knows?

He was forty-two at the date of this story, a fine-looking, fresh-faced man, clean shaven, well dressed, and with a voice that told the tale of his Irish descent, but this morning he looked scarcely thirty as he stood on the deck of the *Saigon* coming to her berth across the blue harbor under the blaze of the Javanese sky.

Colored houses, rocketing palms, far blue mountains, the harbor where Western freighters and junks lay at anchor, he took it all in as he stood on the spar deck talking to Van Zyall, the Dutch trader, and two or three other passengers of the *Saigon.* The tepid wind blowing from the shore brought perfumes of vanilla and earth, ooze and a tang of tar from the nearing wharves — sights, sounds and smells absolutely unnoticed by the others, who were talking of the Borneo tobacco crop, the customs, the price of sugar.

"You stay at the Amsterdam Hotel," said Van Zyall for the twentieth time that morning. "Tell them Van Zyall sent you. Hoffman will put you straight."

"I'll remember," said Cassidy. During the run from Malacca, he had lost money to Van Zyall. The play had been trifling for him, and it amused him to think that the Dutchman was trying to make amends for his winnings by offers of good advice.

Then came along Connart. He had lost money to Connart, too. Connart was a man of dubious nationality, about as old as Cassidy, a fragile man, worn by the climate, pale, and with a brown Vandyke beard. He was well to do, owning a big place near the town, and he interested Cassidy a lot.

Connart hated to lose and loved to win. Most men do, but in the exhibition of his hatred and love, in his general manner of play and in something recondite and illusive in the man's character and appealing only to some sixth sense, Cassidy had formed the opinion that here was a gambler of the first water.

Very few men are that.

Cassidy had also formed the opinion that Connart was an uncut jewel, that his passion for play had never been fully developed, either from want of opportunity or self-restraint. Last night, in a conversation with Connart, he had discovered that lack of opportunity was the probable cause, the ingenuous Connart declaring that it was quite impossible to play high outside of Monte Carlo without being swindled.

"Of course it is different with you," said he, meaning to say that Cassidy's probity was beyond reproach.

II.

"Where are you putting up?" asked Connart.

"The Amsterdam Hotel," replied Cassidy. "Van Zyall says it's the best."

"He's right," replied the other. "How long did you say you were staying here?"

"A week. I'm going on by this boat and she'll be here a week."

"Well, you must come and see me," replied the other; "come to dinner or something. My place is not far out, and I'll run in and fetch you tomorrow, if you'll come. I'll run in about five and you can dine with me — will you?"

"Yes," said Cassidy. "I'll come."

The *Saigon* was close in to the wharf now, moving almost imperceptibly with the engines rung off and the fellows waiting with the hawsers. Cassidy, collecting his luggage, did not see Connart again and, when he reached the Amsterdam Hotel, had almost forgotten him.

Here in Batavia in the hot season, one does a lot of forgetting. Seated in the veranda with a whisky and soda at his elbow, he fell in conversation with a trader who spoke English like an Englishman and who gave him the news of the place. Van Amberg was the trader's name, and his news was mostly about crop prospects, the rate of exchange on London and the pictures showing that week at the chief cinema palace. Then Cassidy gave his news, the bad cooking on board the *Saigon*, a storm they had run into after leaving Malacca and other trifles including the names of some of the passengers.

Van Amberg knew some of them personally, including Connart.

"I'm going to dinner with him tomorrow night," said Cassidy.

"Oh, are you," said Van Amberg. "Then you'll see Daia."

"Who's Daia?"

"She's his wife — well, call her his wife — Dyak girl."

"Dyak?"

"Just so. Not from Borneo. Dutch Guinea coast. Some sea Dyaks have settled there up a river, and that's where Connart fell in with her. He was up there prospecting for gold and nearly lost his head, for those chaps go in for head collecting still on the sly. I had the whole story from Ollsen, a man who was with him in those parts on the gold hunt. There were six of them, with a few Javanese chaps to help working the schooner they hired, and they pushed her up the river as far as she would go and then took to the bank, leaving the ship in charge of the Javanese.

"Ollsen was the man who had the location, and a three days' tramp took them to it, and they found gold but not in paying quantity. They found rubies, too, but small and not of much account. Then they fell in with the Dyaks, who were friendly at first, or seemed so, till one night there was a row. I don't know what about, but the Dyaks broke up the camp and killed every one but Connart and Ollsen.

"They tied these two chaps up and put them in a hut — meaning to kill them later on most likely, but Daia had taken a fancy to Connart, and she cut them loose in the night and showed them the way down the river back to their ship. Connart couldn't send the girl back to her tribe; they'd have killed her. So he took her with him and brought her here. Sounds like a story out of the pictures."

"What sort of fellow is Connart?" asked Cassidy.

"Oh, good enough," said the other, "a bit close and keeps to himself. It isn't often that he invites people to his place, must have taken a fancy to you."

"Does he gamble?"

"Not that I know of."

Then Van Amberg, remembering business, went off downtown, leaving Cassidy to his thoughts undisturbed except by the rustle of the tepid wind in the palm trees by the veranda.

Connart knew Cassidy by repute as well as personally. Pat Cassidy, the gambler, was even a bigger figure in the East than in the West, not only because of his reputation for straight dealing and high play, but by the fact that he had won the Calcutta sweep two years ago. It was the gambler, not the man, that Connart had taken a fancy to.

Sure of his money if he won, with all his latent gambling instinct magnetically aroused, Connart was anxious for play, and play on a big scale. So Cassidy fancied, as he sat in the great cane armchair, smoking and listening to the wind in the palms. The more he thought of the matter, the more sure he was that Connart was no "sucker" anxious to win a few pounds, but a gambler worth engaging in battle.

Cassidy, in his long experience, had only met two dangerous men. Men who had fought him to the death and threatened to destroy him. Cedorquist of the Amazon Plantation Company, and Bowater, the wheat speculator. Men, in these little days, play as a rule for amusement or to win a few pounds; the great gamblers of the past belong to the past. But occasionally one finds a throwback.

Some instinct told Cassidy that Connart was the third dangerous man he had met, but he was not yet sure. Tomorrow would tell.

III.

A little before five o'clock, next day, Connart's car, driven by a Chinese chauffeur, drew up at the hotel.

Cassidy was waiting in the veranda and they started, taking a road that led by banks of tree fern, palms, and gray-green cactus under a sky losing its glare and against a wind warm and scented with the fragrance of trees and flowers.

Then fields of cane took the place of palms and ferns, and beyond the cane fields, groves of orange led them to the home of Connart, a wide, spaciously built, verandaed dwelling amid gardens haunted by tropical butterflies and birds gorgeous as the flowers.

"Well," said Cassidy, as he looked around him, "you ought to be happy here."

"Oh, it's well enough," said Connart unenthusiastically, "the only thing against it is it's not Europe."

"Faith, that's true," said the other. He was thinking more of the Dyak girl Van Amberg had spoken of, than his host, but there was no sign of her. They took their seats in the veranda, and the Chinese servants brought drinks and cigars and they talked of a hundred things, but never once did Connart hint of a wife.

At dinner it was the same. The iced champagne did not loosen Connart's tongue as to himself and his affairs, and, after dinner, they had no need for conversation. The thing had happened. They had drifted into play, and, seated opposite one another, were barred out from all things mundane, but the chances of the game.

The great moon rose and cast its light on the palms and flowers of the garden and laid a square of white on the matting of the room where a blue haze of cigar smoke hung above the lamps; white moths entered and cast birdlike shadows on the table and walls, unheeded by the players. Past midnight the grass curtains dividing the room from the next were pushed aside and the figure of a girl appeared. It was Daia.

Van Amberg had forgotten to mention that she was beautiful. The bangles on her bare arms glittered in the lamplight, her feet were bare, and the robe of gauzy, ghostly white material, half veiling the lines of her figure, added to the strangeness of the picture.

Cassidy looked up; then Connart turned.

"Daia," said Connart. Then turning to Cassidy, "This is Daia." He picked up his cards again, the girl glided up and stood behind his chair, and the game went on without another word.

The beauty of the girl and the strangeness had no effect upon Cassidy. He had wished to see her as a curiosity, nothing more. Women had no part in his life. Without being a misogynist, he was absolutely cold as far as the other sex was concerned, rather antagonistic, if anything. Women were a nuisance. Yet he was attractive to women.

Daia, standing behind Connart's chair, seemed to find him attractive now. Her eyes were fixed upon him, eyes deep and mysterious as the sea, dark as night in the forests of Borneo. Cassidy continued his play. A stone figure standing behind Connart's chair would have moved him as little as the figure of the girl. The game held him entirely.

Then, chancing to look up, he saw the curtains swaying. She was gone.

The play continued till the clock, standing on a little table close by, struck two. Then he broke off play. He had lost seven hundred pounds. He took a fountain pen from his pocket and wrote out his check on

Mathesons' bank which has a branch at Batavia, and handed it to Connart.

"They'll tell you my check is good for any amount," said Cassidy.

"That's all right," said Connart. "Have a game tomorrow night?"

"Just as you like."

"Right! I'll send the car for you. You'll dine here? Right!" He called a servant and ordered the car to be brought round. "It's pretty late," said Cassidy. "Oh, the hotel keeps open all night," replied the other. "We're used to late hours in this place."

IV.

On the way back to the hotel Cassidy felt elated. He had six days before the *Saigon* started, and he reckoned on a big fight with a worthy antagonist. The stakes of tonight would be nothing to what was coming, and Connart had the money to back his elbow. He had made inquiries about him.

Games where skill entered into the business did not appeal to Cassidy; pure chance was his favorite field and the bones his favorite weapon. He played bridge, just as a golfer plays clock golf on a lawn, but he looked down on the game, and the highly respectable men and women who make an income by their sharpness as bridge players, were for him pedicular.

Just before closing his eyes that night, the figure of the girl, Daia, framed itself, for a moment, before him. Was Connart married to her? The question came with the picture. He could not tell and he did not care.

Next day at five o'clock the car arrived and Cassidy took his departure for the plantation. Connart received him in the veranda; dinner was dispatched, and the business of the evening began.

Midnight struck unheeded by the players and again, as on the preceding night, the curtains parted, the figure of Daia appeared, stood for a moment, and then glided behind the chair of Connart. Cassidy looked up and bowed. The girl inclined her head slightly, then she stood, motionless as a statue, seeming to watch the play, but, in reality, watching Cassidy. He seemed to fascinate her.

Perhaps he was for her a new type of man, perhaps his absolute indifference toward her was the charm. Her eyes followed every movement of his hands and every expression on his face. Instead of withdrawing as on the preceding night, she sat on the arm of a great basket chair near by, still watching and absolutely unheeded by the object of her gaze.

Cassidy was winning tonight. He had wiped off the seven hundred. Fortune had deserted Connart, and was standing behind the chair of his opponent. When the little clock on the table near by struck two, Cassidy laid down his cards. He had won two thousand five hundred pounds.

Daia had vanished.

"Let's go on," said Connart.

"Well, then, till half past," replied Cassidy.

They went on, but the luck still held, and at half past two the play stopped, Connart three thousand pounds to the bad.

"You've struck a bad vein," said Cassidy. "It would have been better to have stopped. Oh, don't bother about a check. We can settle up before I go. You'll want your revenge."

"Tomorrow night?" said the other.

"Right," said Cassidy. "But I'm straining your hospitality; why not come and dine with me at the hotel and play there?"

"I'd just as soon play here," replied Connart, "if it's all the same to you. It's more comfortable here, and quieter. Besides, hotel people talk."

"That's true," said Cassidy; "but what do you mind about the hotel people?" Connart, helping himself to a whisky and soda with a steady hand, despite his losses, did not reply for a moment. Then he said:

"Oh, I don't know — one has to keep up a name in a place like this. I know the best people, and you'd be surprised how old-fashioned and stodgy they are. There are only two circles here, the best and the worst, and I've strained the best with Daia. I don't want to add late gambling at the Amsterdam to my sins. I never gamble — that's my reputation here."

Cassidy took a whisky and soda; then, while the car was being brought round, and to make conversation, he asked about Daia. "A man at the hotel was talking about you," said Cassidy, "and he mentioned that you were married."

"I'm not."

"I see."

"No, you don't. Daia is no more to me than a daughter."

"You mean —"

"I mean exactly what I say. Did that man tell you how she came to me?"

"Yes."

"She got me free of those Dyak people, risked her life for me, and she lives with me, and, of course, not being married to me, people look on her as my mistress. She's not, she's my dog. She became violently attached to me up in that camping place just as a child or a dog might; she led me as a dog might, and she lives with me as a dog might live with me.

"There is nothing at all between us but that. People don't know that. It's no use in telling them, they couldn't understand. I've never even tried to tell them. I did tell one man, a Dutchman, that there was nothing between us, that Daia was only living here as a child might live with me, and he winked at me and grinned."

"I can understand it easy enough," said Cassidy; "but it's queer. D'you care for her?"

"Very much, but only as I might care for a dog. She's undeveloped, or, rather, not quite human. Still, I care for her very much. You see she cares for me in quite an extraordinary way — as a dog. Can anything care for a man as much as a dog does?"

"Faith, I don't know," said Cassidy. "I've never had a dog and I've never cared for a woman."

Then the car came round and he drove off for the hotel with, somehow, a better opinion of Connart than he had before.

Connart was weak. Cassidy, like a physician, had diagnosed the great weak spot in his character. He was an A-1 gambler without the special genius of a Cassidy, and without the moral or immoral courage to gamble openly. Fortune hates a man like that who hangs on to her skirts in the dark and ignores her in the daylight. And Cassidy, the spoiled child of Fortune, could not but despise him. But he was at least leading a clean life and he had not wronged the woman who had loved him.

Next night the proceedings took place as usual, and the next. It might have been a play that was being acted over and over again, with a slight difference each time; the dinner, the game, Daia gliding in and out again, the settling up and the departure of Cassidy.

Fortune played with the players; huge sums were lost and won; but it was not till the fifth and tragic night that the real struggle came. Cassidy was due to depart in the morning. The *Saigon* left at eight o'clock. His luggage, all but a few light things, was on board.

They had flung the cards away. The dice had taken their place, and the players sat opposite one another flushed, bright-eyed and heedless of everything but chance. They had drunk more than enough, and long glasses of iced brandy and soda stood on the table at their elbows.

Daia was not present. She had looked in and vanished. The clock pointed to seven minutes to two. Cassidy rattled the box and cast. Then Connart pushed his chair back.

"That does me," said he. He had lost fifteen thousand pounds.

Cassidy picked up the cubes, dropped them again, and leaned back in his chair.

"Are you cleared out?" he asked.

"Absolutely."

"Damn!" said Cassidy.

The tension removed, the drink was getting at him. He suddenly hated the business. He had never played quite like this before, calling night after night and accepting his opponent's hospitality. The victory had drawn all his teeth. He would have handed back his winnings straight across the table, but he could not do that. They had played; if he had lost, he would have paid. The fifteen thousand was his and Connart was not the man to accept charity.

"The plantation is tied up," said Connart, "and there's no more cash, and that's an end of it."

Cassidy, leaning back in his chair, hands in pockets, seemed thinking profoundly. Then he sat up. The whisky had given him an idea.

"I'll play you double or quits," said he with a hiccup.

"I told you I had nothing more," replied Connart.

"Put up Daia," said the other with a laugh. "I'll play you for Daia or quits. Go on, you d — fool, you're going to win."

"Daia!" said Connart.

On the crest of disaster, a lifeline seemed flung to him by Satan, though Cassidy was Satan by no means. Cassidy was just a man who wanted to get out. He had fancied Connart a very wealthy man; he wasn't. He was broken at fifteen thousand, and all those dinners and all the hospitality he had received rose up, backed and flushed with whisky in Cassidy's mind, crying, if you will permit the stretch, "Give the chap another chance."

He did not want Daia. If he won her, she would be of no use to him. It was like saying, "I will play you for that big euphorbia tree in your garden." He could no more take Daia off with him, than the tree.

But to Connart, whose mind was in a whirl, the lifeline seemed cast to him by the devil. Still there was the chance! Had he stopped to think, he might have refused. Cassidy gave him no time. He cast, handed the box to Connart, who cast.

"You've won," said Cassidy. "We're quits."

"God!" said Connart, with his elbows on the table and his head between his hands.

Gambling teaches one a lot of things. He had gambled with her as a counter and might have lost her to this man — this devil! and the thing he might have lost disclosed itself to him. He loved the woman who had saved him. She had saved him twice — saved his life, and saved his future.

Cassidy, well pleased, poured himself out another whisky, lit another cigar, and sat down again. Connart neither moved nor spoke, then he rose up, went to a desk in the corner of the room, opened a drawer, and took something from it. Then he wrote for a moment.

He came to Cassidy with a slip of paper in his hand. Cassidy took it. It was a check for fifteen thousand. Cassidy tore the paper in two, then in four, and cast the pieces on the ground, the whisky turning to vinegar in him.

"I'd give you to understand that I'm a gentleman," said Cassidy. "Good night. I don't want the car. I can walk."

V.

Nothing is more unreasonable than whisky stopped in its convivial and warming work, especially when its workshop is the mind of an Irishman.

For a mile down the road Cassidy walked absurdly raging. Then the night wind and the moonlight and the palms and the exercise began to tell on him, and he reached the outskirts of the town, calm, and almost regretful. At the hotel the Chinese night porter saluted him, and he went up to his room, turned on the electrics, and began to pack the few things he carried in his light luggage.

He could not sleep, so he did not undress. It was after four in the morning, and he would have to join the *Saigon* at seven, so he lit a pipe and sat down at the open window to smoke and think. The whole of this business was a new experience and gave him plenty of food for thought. It came to him now that Connart had actually gambled with the girl, while he, Cassidy, had only used her as a door of escape, a last chance to let Connart save himself. Did Connart actually imagine that he, Cassidy, cared for the girl and wanted her. Undoubtedly. That was why he tried to hand back the money and efface as much as possible the disgraceful deal into which he had been trapped.

Cassidy, considering this matter, laughed to himself.

He would never see Connart again, but Connart would always have that opinion of him, would look on him as a man who had taken advantage of another man's money losses to do a deal in flesh and blood.

He heard voices down below, then the voices ceased. He tapped the ashes from his pipe and was just about to refill it when the door of his room opened. He turned and found himself face to face with Daia.

VI.

She had evidently followed him on foot. The reason why she had followed him, any man could see, even Cassidy. It surrounded her like an aura as she stood gazing at him with those dark, unfathomable eyes.

He neither rose from his chair nor spoke. Behind her, the yellow, clawlike hand of the Chinese night porter closed the door on them.

She came gliding toward him, sank beside him, and took his hands in hers; then, with head raised and her eyes still fixed on his, she began to speak. She spoke in the language of her people. He did not understand a word, but he understood everything. Understood that she had followed him, that she loved him, that she was his slave, that she would follow him to the ends of the earth, and even beyond, to the ghostly country of the Atu Jalan.

With her hands clasped in his, he was no longer thinking, or trying to think, she enveloped him. Then, suddenly, the spell was broken. The sound of a car drawing up outside came through the open window.

Cassidy disengaged himself, swiftly but gently, from the arms that had encircled him, placed his finger on his lips to say "hush," stole to the door, opened it, and glanced back. She was gazing after him, crouched still beside the chair with one arm resting on it. She nodded to him as though to say, "I wait." He left the room, and next moment he was in the hall.

The night lamp showed Connart, and through the open door beyond he could see the car standing in the dawn.

"Ah," said Connart.

"Come outside," said Cassidy.

He got the other into the street. Connart, in the gray-blue light that was breaking over the houses, looked old and shaken. Cassidy, hatless and dazed, stood for a moment, then, pointing with his thumb to the upper story of the hotel, he said. "She's up there. In my room."

"You tore up my check, for money was not your game, and you pretended to be angry and refused the car, and spoke of yourself as a gentleman!" said Connart. He took off his hat and held it in his hand for a moment as though to let the land wind which was beginning to blow, reach his head. Then he dropped the hat on the ground, and folded his arms and inclined his head slightly as if in thought.

"You are absolutely wrong," said Cassidy. "She has only come this minute."

"I know that," said Connart, "an honest man told me — the hall porter."

Cassidy swallowed the insult.

"She followed me without my knowing, I had absolutely nothing to do with it. I do not care for her."

Connart laughed.

"How could she follow you? She has been scarcely ever in this town, and she did not know where you were staying."

Cassidy seemed to consider the proposition for a moment. The unfortunate man could not tell whether she had followed him by some Dyak tracking instinct or how. He only knew the facts of the case, and the hopelessness of trying to explain the position; also the absolute necessity of getting away at once lest Daia should suddenly appear.

Then he remembered that he had no hat, that he would have to go back for it. That was the last straw.

"You can think what you like of me," said he; "she's innocent. Go up and take her away. I'm off. Curse this place. I'm going aboard. I have no hat."

He picked up Connart's hat, turned and walked off with it.

At eight o'clock, the *Saigon* put out, and Cassidy, on the deck with Connart's Panama on his head, stood watching the receding wharves. Not a word had come from Connart to the ship, not a whisper through the clear air of all that fantastic business. The town with its palm trees and houses flooded by the blaze of morning light, had about it an extraordinary air of peace and contentment, silence and detachment.

What had happened at the Amsterdam Hotel? Had she gone back? What did she think of him? What was Connart thinking of him? Was Connart wearing his hat? What would the hotel people do with the few inconsiderable articles he had left behind? What would they think of his leaving like that?

Suddenly, a great and forgotten fact wrote itself in letters of fire from the blue hills to the sea:

"You have not paid your hotel bill!"

A week's board and lodging, champagne, cigars, drinks to all and sundry, tips —

He left the deck and sought the bar of the *Saigon* where a dusky gentleman was setting out bottles. Above the bottles, across the Venesta paneling, the words regrouped themselves:

"You have not paid your hotel bill."

He could liken the whole situation to nothing earthly, till —

"Cocktail, sar?" asked the dusky bartender.

Cassidy nodded.

"GLUED"

BRANDT IS a hunter. I met him at Seattle before the war, and, a few days ago, I met him again on the boat from Calais to Dover. Hunters are getting fewer and fewer these days. I mean men like Selous and Brandt. The wild parts of the earth are getting more settled, the big herds are thinned or destroyed. Look at elephants — I mean, look for them. Places where twenty years ago they were a natural feature of the scenery, now deserted. Listen for the organ-trombone voice of the hippopotamus by the old rivers where once the hippo sang and bathed. If you hear it, it will be from some upper reach. Tomorrow or next day, you will not hear it at all.

Then again, the markets and museums are against the hunter these days; rare beasts are not so rare, and the price of furs and skins, barring sable and fox, has not increased in proportion to the higher price of living and the fitting out of expeditions. I gathered this from Brandt. He is a bit of a pessimist, and may be wrong; but, anyhow, when I met him the other day, he had "chucked hunting for good," taken up with rubber, and was able to travel Pullman.

On the train up from Dover we fell to talking of the war. Although over forty when the fighting broke out, he had served with the Canadians. That he was a German by extraction did not matter a button to him. He was more than a good shot. He was inevitable with the rifle. You can fancy the execution done by this deadly man as a sniper, till a German got him and smashed up his elbow, and turned his attention to rubber.

"How many did you kill?" I asked.

"It may have been a hundred," said Brandt; "it may have been more. I had good luck. Well, it is over now, and I will never hunt again, except for dollars."

"Are you sorry?" I asked.

"Well, I don't know," said he. "Sometimes I am sorry, and sometimes not. When I was out there in the bush or jungle I was free. I had no money to speak of. Now I have suddenly got money — and I am no longer free. Money makes a man a slave. Money is business, don't you forget that.

"Lazy people say to themselves, 'Oh, how I wish I were rich.' forgetting that if they were rich they would have to guard their wealth. You buy a stock, and it goes down. Your brother says, 'Oh, that doesn't matter, it is a good investment.' Just so, but, meanwhile, your capital has shrunk, and that is not very pleasant. You buy a stock and it goes up, and you say to yourself, 'Now, I ought to get out and take my profits.' You have seen the rubber boom and the oil boom. I was in them both. I tell you, there were times when I felt afraid."

"Were you ever frightened in the old days?"

"Once."

"How was that?"

"Well, I am not a man given to talk big, as you know, or to brag. Of course, all old hunters are apt to brag a bit as to the size of beasts or the price of pelts and so on; but they don't brag of courage, because they are not proud of it. The thing comes as a necessity, just like breathing. Without courage, as people call it, a hunter would not live a month, in some places, and would not hunt long in any place — except, maybe, where there were only rabbits. He has it always with him, like his rifle.

"All the same, I lost my courage once, and I will give you a hundred guesses as to what sort of a beast or thing it was that made my heart go down into my boots. Elephant, no — lion, no — tiger, no. Something more terrible than that. What could be more terrible than a tiger? Well, to my mind, a snake is more terrible, but it was not a snake. No, it was something worse than a snake. Give it up? Well, I will tell you, and if you doubt my word when I've done, ask Tangze. You will find him at the South Kensington Museum. He has given up collecting this fifteen years, and he has got a fixed post now — a sort of professorship, and has got married and fattened up wonderfully since I knew him out in South America.

"He was a bit of a stick of a chap in those days — looked more like one of those dried orchids he was always packing off to Europe than anything else; but there wasn't a man in the two hemispheres that knew more about tropical flora. Beasts were nothing to him; he was a vegetable hunter and nothing else — he didn't even bother about butterflies, I doubt if he would have taken the trouble to catch one, not if it was labeled as being the newest specimen.

"I met him by pure chance. I was in Para, just come back from a trip upcountry with a chap, Lord Wearmouth, who was prospecting for gold with a little hunting thrown in. I don't know who sold him the gold prospectus, but whoever did, sold him a pup. There's no gold south of the Javary. I told him so, and he wouldn't listen to me; but he was a nice chap, and the pay was big, and, as I said, there was hunting of sorts to be done, so I had gone. I was paid off in Para, and that same night I went into a gambling shop kept by a Peruvian and lost everything I had but ten dollars and my equipment.

"I suppose I'm a gambler born, and, anyhow, I've got it back in rubber and oil. But that night I felt pretty bad. It was *trente et quarante*, played in quite a decent shop with women in evening clothes eating ices, and fellows from the upper Amazon dashing down their money by the fistful. But the place seemed like hell to me when the croupier raked in my last off the red. I'd backed red right through.

"I had enough for a drink and something to clink in my pocket, and I stood there for a few minutes when all was done watching the play. Then I went back to the hotel.

II.

"I went up to my room, turned on the electrics, and sat down in an armchair to have a smoke. I hadn't intended to risk more than twenty dollars when I went into that shop, but card gambling is like quicksands; you get up to your knees, and trying to recover yourself you get up to your waist — and then you're done.

"Well, as I sat there smoking, I had lots to think about. I couldn't pay my hotel bill without selling my equipment, and how to get away I didn't know. But I did know that the worst will do its worst, and that a man, to tackle his luck, isn't much good unless he's had a night's sleep behind him. So I finished my cigar and turned in, and woke next morning with the waiter bringing in my early coffee and a letter.

"It was from a chap in the same hotel. His name was Tangze; he was out on a commission from one of the Rothschilds, if I remember rightly, and his chief man had failed him. Lord Wearmouth had spoken of me to him. He was in room No. 14, and would I call and see him any time that morning? Then there was a postscript, half apologizing for saying that terms would be easily arranged, as money was not the main object of his principal.

"Well, I lay back on the pillows and laughed to think of how I'd given bad luck the slip, leaving only a few dirty dollars in his hands; for there's many a man would have left his sleep behind him, finding himself in the same fix, or maybe put a bullet through his head.

"Soon as I was dressed, I popped in on Tangze. He was a little dried-up chap, as I have said, and he was in his pajamas, writing letters. He jumped up when he heard my name, and under five minutes, from start to finish, we'd fixed terms. They were big terms for a big job. Rothschild, or whoever it was, had fixed his avaricious eye on the flora of the upper Amazon. He wanted to ransack that place, chiefly for orchids; expense was no matter — within limits, of course, and a gunman, being necessary to deal with big game, could ask his own figure.

"It was a week later that we started, taking a Royal Mail boat up the river. I only knew the lower Amazon, not far from Para, and that's as much as to say I didn't know the Amazon at all. The thing isn't rightly a river. It's a world. A world always slipping away to the sea. Day after day and day after day and day after day, pulling against the stream, it was always the same; the great forests and the birds, tracts of swamp where the 'crocs' lay like logs.

"But the one same thing that got on our nerves was the width. It never got narrower. Always the same old sea when one came on deck of a morning. It was in flood, or, more truly speaking, near the end of flood, and the Ithecraly and Javary and half a hundred streams that would have been big rivers in Europe were sending down assortments — tree trunks and dead cattle and suchlike. The water came brown as porter by the banks, and swirling as if the river was alive and in trouble.

"'It will be all right when we reach Remat des Males,' said Tangze. 'The river is sinking now.'

"'I'm thinking that we'll find the going rather stiff after these floods,' I said. 'It will take a lot of sun to dry the forests, to say nothing of the swamps.'

"He hadn't thought of that. There's an awful lot of clever people who don't do much thinking outside the line of their circle. The expedition had been timed wrong for the upper Amazon — and it had been timed by Tangze, who ought to have known better. I told him so, and he agreed. That is the sort of chap he was when he hadn't a touch of liver on him. When his liver woke up he was a different person.

"However, there was no use bothering. But you'll see our position when I tell you that just then whole tracts of country were under water, thousands and thousands of square miles. In fact, the Amazon was a lake as big as Europe in its upper part, a lake maybe not more than three feet deep in places, with forests sticking out of it. Well, when we got to Yaniero, that is to say fifteen hundred miles from the mouth, we found a town on stilts. Being built on piles, the houses in Yaniero have landing stages as well as steps.

"Lord, it's a cheerful place, especially just after the end of the rain, with the forests smoking and big, filthy clouds rolling away overhead. There's nothing fit to eat, and nothing fit to drink; sardines are five dollars a tin, and tobacco a dollar the two ounces — when you can get it. What do the people live on, there? Rubber!

"I don't mean to say they eat it, but, by Jove, they spend it! Big money they make tapping the trees on the estates roundabout. Then they come into Yaniero and bust their earnings on sardines and whisky and top boots and Henry Clays that never saw Havana, and suchlike — and gambling. There was a hotel, and we stayed at it, for there was nowhere else to stay. We had nothing to do but sit on the hotel landing stage and watch the floods go down and shoot at passing alligators. Then we met Ramon.

III.

"Ramon was a sort of Serang. He bossed the rubber lands on the estate next above Yaniero on the same bank, and he used to come to the hotel to get drunk. He led two lives, did Ramon. His sober life and his drunken life. At work, Pussyfoot J. would have hugged him; at play, he couldn't. He drank gin mostly, when he could get it; when he couldn't, he would drink shoe varnish, if that was all he could get. But, mind you, when I say he got drunk, you mustn't take me as meaning he made a beast of himself. No, sometimes he'd be fuddled and dull, and sometimes he'd be talkative, but he was never objectionable; and when he was talkative, he was the most interesting Spaniard I've ever come across — that is to say, when he kept clear of politics.

"He wasn't long in finding us out and our business, and he took a lot of interest in Tangze. It turned out that Ramon was of the same sort of build of mind, a sort of born naturalist, with his tastes running to vegetables. He knew all about orchids. Perira, his master, and the owner of the estate, was worth maybe a million dollars, and took an interest in orchids, and did a lot of collecting through his rubber gatherers, including Ramon.

"You may fancy how this news flattened out Tangze. He had come fifteen hundred miles up the Amazon orchid hunting, only to find that a millionaire Portuguese had been combing the forests for Lord knows how long. It was plain as a pikestaff that all round there the place must be skinned, and that there was nothing likely of interest to be found that had not been found by Perira and sent off to the botanical gardens of God knows where. There's no use finding new specimens for a Rothschild if some son of a gun of a squatter of a Portuguese pops up and says, 'I've got that and stuck my name on it already' — see?

"Well, there we were in that fix, looking up the river and thinking of our new move, when Ramon turned up trumps and took us to his heart. He was pretty sick of Perira, and said so — giving us to understand that he had never done orchid hunting for Perira with any enthusiasm, so to speak. Perira was one of those rich men who'd be richer if they weren't so mean. Instead of giving Ramon full pay for orchid hunting and nothing else, he made him do the hunting in his off time and only gave him a few dollars for his trouble.

"Ramon got Tangze aside now and proposed to lead us into a part of the forests beyond the Javary which he said was no use for rubber but rich in everything else — sand box, euphorbias, matamatas, and all such, to say nothing of climbers and orchids. He said he'd take a month's holiday which he was entitled to, and lead us, asking only a dollar a day and a commission on anything new we should find.

"Tangze asked him what the commission would be, and Ramon said he'd fix it at a quarter of the market value, that is to say at the market value estimated by Tangze. That was the sort of chap Ramon was. A good bit of nobleman, though as brown as a coffee berry, and with the reputation of having killed three men in quarrels over their wives.

"It was settled that the commission should be paid for anything found on the month's march, and, of course, we fixed it that the commission only held good for things above a certain fixed value. Tangze explained this to Ramon, and Ramon said, '*Sí, señor.*'"

IV.

"When the floods had gone down, we started. We were six altogether, Ramon, myself, Tangze, and three porters to carry tents and grub. I took a cordite rifle, a Luger pistol and a gun I've found the usefulest of any for everything bar big game; it was a double barrel, one barrel choke. I reckon that was the narrowest choke bore ever drilled; close to any big beast, I believe it would have been deadlier than a rifle. I've never measured, but I judge that at ten yards you could have covered the scattering of the shot with a penny — so to speak.

"We left Yaniero on a Tuesday morning at sunup, with the toucans yelping above the trees and the mist blowing away in the morning wind, and every prospect of another hot day. We left in a steam launch we'd hired, with a chap to run her and take her back, and in two minutes we'd turned a bend of the river and Yaniero was out of sight. It was the Javary we were navigating, and you should see that river after the rains, with the last of the dead logs drifting and the alligators sunning themselves, and the smell of river mud and rotten leaves and decaying vegetation and dead bodies of things that'd been drowned months ago.

"It's not a good river at any time. I'm not saying that any tropical river is good; but the Javary beats the band. It's lonesome, it's got a feeling of being tucked away, and it's ugly. Gets on one's spine. However, we weren't tied to it for life, and the place Ramon was seeking for was only thirty miles or so above Yaniero.

"We struck it about two hours before sunset on the second day, landed, camped, and sent the launch back with orders to come again in a month and stick till we turned up. Then we lit our fire and cooked supper, while the porters built a *tambo*. A *tambo*'s a shack; they don't take more than a few hours to build, and on a march, unless you're moving on a track where they are already built, you put one up every night. It's like putting up an umbrella. Then, you see, on the return march, you have them ready built for you.

"That night, as we sat round the fire talking and smoking we heard the howling monkeys as we'd never heard them before. The brutes kept pretty shy of Yaniero, but ten miles from houses they came down most to the water's edge, and sang. And they don't really howl — they roar. If you can fancy a couple of dozen children turned into giants and roaring over some broken toy or another, you can fancy a howling monkey concert. We fired a few shots and drove them off a bit, and then when we could hear ourselves thinking, we went on with our talk.

"Ramon was letting himself loose on his pet subject, and I will say that, though I don't take much account of vegetables, his talk interested me a lot. He was a tree doctor as well as a rubber hunter. He seemed to know all about trees and their ailments. He said they suffered just as humans do, got cancer and consumption and so on, and that they had their likes and dislikes. He said also that they fought with one another, and from what I've seen of the jungle above Yaniero I believe he was right. They don't hit out and pelt each other over the heads, they fight with their roots.

"Ramon said that all over the jungle there was always a great battle going on underground between the roots of the pachyuhas and matamatas and rubbers and euphorbias and so on. He said that it wasn't so much tree fighting tree as species fighting species, and where you find great tracts of matamatas, f'rinstance, that was where the matamatas had won a victory long ago and taken up the land for their own people. I believe he was right.

"Well, this chap goes on talking of climbers, air shoots, and water shoots and so on and telling of their ways; and then he tells of an orchid he found and lost more than a year before. He came on it somewhere about that spot. It was hanging between two trees, and it beat creation as far as orchids went, for it had six or seven things like feelers out of it, and at the end of each feeler was a butterfly, a real butterfly as far as looks went, all different colors, yellow, blue, red, striped — and any movement of the air made the butterflies' wings go as if they were flying.

"'Oh, come!' said Tangze at this point. If he'd given Ramon a blow in the face, Ramon couldn't have taken it worse, without hitting him. Tangze had to apologize, which he did handsomely, and the orchid man gave us the end of the yarn. He'd been wandering a bit from camp when he found the thing, and he went back for a companion to help him to hive it. Then when he came back, he couldn't find it again. It had been so high up, hanging from a tree branch, that it wanted two men, one standing on the other's shoulders, to get at it. That's why he went for his companion.

"They hunted here and they hunted there, but still they couldn't find it. They got all the rubber gatherers in and offered a reward of ten dollars to the chap who would spot its whereabouts. Lost time. Then they gave it up as a bad job. Their main business was getting rubber, anyway.

"Ramon hadn't well finished before Tangze struck in with a yarn about the Malay jungle. I went to sleep under my mosquito net in the middle of it, and didn't wake till I was kicked.

"Dawn was up, and we'd got to start. Ramon said we had to negotiate a bad place. But that was an old rubber road which he thought was still open — but wasn't. Not a sign of it. I tell you in that jungle you can cut a road twenty feet broad today, and in a month you won't find it. It's not a matter of quick growing, but of quick flowing — the vegetation spreads like water. I'll give you an idea of what it was like just there where the old road had once been. First there were the trees. Big trees and little trees and thick ones and thin ones, tree ferns and bushes. Looking through the air at noon when a chap'd have got sunstroke in the open if he'd showed his nose without a hat, it was like the inside of a cloud getting along toward evening time. There was something solemner about that bit of jungle than I'd ever struck among trees, and I've seen a good many tracts of forest.

"Looking about you could see far and near as if the air was hung with lace high up. It was the liantasses, and across the lace shooting up like rockets you could see the shoots of the wild pine — air shoots and water shoots. To get a drink, you'd only to cut one of them. Then there were cables of creeper, thick ship's cables; and hanging sagging between the trees and on the cables, here and there, were orchids. Orchids by the hundred, hanging in that steaming heat. You've smelt a glass house when everything is growing, and the furnaces stoked — well, that's the smell that I'm smelling now when I think of those orchids.

"So much for the trees, and everything six feet above ground. If that had been all, traveling would have been a picnic. But Lord! — the undergrowth! It wasn't so much that things grew, but that nearly everything grew thorns. Thorns half a foot long, and thorns you couldn't see till you felt them. Wait-a-bit thorns that had hooks on them same as a fishhook held you back, and while you were dealing with them, good old lazaret thorns jabbed you here and there to make you hurry up.

"Under the thorns ran ground vines to trip you up, and where there weren't vines there were boggy patches to trap you. I'm telling you all this to show you that the Amazon forests — at least, the forests of the upper Amazon — aren't as much forests as strong houses, and that a hundredth part of the things they hold in the way of new species of plants and insects haven't been tapped by naturalists. Why, already on our first day's march, Tangze was finding all sorts of new mosses and suchlike, for the ax men were going before us cutting and slashing with cutlasses to make a road.

"That's how we traveled, cutting our way before us; and I've never felt sicker than I did the first few hours, with the smell of sap and cut, green things. You'd see the sap spurting, sometimes; and when it wasn't spurting, it was always oozing; you'd see the green stuff curling away like snakes cut across. Then after the first few hours, I got used to it, and didn't care. But somehow, ever since that, it's been in my mind that growing things are as much alive as walking things and crawling things, and a forest is almost, as you may say, a living body.

"I didn't get much use for my gun. Vegetables were what we were after, and it came in on me, making me burst out laughing once, that Tangze was a vegetable hunter and nothing else. He was after big game in the way of vegetables. I laughed at the time, when I thought about it; but it wasn't a laughing matter by any means.

"Vegetable big game sounds funny, but it's not funny when you come up against the thing itself. A pachyuha tree's as dangerous as a snake if you come up against it suddenly and feel its teeth before you see them; and there are worse things in the jungle than pachyuha trees. We weren't long in finding that out.

V.

"I'm coming along now to the thing that scared me. Scared me stiff for fifteen seconds or so before I got the clutch on my nerves to deal with it.

"I've found out it's the new things that matter in this life. The old things don't count, as far as nerves go. Put a man right in front of what he's never seen nor realized, and his courage — well, it isn't there, just for the minute. You try an earthquake if you want to see — a good old South American seaboard earthquake — or come on what you think is a ghost! Well, it happened this way. Ramon hadn't said anything about fever in his talk at Yaniero. I suppose it was such a common thing in those parts that he forgot to mention it. And the upper Amazon jungle fever is a thing that's best forgotten, anyhow. It's not malaria, as far as I can make out, but a sort of twin brother, and you can catch it without being bitten by mosquitoes. Two days after we left the river, a man went down with it. And who was that man, do you think? Ramon. You'd have sworn that if one of us three went down, it would be either Tangze or me. But it was this chap who you'd have thought to be salted.

"We'd built our second *tambo* and there was nothing for it but to settle down till the chap was better. It took him three days to get his pins under him, and then they were so shaky we decided to stay for another day before pushing on. The *tambo* was built in a clearing, and the jungle round there was thinner than we'd met for some time. That day, having seen that Ramon wanted for nothing, Tangze and I settled to go off on a little prospecting trip of our own; nowhere far — just round a bit to see what we could pick up in the way of plants and animals. We blazed a trail and on top of that we kept the camp within helloing distance; and on top of that I'd got my compass. I'd also taken the double barrel. Of course, we were to stick together and not lose one another.

"Well, now, would you believe it, we hadn't been gone five minutes when I startled a bush pig and was after it, forgetting Tangze and every blamed thing but the game ahead. These bush pigs run queer. Give them clear ground, and they'll beat the band for running; but right in the thick jungle, they'll lie up as often as not, and let you go by them, if you haven't the eyes to spot them.

"This part wasn't specially thick, but there were thick clumps. I could see the beast ahead, or thought I could, till all at once it came to me that I'd gone too far. I stopped in my tracks and shouted. Tangze replied, and he wasn't so far off by the sound of his voice, so I took things easy, and didn't hurry to join up, for there were those patches to be avoided, and the ground was pretty soggy.

"I'd stopped for a moment to look at a water vine that ran double like two tubes connected together, when I heard Tangze's voice to the right of me, and more distant than I'd heard it last. I heard him cry out, 'Hello!' but not louder than if he was talking to a person he'd just come across. Then it came again, quick — 'Hello! Hello!' Then I heard him cry out to me — 'Brandt — help! help! help!' Just like that. Then I heard him scream. Scream like a stuck pig. I knew it was either pain or terror or both that made him scream like that, and I was into the thick stuff, like a bullet, in the direction of the sound.

"It was all thorns and tangle. If I'd had time I could have got to him quite easy by beating a way round, for, as I was saying, this part of the jungle wasn't bad compared to the rest; but I had no time. It was life or death, and I knew it.

"I hadn't reached him when the screams stopped, but I was right on to him, and the sound of his struggling gave me the last directions. I broke from the tangle into a clearing, and then I saw Tangze. He was standing and struggling there in the twilight, fighting dumbly with something — I couldn't tell what, till I saw it was a spider.

The thing was hanging between the trees and the body of it wasn't more than twice as big as a coconut, but it seemed to have fifteen hundred arms, and a lot of them seemed tangled round Tangze. That was my first impression. Then, in the next flash, I saw that the arms were all curled at the ends like tendrils, and I knew for certain that the thing was no spider but a plant made in imitation of a spider — only ten hundred times bigger. I didn't notice the heap of bones of bush pigs and monkeys the thing had been feeding on, but I did notice that Tangze was being lifted off the ground by the tendrils that had got him.

"He was in a Venus flytrap, only made different, and a hundred times bigger. A trap for catching monkeys and pigs and jaguars.

"What did I do? Well, I had no time to think, but by instinct I treated that vegetable as if it had been an animal. I took aim at the body of the brute as it hung there between the trees and sent the contents of both barrels through it. Killed it. The tendrils curled down, and Tangze was dropped on the ground. But that didn't mean he was free.

"When I got up to him, he began to come round, and he shouted to me to keep off, or I'd get stuck up, too. Then it broke on me without any more explaining what was the matter, and how the thing had seized him.

"As he told me after, it was like this: He was working along through the thick stuff when he came to the clearing. He wasn't looking up, else he'd have seen the thing above him. What he did see was long, green tendrils hanging down and curled a bit at the ends. He hadn't more than noticed them, when, making a step forward, his leg touched one of the tendrils, and it stuck to his trousers as if it had been glued. He bent down and caught hold of the tendril to pull it away. It stuck to his hands. He got it away from the cloth of his trousers, but somehow, in doing so, it had glued itself to his coat sleeve — right coat sleeve. He twisted round, trying to free the sleeve, and found he had blundered into another tendril that was round his left leg just above the knee.

"You understand, the plant didn't do a thing, or make a move. All the trapping was done by the chap struggling to free himself. All the same, and it's a pretty grim fact, the plant must have been constructed so's to take advantage of the nervous terror of animals that find themselves trapped.

"A bush pig or a lynx, for instance, passing along there, would have almost sure been caught by the leg. Having no hands to free itself, it would try with its teeth, and get properly glued, for the thing sweated glue from its tendrils when food was near it, just as a man's mouth waters at sight or smell of a good dinner. A monkey caught would have carried on same as Tangze did. The more he struggled, the more he was tangled, and he said it wasn't so much the feeling of being trapped as being glued that made him shout and lose his senses and fight like a maniac. He said the feeling of being caught by stickiness was a lot worse than the feeling of being caught by a tiger.

"Well, with the help of caution and using big leaves to get a grip of the tendrils, I managed to undo him, though I nearly got stuck myself once. Then, when I'd got him free, I looked up to where the rags and remains of the body of the beastly thing was hanging in the air and, putting in two more cartridges, I shot it away.

"I've often thought of what its anatomy must have been. That body and head combined would have sure sucked Tangze's blood when the tendrils had raised him up to it. But I wonder what the mechanism was. Probably not more than the inside of a leech.

"Quite simple, and yet, as I've told you, it was the only thing I've ever shot that frightened me, and I've shot a good few things in my time in the way of beasts and men.

"Here's Victoria."

THE CHILEAN GIRL

"TALKING of girls," said Dolbrush, "I'll tell you a yarn about a Chilean girl. Ever been in Chile?"

"No," I said, "and I'm rather in a hurry. I've got to catch the Oakland boat."

"You've got half an hour," said he, "and you'll only be kicking your heels on the wharf. Pass me those matches. What I'm going to tell you happened when I was working with Tod Robinson. Ever hear tell of Tod?"

I replied that I had not. I could have added that I wanted to know nothing about him or the Chilean girl, but the old sea trader was not listening. He was away in the past, and then the yarn began and pursued its course, unreeling like a ribbon, without a lift of the narrator's bushy eyebrow, or change of his expression, to its curious termination.

"Well, he was a chap from Aberdeen or somewhere there, struck Frisco young and innocent and was hooked by a San José woman for his good looks. Married him, she did, and then lit off with a Greek from the upper bay without waiting for him to divorce her. He and me met after that and we made big money one way or another with clean hands, till it come to a question of smuggling, if you can call gun running smuggling — which it is, but it's a better game than running dope or drink. I've done both. I've run opium and I've run spirits to my sorrer and my shame, but mostly to my sorrer. It don't pay, not when you add the risks you run to the rotters you deal with and reduce the answer to shillings and pence. No crooked game pays, and I'll tell you why — it's not the crooked game so much that does you in as the crooked players.

"The lowest-down thing ever written up for school children to read is that dope about honesty being the best policy, but it's dead true.

"But guns is different if you pull it off. There's big money in it and you're generally dealing with straight chaps, same as Scudder. Scudder was a marine store dealer in a small way and his place was foot of Fourth Street, close to Long Wharf.

"Scudd was six foot two and mostly bones and one night he came in to where we were living and folded himself double and sat down on a chair and told us he'd struck oil in a new place. He said Chile was going to revolute and wanted guns.

"Scudd was nowhere if he wasn't particular in his details, and he gave us a history of Chile from the hoof up. How it had a president and council of state and a conscript army and a national guard. He gave us news of the length of the Valparaiso-Santiago railway and the size of the public debt and the revenue, all about the gold mines and silver mines and copper mines and salt mines — and, 'There you are,' he finishes. 'The place is rotten with money and they want guns.'

"'Who want guns?' asks Tod.

"'The chaps that are revoluting,' says Scudd.

"'And who may they be?' I questions.

"'Search me,' says Scudd, 'but they've got the money and they don't want guns for shooting rabbits. Them new Winchesters is what they're after, and they'll pay their weight in gold. I've got in with a Spanish chap who's the agent, he's here in Frisco now with the money in his fist. The thing's as easy as pie! They don't want no shipload, only two hundred guns all told, for street fighting, with the ammunition; why, you could stow them in a hat case. A rowboat would carry them, and they'll pay ten thousand dollars to the men who run them, leaving out the cost of the weapons and the carriage. Ten thousand dollars just to run them.'

"'Net profit?' asks Tod.

"'Net profit,' says the other, 'and paid before you start.'

"'But that ain't business,' says Tod.

"'No,' says Scudd. 'Revolutions aren't run on cash-on-delivery lines; it's pay cash and take your chances in that shop. But they'll trust to the honor of any chaps I put them on to for the business. Will you take the job? I'll only ask a thousand commission so there'll be nine to divide between you two.'

"'Well, as a matter of fact,' says Tod, 'our old shark boat is out of commission. She's going into dry dock tomorrow for calking.'

"'And let her stick there,' says Scudd. 'She's not the boat you want. You don't take cows hurdle racing. I've got the barge that will do the job, she's lying at Faulkner's over at Berkeley. She's an old U. S. torpedo boat out of commission and sold for breaking up. They've taken all her teeth out but the engine runs and I reckon you can get fourteen knots out of her. Will you come and have a look at her?'

"'I will,' says Tod.

II.

"We dropped over to Berkeley that night, the three of us. Faulkner's Wharf isn't more than a boat stage. You get oyster fishers putting in there to clean themselves and the Greeks from the upper bay use it a lot. We came along across the planking and there, sure enough, moored next to a Whitehall lay the torp.

"G'strewth, I didn't like the look of her as I stood on the wharf edge. The little narrow deck looked more like the deck of a child's toy than anything else, and its length seemed to make it look narrower. I couldn't imagine taking that thing out through the tumble at the bar, but I didn't say anything, leaving it to Tod to make all objections.

"We dropped on deck and examined the fittings and climbed on the bridge and felt of the wheel. We dropped below to the engine room and stokehold where there wasn't room for a cat to pass and then we went into the cabin which was like the inside of a coffin. Then when we'd made our overhaul Tod turns to Scudd and 'I'll take her out,' he says, 'on the terms you name. Me and Dolbrush here will do it. Ten thousand dollars and all expenses paid including the hire of this sardine tin. Is that the figure?'

"'No,' says Scudder, 'you'll have to pay me a thousand commission, you forgot that.'

"'Not me,' says Tod. 'The other party pays the commission. If you want revolutions you've got to pay commissions. You go and tell Diego What's-his-name that and say if he don't, I'm off. Eleven thousand it will cost him, not ten.'

"Back we goes to Frisco, and next morning Scudder turns up and says that the other parties have agreed to pay the eleven thousand and that the guns will be ready for lading inside the week.

"That's the way we used to carry on in the old days. Never thinking nor caring what we poked our noses into if we smelled dollars and not for the dollars so much as the fun. When I tell you we were both fore-and-aft sailors with little knowledge of steam, you may guess what this job was like to us. We were to have an engineer, of course, and a complement of chink stokers and a Spanish chap to help with the steering and show us the spot to run the stuff. All the same we were to be in command and us not knowing the difference between a crank shaft and a clinked bar.

"I remarks on this to Tod and he only says, 'Oh, we've done worse in our time than that,' he says.

"There was no use in arguing so I let things rip, and one morning having got the chinks on board and the guns smuggled in with the coal and ten thousand dollars safe in the Bank of California to pay for our funeral expenses if we were drowned or more likely shot, we pulled out, Tod steering, and Alphonso — that was the name we give the Spaniard — on the bridge with us.

"We'd told the port authorities we were taking her down to Santa Barbara to break her up and they raised no objections though by rights she ought to have been broken up at Frisco, seeing the facilities there were.

"Hellbrow was the name of the engineer and he was worth his money. All the same we hadn't more than got free of the wharf than I was wishing myself back again. Tod was steering and I could see by the set of his jaw he wasn't happy. Steering a schooner is one thing and steering a tin coffin like the *Bolivar* — that was the name we gave her — was another.

"Chaps laugh at the old torpedo boats, but they had their points and speed was one of then. Size for size the old *Bolivar* would have beaten any destroyer going. Hellbrow down below was whacking up the engines for what they were worth and we were making a plume of smoke that carried — the wind being sou'east — from us to Tiburon.

"'If any darn thing gets in my way,' says Tod, 'don't wait for the smash but take a header. It's like trying to steer a runaway horse,' he says, 'and I reckon it's more a jockey's than a sailor's job. Nix on the steam, Hellbrow,' he shouts down the speaking tube, 'the bay ain't afire and we're closing down on the ferryboat lines.'

"We were. We had Angel Island to starboard and Alcatraz to port and the ferry tracks from Sausalito and Tiburon direct ahead. There was also a Chinese junk making as if to cross our course and away near Lime Point a big Cape Horner was coming in with everything set up to the royals.

"My teeth were chattering to the tune of the engines and I was holding on to the siren rope giving it a chug every half minute between my prayers, but nothing seemed to frighten that junk. Along she came, the big eyes staring in her bow. Within twenty jumps of her we were aiming to hit her right amidship when Tod put the wheel hard a star-board and we lay over with the turn, the foam roaring down the deck that was half awash, and a ferryboat jumping ahead of us now, not three cable lengths away and full of passengers. Couldn't shift your helm in that place and going at that speed without aiming to hit something and hit it quick.

"With helm hard aport we shaved that ferryboat so close I could see the name on a paper bag a woman was eating buns out of, then we tried to hit Fort Point, next to near killed ourselves on a dredger, tried to abolish Point Bonito and got nearly smothered in the tumble at the bar. We were going half speed by now and the big, green seas were meeting us with the gulls and the wind and Tod hands the helm over to me with the whistling buoy on our port quarter and the Farallons showing over the sky line on the starboard bow.

"'Done it,' says Tod, and he had. Most of the troubles I've seen at sea have been come across getting in or out of some darn port or another, and it was the case with us. Outside the Gate we laid a course near due south, keeping San Pedro Point six or seven miles to port.

"We were used to the Pacific but we weren't used to coastline business, and we didn't know the Americas were as big as they are.

"To run along the coast down to Chile sounds all right and looking at the map it don't seem far, but you try it in a torpedo boat, old pattern. We kept along with the Kiro Shiwo past Santa Barbara — where we coaled — and the islands and Lower California, then we crossed the big bay Central America makes in the earth and the next land we hit was Cape Blanco. Then we got across the Gulf of Guayaquil limping, though we'd coaled at Acapulco. We got to Bayovar with swept bunkers and Hellbrow was just putting the last cinder on with the tongs, so to speak, when we dropped anchor.

"We got enough coal at Bayovar to take us along down to Callao, and there we filled up and scraped the salt off the funnel and shook ourselves and went ashore to have a look round. You can kill a man and go to Callao and never be caught, for there's no extradition or wasn't in those days, but chaps don't stay there — they prefer being hung. So we lit out the second day after coaling and bumbled along to Antofagasta where we took another scuttleful of coal and had a propeller blade straightened, leaving next day for our last destination which was Papudo, a town on the sea just above Valparaiso. It's only fifty miles between the two and there's a railway between them. The goods were to be laded on the beach at night and Alphonso said there would be men waiting to receive them, get them on to the rail for Valparaiso and from there they'd be easy sent by rail to Santiago. Well, it wasn't all as easy as that.

III.

"One evening Tod comes down and pulls me out of my bunk.

"'Papudo,' says he. I come on deck and sees nothing but half a million miles of sunset and near the same number of gulls; then on the port beam I picks up the coast. Up on the bridge I could see a beach that looked a hundred miles long and a town I could cover with my thumb nail, and back of the town hills with the last of the sun on them.

"Alphonso orders the engines dead slow and we squatters along, the dark setting in and the stars coming out, same as if a chap was running about lighting them. Then the lights of the town began to show up across the water and we hove to and ran up a red light.

"Alphonso had sent a code message from Antofagasta and he said chaps would be watching out and would answer with a green light, and sure enough five minutes later from the beach to south of the town a green light showed. It was pretty to see it answer up like that, but we'd scarce time to admire it when Alphonso spoiled the show by saying it might be a trap. He said f'r instance if any one had turned traitor for a packet of cigarettes and given the show away the authorities would answer up with a green light so's to get the guns ashore.

"That chap was as cunning as a bagful of weasels. He said he'd row ashore with two of the chinks and some old dunnage in the boat. The *Bolivar* could put in close, as it was deep water and steep beach right up to the surf line. He'd yell if he was seized and if he did we were to put right out, dumping the guns and ammunition overboard as we went.

"'Right,' says Tod and in we put, dropping the boat with Alph and the chinks and some old dunnage covered with coal sacks, two cable lengths from the beach. Then we hung, riding the tide and flapping our propeller, listening and looking and Hellbrow below waiting for the word. We saw the boat take the pebbles and chaps swarming round her and we heard Alphonso yell same as if he'd been knifed.

"'Whack her,' shouts Tod down the tube to the engine room, shoving the helm hard aport, and round goes the *Bolivar* on her heel, as you may say, shooting out to sea with the sparks coming from her funnel and a bow wash near as high as her gunnel.

"Now those Chileans as we found out afterward hadn't been content to send a shore party along to nab the guns. They'd got a sort of jackass destroyer at Valparaiso, one of the first destroyers ever invented, and invented before her time, called the *Maipu*. They had several good ships like the *Esmeralda* and the *Covadonga*, but they laid most store by the *Maipu* as she was the fastest. They sent her out and she'd gone up north to meet us and missed us, and now she was coming back. Alphonso had warned us that she might be about and when we saw the triangle of her lights, for the fools on board of her had never thought to dowse them, we knew she must have seen the shore signals for she was steering straight for the beach.

"'Look out, Tod,' I says, and he turns the spokes of the wheel and heads the *Bolivar* due south. We hadn't been running five minutes when we saw the lights behind us, same old triangle only dead astern.

"'They're after us,' I says.

"'Sure,' says he. 'It's this damn Spanish coal, all sparks and clinkers — we're leaving a trail like a firmament. No matter, it's forced draft or nothing.'

IV.

"We kept at it the whole of that night; at daybreak we saw her. She'd closed up to a mile away and she was a warship right enough. She didn't wait longer than till the sun took her bridge canvas before she began target practice. It wasn't that which worried us but the fact that she had the pace of us, and half a mile away from her when the shells were shaving our heads, we stopped the engines, hung out a white shirt as token of surrender, and lay wallowing. Then as she hove to and a boat was coming aboard, I said to Tod, 'Lord, Tod! we've forgot to dump the guns!'

"We had that, but it was too late to bother, for the officer man from the *Maipu* was coming aboard, a little, dark, good-looking guy and the nicest-spoken chap I've ever fell in with.

"He could talk English without making a fool of himself, and Tod, to cut the matter short, told him about the guns. The other, Captain Valores was his name, thanks Tod for his frankness and there they stood paying compliments and bowing to each other, and there I stood watching them with my mouth banging open till I remembered that one was Spanish and the other Scotch.

"It's astonishing how the Spanish and Scotch get on together in friendship or fighting, but all the same Valores was a man of business, for he told us straight that when he got us to Valparaiso we would be tried and if we were condemned we'd be either shot or put to work in the copper mines.

"Then he went over the side back to his ship telling us to get along ahead in front of him and that if we tried to do a bolt or were up to any monkey tricks he'd sink us. He hadn't men enough to put a prize crew on board us, so he took us like that, same as a constable marches a tough to jail with a pistol to his head.

"The weather had changed with more wind and a bigger sea and off we trotted, slushing through the green half speed, and them a few cable lengths astern. I turned in to do a sleep, leaving Tod in charge, and was pulled out half an hour after.

"'What's the matter?' says I.

"'She's broke down,' says Tod.

"I knew he wasn't meaning the *Bolivar*, for the engines were going, so I got on deck and there was the *Maipu* rolling in the trough, the wind and the sea drifting her ashore, and the waves breaking ten foot high on the rocks. We were heading back for her.

"'What have you shifted your helm for?' I asks him.

"'I'm going to help her,' says he.

"'Help her to take us to Valparaiso?" I questions.

"'Help her, anyhow,' he says.

"It was sure death for her if she was left, but it was damnation for us if we were taken. However, there was no use in arguing with a chap like that so I keeps my head shut and we closes with her. There was no time for boat lowering or frills, she was rolling gunnel under nearly and we flung her a line as we passed, pitching the seas over ourselves. They grabbed it and we passed a hawser.

"Then we headed sou'west, she after us with a string of bunting flying which we couldn't make out.

"She towed like a drogue and the *Bolivar* wasn't built for the work. Still, we managed. Seamanship begins where plain sailing ends and Tod was a seaman. He was as happy as a woman up to her arms in soapsuds, all the same I wasn't any too easy in my mind. Chile is near two thousand miles long and about an inch broad — how they ever made such a ribbon of a country gets me — and here we were, gun runners condemned and certified, towing a Chile warship Valdivia way with Juan Fernandez the nearest port on the west and Cape Horn the only safe spot to the south.

"I said so to Tod and he only laughed. I said to him, 'But where are we taking her to?' and he said he was taking her nowhere, only towing her till the weather moderated or she'd tinkered herself up. He asked me what else was to be done and I couldn't tell him. It was the living truth that if we didn't leave her to be driven ashore we had to keep towing and from the nature of the case we had to keep in Chilean waters. So we bumbled along, making due south all the time and all that day, till next morning when she fired a gun and let off a blast on her siren to let us know she'd tinkered herself and was able to go without crutches. Then we pulled in the loose end of the tow rope and turned our nose south full steam ahead.

"We were level with a place called Vichuguen where the Mataquita River comes down, and the sea had quieted a lot; I was at the wheel and as I steered I turned my head and there was the old *Maipu* still after us, making signals and waving her arms for us to stop.

"'Well, of all the cheek,' says Tod, 'after what we've done for her — what's the Spanish for gratitude? Ain't such a word, I do believe, in the whole of their dictionary. Whack her up, Hellbrow,' he shouts down the tube to the engine room that was shouting up that the coal was rubbish and the pressure falling.

"'Never mind the coal,' he says. 'Stick a chink on, blow the cylinder heads off, bust her, but beat that darn Spaniard.'

"But it wasn't any use, she'd strained herself in the towing or the engines had taken it into their heads that they were doing too much work considering their age, anyhow the pressure was falling, gradual at first and then like a fellow tumbling downstairs when he's kicked.

"'We're done,' cries Hellbrow up the tube and we were.

"One hour and twenty-five minutes after that we were safe on board the *Maipu*, prisoners of war or simply caught smugglers, whichever you like to make it, all but a chink that had been crushed in disembarking. Then to put a tassel on the cap of the whole business Valores makes a target of the *Bolivar* and sends her to the bottom nose first.

"Then he invites us down below and gives us cigars and wine and after drinking our health, 'You're shipwrecked sailors,' said he. 'May I ask what was the name of your ship and where you were bound?'

"I begins to think that Uncle Valores had been getting at the wine before we arrived, but Tod, who had a headpiece twice as good as mine had tumbled to the other's meaning and, 'We were the *Sea Horse*,' he says, 'bound from San Francisco to New Orleans with a cargo of grain.'

"'With apologies,' says Valores, 'that won't do, for at Concepcion, to where I am taking you, there is a telegraph line and were I to bring you into port with such a story, San Francisco would be at once notified that the *Sea Horse* had been lost at sea and she would reply, "What *Sea Horse*?" and there would be trouble. Better make her a whaler, captain, no one troubles about whalers, and make her from an English port.'

"I began to see now that the little beggar hadn't sunk the *Bolivar* out of spite. He'd sunk the evidence against us and was going to repay us for our tow by landing us at Concepcion as shipwrecked mariners he'd picked up. A dangerous business for him, but the saving of us, for we'd run out of coal on the *Bolivar* — our bunkers were near swept, so where could we have gone?

"He told us right out that when we might have run away and saved ourselves we had stuck to him, and he said he would stick to us now even at risk to himself. The Chilean admiral had ordered him to take us at any price, but he said the admiral might go be damned.

"He was a proper sport and we were all thick as thieves before we raised Concepcion. Tod and him got on specially well together. He'd taken a great liking to Tod and when we got to port and before he landed us he offered us a loan if we were hard up. We weren't. We had plenty of money in our belts, all but Hellbrow, but we had enough for him and we said so. The chinks might have been dangerous and have given the show away but Valores took them under his care. I don't know what he did with them, boiled them for all I know — anyhow we didn't see them again. Maybe he sent them to one of his estates, for we soon found that Valores was no two-cent officer of a jackass destroyer. He was a naval officer right enough, but he was a millionaire as well, owned estates and mines all over Chile and did the naval business for fun. He had a queer history, for he wasn't a Chilean to begin with; he'd just come there some years ago with tons of money and invested the lot in real estate and left it to grow. Then he'd joined the navy and got command of the *Maipu*, being a capable sailor.

"We found out that from the hotel keeper where we put up, but we didn't bother whether he was a Chilean or what was his history, we only knew that he was giving us the time of our lives. He opened up Concepcion for us, introduced us to all sorts of folk and after we'd got a few decent clothes we found ourselves hobnobbing with the best people who thought we were ships' captains, and didn't care what we might be, seeing we were friends of Valores.

"The *Maipu* was being tinkered up all this time and I expect he gave orders to the dockyard chaps to tinker her slow while he had a lazy time on shore, for the weeks went by till one night he took us to a ball.

"I shan't easy forget that ball. Valores had been dancing with a peach of a girl with black hair and flowers in it; then Tod got her, and he and she stuck together like treacle for the rest of the evening.

"I've told you Tod was a handsome chap and she was a beauty. It was a pleasure to watch them and I was watching them canoodling toward the end of the evening when I caught sight of Valores. His eyes were on them and I've never seen a more devillike look than there was on that chap's face. Tod had got his girl, and he was looking at him as if he could knife him.

"We got home and I said nothing. I said nothing next day when I found Tod was after the girl again, visiting her, and I knew Valores had gone sour on seeing he did not turn up. Then on the third day the hotel man took me aside and he said, 'There is a steamer, the *Papua*, sailing for San Francisco tonight. Take your friend away, for Concepcion is not healthy for him,' and he drew his finger across his throat and winked.

"I said to him, 'I'm not going to inquire into the workings of your happy town — but is it Señor Valores that is the trouble?'

"'Sí,' says he, which means yes.

"Then Tod comes in and I says to him, 'Look here,' I says, 'you're a married man, though your wife's run away from you or you've run away from her, which is all the same. Quit fooling with that girl and let's get. Valores is after her and you've made a mortal enemy of him and he's going to have your throat cut.' I put him wise as to the position and that sobered him. He didn't care for the girl, only fooling with her, but he was mortally hurt at having knocked Valores in his affections and out he put to find the don and apologize and back he comes in an hour raging, for Valores, who'd shut himself up on board the *Maipu*, which was out of dock, wouldn't see him — only sent an insulting message that he never wanted to speak to him again.

"That night we put out on board the *Papua* which took us back to Frisco and we thought the business closed and done with. We had lots of other things to think of. We took our boat up to Seattle on a job, and when we got back we found, one day, the papers plastered with an advertisement asking would the sailors rescued by the *Maipu* communicate with Captain Valores at an address in Valparaiso.

"Tod laughed. 'That's Spanish all over,' he says. 'He wants to nail us over the gun running. Pretty thin, ain't it?'

"'No,' I says, 'it's not that. He's a gentleman. Besides it would never do for him to tell he'd let us escape. He's sorry and wants to make friends again.'

"'Well,' says Tod, 'he insulted me, and I never forgive an insult. You know that.' I did. And we left it so."

The captain fell silent and started to light a cigar.

"Is that all?" I asked, feeling somehow that the yarn was incomplete.

"No," said he, "it's not. A matter of eighteen years went by when one day I read something in the paper that raised the hair on my head. We were at Sydney then and I went to Robinson and, 'Tod,' I said, 'do you remember Valores?'

"'Oh, that chap,' he says.

"'Well,' I says, 'he's dead. Died an admiral in the Chile navy, but that's not all — after he was dead they found he wasn't a man.'

"'Then what the devil was he?' asks Tod.

"'A, woman,' I says. 'Been a woman all his life masquerading as a man; it's not the first woman that's done the same trick, according to this newspaper guy. There was a British woman who died an army surgeon, and a lot of others — but that's neither here nor there. Thing is, she was in love with you, Tod, and turned sour because you took up with that other girl. Lord! What you lost not answering that advertisement of hers, for she'd have been a peach in petticoats and she was worth millions.'

"Poor old Tod. He looked as if he'd got a knock on the head.

"He took refuge in saying she'd never have married him, seeing he was married already, though he didn't know where his wife was, but I countered that by saying if I knew anything of Chile laws that wouldn't have mattered to the lawyers, and if I knew anything of women it wouldn't have mattered a row of pins to her."

"You think she was in love with him?" said I, fascinated by this strange old story of the long ago.

"Sure," said the captain, "enough to make her want to kill him for fooling after another woman; enough to make her advertise after him. Sure as certain."

THE END
OF THE ROAD

IN THE YEAR 1913 I was on a walking tour in Italy. If you want to see a country you must walk through it. Speed blinds, and every one traveling over four miles an hour wears goggles.

I had no special destination. Rome lay behind me and before me autumn and the Apennines; no luggage except a knapsack, no worries, no letters to follow me.

If you want to see a country you must not only walk through it, but walk through it alone. Then it talks to you without interruption. You must have no worries to join in the conversation, no present but that which lies around.

So, day after day, with no companions but the vineyards and olive groves, the hills and the blue sky and the berry-brown country folk, Italy became a reality for me; and the fact is that Italy, despite the railways and the doings of Marconi, is still the Italy that the Borgias knew — the same passions, the same blue skies, the same people; though maybe outwardly altered a bit. It has the same fleas, also, I should imagine, to judge from my experience of the taverns where I put up at nights.

One evening before sundown a turn of the road brought me to an inn, a solitary building, standing on the right-hand side of the way, with not another house in sight, and placed there as though in defiance of custom. Buildings have for me almost as much personality as people. There are houses that repel, houses that attract and houses that leave me absolutely indifferent. This old inn standing there in its naked loneliness seized my imagination at once. Repelled me, yet attracted me. Over the door, in vague blue letters almost burned out by the sun, appeared the words Osteria del Sole; on a long bench to right of the door an old man was seated enjoying the afternoon warmth, and by his side was a black cat.

I asked for the landlord and he told me that he was the landlord, giving his full name as one gives a visiting card — Alfredo Paoli. With a half flask of Chianti to help the conversation we sat and talked in the warmth of that delightful sunset. We talked of Italy and the grape harvest and the taxes, and a reference to Garibaldi brought out the old fellow's age. He was eighty-five. Then, when I discovered that the town for which I was making lay more than six English miles away, he proposed that I should stay at his inn for the night. "You are welcome," said he, "and the place is clean as you will see for yourself. This is not an ordinary inn, and we who live here do not set ourselves out to entertain travelers except those who stop for a glass of wine, but your conversation pleases me, and I like you for yourself."

Now that invitation in that lonely place to a traveler on foot and with money in his pocket might have savored of robbery and murder to a suspicious mind. But I am not suspicious by nature, and old Paoli was plainly and evidently a person who wanted to rob and murder no one.

All the same he robbed me of a night's sleep and murdered my rest.

I agreed to his suggestion. He rapped on the bench with an empty glass and called out "Giovanna!" A woman's voice replied from the house, and in a moment Giovanna appeared at the doorway in the last rays of the sunset, a woman bent with age and incredibly wrinkled.

He ordered supper, and "the room" to be prepared for a guest, and then, Giovanna vanishing, relapsed into conversation about Garibaldi.

II.

Later that evening as we sat on the bench before the door, he told me his story, or rather the story of his youth. He spoke with the detachment of a man telling another man's story, as though age had made him indifferent to all personal things, and yet with the vividness of an artist in words stirred by an interested audience and warmed by wine.

"I was born in Perugia," he said. "A different city from the Perugia of today. My father was an antique dealer — his shop situated at the top of that steep street leading from the Piazza del Papa to a Piazzetta from where you can get a good view of the Umbrian Hills.

"His shop, at the top of this street, was in a bad position for business you will say. But my father was not a man to spread his net in a bad position; he reckoned to get as customers all the visitors — and they were many — who climbed the street to see the view. His family consisted of only two sons, myself and Arturo. We were twins, alike both in faces and dispositions; but Arturo was the more adventurous spirit and, having a passion for the sea, he became a sailor, while I, the eldest by some fifteen minutes, fell into the antique business as assistant to my father.

"That business requires a great deal of knowledge both of men and things, for who knows anything of tapestry who knows nothing of St. Florent of Saumur — or of bronzes who knows nothing of Gallien? But all knowledge is useless without the flair. This my father had and this in some measure I possessed. Things cried out to him their worth, and the most skillful forgery could have made itself known to him in the dark. Now why was this so? Very simply, because he had descended from generations of men who had dealt with art, both as artists and dealers. Old Italy lived in him, as in me. Old Italy with its passions and, alas! its power of hatred. So things went on till I had reached my twenty-second year.

"Then one day my life changed. One day in the Via dei Bontempi I met a girl.

"Now I had met this girl many times before. She was, indeed, distantly related to my family, and lived in a street close to where is now the Piazza Vittorio Emanuele. Her name was Giovanna Batista. She was of Genoese extraction, blonde, like so many of the Genoese women, and very beautiful. Hers was the beauty of a spring morning — the beauty of youth.

"Yet, though I knew her, it seemed to me that till that day I had never met her before. Though I had recognized her beauty it had never given me more than a passing thought. But today she looked at me differently. She had, in fact, suddenly chosen me. Just one glance of her eyes and her beauty fell on me like an avalanche, and I was hers. A moment before if I had heard of her death it would have left me almost unmoved.

"But I said nothing that day to her. I was like a man who has suddenly found a treasure in the street and who hides it under his cloak and hurries home with it.

"Next day I met her again, and again her eyes told me what I dared scarcely believe. I was new to the business. I did not know what to do. Alone with her in some country place I could no doubt have brought things to a conclusion very quickly, and almost without speaking, but, as I was, there in Perugia, there was nothing for me left but to call at the house where she lived or tell her of my love for her in the street — in cold blood! Anything seemed easier than that, and so I let things drift. And then she left Perugia.

"She had only gone away for a holiday of a month, but her leaving nearly killed me, and increased my love for her tenfold, if that were possible. Every place where I had seen her became for me a place of torture, and, at night, under a moon, full as it is now, I would stand on the opposite side of the way before her house, torn between sorrow, hope and passion. Surely love is a madness!"

He ceased for a moment to drink, and as he raised his glass in the light of the great broad moon, the old woman's croaking voice came from some room in the interior of the inn.

"Alfredo, the hour is late."

He laughed, called out to her to be still and leave him to his own affairs, and went on:

"Love had so completely taken me and eaten me that I was not more than the shell of a man. I had no head for business, nor eyes for art. I quarreled with my father, who could not make out what was wrong with me, and I lost five hundred lire over a deal on a spurious bronze that was palmed off on me by a trader from Florence.

"If things had gone on like this, I would have left Perugia and my home and business. But one day I recovered. Giovanna returned to Perugia and seemed to set all the bells ringing and the whole town *en fête*. I had news of her return through my relations. I met her in the street and I no longer delayed. I told her of my love for her, and she listened with head half turned away, then she turned to me and looked me in the eyes and smiled. She was mine.

"After that I was a new man. My prospects were good, and there was no opposition from Giovanna's parents; we would meet of an evening and stroll outside the town, always in the same direction, toward a grove which was a veritable lover's walk, filled as it was with paths leading nowhere. Here we would sit on a fallen tree trunk we had made our own, not minding if the weather was cold, and talk of the future, of our love for one another, and of the hundred nothings that make up the conversation of lovers.

III.

"We were to be married in the summer. And meanwhile came Carnival.

"In those old days Carnival was perhaps a more joyous affair even than now. There was more joy in the old world, I think, than in the new. Men forgot their businesses and women their houses and children their toys. King Carnival ruled them all and made them forget even Lent.

"It was the last evening of Carnival, and I was to meet Giovanna at a selected spot near the Duomo. She had chosen a Spanish costume, and as for myself I had chosen a suit of motley and a crimson mask.

"Now mark how things happen in life.

"My father, who had not been very well for some time, remained at home that day. Knowing of his ill health and wishing to be in touch with him without returning home, I had given him the places where I could be found at certain hours. I would be at my friend Manfridi's at noon, I would be in such-and-such a place at two o'clock, and at ten minutes to six I would be at the Fonte Maggiore close to the Duomo to meet Giovanna. You would have said that this last appointment would have found me at the place before the time, and yet I was late.

"The clock at Manfridi's house was slow. There were many robbers about, that year, and I had left my watch at home rather than trust it among the crowd of Carnival, and, as a result, when I finally reached the Fonte Maggiore the bells were striking. I had not heard the quarter chime, and I could scarcely believe my ears at hearing the hour strike nor my eyes when they did not show me Giovanna.

"Then I knew. I had offended her. She had come and, not finding me, had gone away. If I had thought for a moment, I would have seen the impossibility of a young girl waiting there by the Fonte Maggiore alone; and I could have put the blame entirely upon myself. Instead, anger and bitterness filled my heart.

"I knew for a fact that Giovanna, for all her soft ways and looks, had a temper sharp as steel. I stood there looking about me filled with this thought and the anger of a disappointed man. People were passing, all making for the Corso, all talking, laughing and with an air of festivity and enjoyment that increased my anger and irritation till it seemed to flow against the whole world. I crossed the way and entered a wine shop. Here I took my seat and called for drink, heedless of the other drinkers.

"I did not notice a dark, slim man seated at a table near by. I drank. In those days a very little wine was sufficient for me. I had not a good head for the drink, but this evening it seemed to me that were I to drink a ton, it would not drown my wits; and I was not drinking wine but Lambec. It was a Gambrinus — Lambec laced with cognac.

"Men talk of magicians, but where will you find a magician like to alcohol? In ten minutes I had passed from anger to a sort of despair and from that to recklessness. Then of a sudden I had all but forgotten Giovanna. I was talking to the thin, dark man who had recognized me and who spoke to me by name. He was an art dealer from Pisa. I had seen him at my father's shop, and he had called there that day to do business despite Carnival time, but could not gain admittance owing to my father's illness.

"He had several things to dispose of at a marvelously low price — things most likely the product of some robbery received by him and dangerous to traffic within Pisa. We had often customers like this. It was not our business to inquire into other men's morals or the morality of their transactions, and as long as we did not suspect them to be robbers themselves, we took their goods.

"He had with him, this man Bodini, a cross of pure gold studded with small stones, a pair of earrings, and a dagger of Florentine work with a silver hilt. He offered them and told me the price. I had not that amount of money with me, but that did not matter to Bodini; our business was as good as a bank and our name good for a thousand times the amount he asked for — which was seventy lire for the cross and earrings and twenty for the dagger. I placed the jewelry in my bosom, and the dagger in its sheath I placed in the single pocket that the costume maker allowed a fool. Then Bodini took his departure and, just as though a cord had snapped, I plunged back into trouble and misery of mind. I left the tavern.

"The lights were now springing alive and the stars breaking out overhead. The noise of the Carnival rose through the evening like the sound of a sea.

"I stood undecided. Should I go to Giovanna's house on the chance of finding her there? Then still undecided I turned toward the Corso. Perugia seemed mad that evening. The spirit of Carnival had flared up like the flame of a lamp, all sorts of conditions of people went to make up the mob into which I now plunged, but they were all in the same condition of mind — gay to the point of madness. Bullfighters jostled fools and Pierrots soldiers. In the crush I half forgot Giovanna for a moment and, carried along by the stream, I acted the part of Folly though I had forgotten my jester's bauble.

"Then, of a sudden, the crowd parting slightly before me, I saw Giovanna.

"She was with a man. Their backs were toward me, they could not see me, though I could almost have touched them. He wore the coat of a Pierrot and a false nose tied behind the ears; taking advantage of the crush, his arm was about her waist. They were laughing. The sound of the last trumpet could not have stricken me as that sight did.

"Now, in my dealings with Giovanna, I had always forgotten one thing, and that was the fact that I was not the only man in Perugia. She had chosen me from a score of lovers and that fact had made me forget the score. I remembered them now.

"The dagger in my pocket jumped into my hand. A moment more and it would have been plunged in the back of the Pierrot, but that moment did not come. A horse, loose and garlanded, came racing down the Corso, the crowd swayed and rushed back carrying me with it, and separating me from my revenge.

"Giovanna and her companion were nowhere to be seen. They had been swallowed up by the crowd.

"You can fancy my position — rage in my heart and a dagger in my hand — jostled by laughing fools — carried hither and thither against my will. But my will was strong, and, though unable to command the movements of the people around, it enabled me to return the dagger to my pocket, to grip the situation with my teeth as you may say, and to regain my calm. I resigned myself to the situation and, though now I could have escaped from the crowd, which had thinned, I let myself drift with the stream.

"Then I had my reward. Close to the Via Piccolo Umberto I saw my quarry. I saw Giovanna and her Pierrot, I came upon them so suddenly that I could have counted the hairs on the back of her neck or untied the tape that held his false nose to his face, yet my hand did not fly to the dagger in my pocket. I was cooler now, I could wait my time, and do my business without running the risk of death by the executioner.

"I followed them along the Via Piccolo Umberto. They never once turned, so interested were they in one another. But, one moment, monsieur —"

He rose and took the empty wine flask and went into the house. I heard him lighting a lamp and poking about, and then I heard his voice asking Giovanna what she had done with the key of the cellar, and Giovanna's voice replying that it was on its nail by the door.

The old woman seemed angry at being disturbed, and I could hear her grumbling. What an hour to be sitting up talking! Had he no sense — and with his rheumatism drinking with strangers like that?

And he was telling her that his rheumatism was his own and that if he chose to feed it no one had any right to interfere. Then he came back with a wicker-covered flask and, taking his seat, continued:

"I followed them along that street and then through another leading in the direction of her home.

"Then they entered the street where she lived, and right before her door they parted. Hiding across the way, I could not believe my eyes. True it was dark, and there were few about, yet it was known in the whole quarter, nay in all Perugia, that she and I were engaged to be married; and here, a few months before our wedding and for a trifling offense on my part, she was saying good night to a stranger, a man who had placed his arm round her waist, a man she had picked up in the Carnival. I saw their heads pressed together, and I heard the kiss. He had removed his false nose to enable him to kiss her, and now she was tying it on again for him.

"They were laughing, then they parted. She went into her house and he turned down the street walking swiftly, gay, and whistling a tune.

"I let him get thirty paces ahead, and then I slipped after him. In those few moments while hiding in a dark entry and watching the parting of those two, I had tried them in my own mind, judged them, and it was now for me to carry out the sentence of the judge. The man with the false nose had to die, the woman with the false heart had to die. But the man first.

"It was quite easy for me to kill him right there in the street. But were I to do so, I would be captured to a certainty, and then the woman would escape. You see my point, monsieur."

He uncorked the flask as he spoke and poured out the wine with a hand as steady as the hand of a young man, albeit the moonlight, now strong almost as the light of day, showed the metacarpal bones separately and distinctly as though it were the hand of a skeleton.

"You see my point, monsieur. I had to be careful, I had to treasure my life till my revenge was complete, and my revenge could not be complete till Giovanna had paid as well as he.

"Meanwhile I followed. My gentleman had picked up a jester's bauble from somewhere and now as he went he used it, striking here and there on the backs of folk with the bladder, laughing and jesting as he went, unconscious of the jester who was following in his footsteps armed with a dagger.

"He seemed to draw mirth and attention to himself just as a magnet draws iron. Girls, young men, old men, clowns, harlequins, monks, all had a word or a laugh for him or a handful of confetti. No one had a word or a laugh for me, eclipsed by his gayety and content to follow.

"Then my gentleman, not content with his affair with Giovanna, must seize upon another girl, taking her by the waist and whirling her off into a restaurant by the Corso. Several of her companions followed, but that made no difference to him. He had plenty of money and meant to spend it, and in a moment the Asti Spumante was flowing.

"You can see me outside, with death in my heart, watching the merrymakers and drinkers. I could not see my man's face for his back was turned toward me, but I could see that he was the life and soul of that party.

"Then it broke up and they all left, departing this way and that, he alone and taking the Via Andria Doria.

"It was there I did the deed. The street was deserted, there was no one to watch; it was so dark between the lamps that as I seized him by the shoulder, I could only see his face as a whiteness, something without form, something to destroy. I was mad. The whole events of the day and evening had come to a point. My love for Giovanna, my jealousy, my hatred — and under all the alcohol working like a serpent. He struggled with me, something stung me in the left shoulder as we fought, it was a knife he had drawn and which he dropped on the pavement as I drove my dagger through his heart.

"He fell and lay at my feet, a white heap. The dagger was still in his body, but I thought nothing of that, my only idea was to hide him.

"Now that was the strangest thing, for my mind was made up to kill Giovanna and then myself. So why should I wish to hide him, why should I trouble to hide him? I do not know. I only know that the mind of man is beyond the comprehension of man, and that in moments of great trial and tragedy it works in ways of its own.

"I dragged the body to the entry of a court and propped it up half sitting in a doorway. There in the half-light given by an oil lamp swinging from the wall it looked like a man drunk who had fallen asleep. Then I walked off, marking the court and where it lay, in my mind, and went home to change to my ordinary clothes — for I had now to meet Giovanna — and then die, and I had no mind to die in motley. I was careful not to wake my father.

"Then I went quickly to Giovanna's house, knocked and was admitted. Her family were still out, keeping up the last of the Carnival, but Giovanna was at home, and had not retired yet. After a moment's waiting she came down.

"I was standing in the room into which I had been shown — standing by the table facing the door. She came in and looked at me in surprise.

"'Why have you come back?' she asked. 'And so changed?'"

"I laughed out loud and looked at her and said not a word.

"Then she drew back and I saw that she was frightened. But what a strange thing is expression. It was driven in upon me at once that her fear was not of the consequence of her infidelity to me. I saw at once that her dread was that I had been drinking or had gone wrong in my mind. I had no weapon, only my hands, but they were strong enough. I looked at her.

"I said, 'What was his name?' She answered, 'Whose name?' I laughed, I said again, 'Where did you pick him up?' She answered, 'Who?' This enraged me and I said, 'Who? Why, the man who left you at this door not an hour ago.' She answered, 'I have met no man this evening but yourself.' I saw at once that she spoke the truth, yet I had seen what I had seen with my own eyes, There could be only one meaning to the business, some man must have impersonated me.

"I said so, and she laughed me to scorn. 'You were with me,' said she, 'and you alone, dressed as a Pierrot, with a false nose which you took off when you met me by the Fonte Maggiore.'

"'But God in Heaven!' I cried, 'I did not meet you there. I was late for the appointment and you were gone.'

"I saw that she either believed me a liar or mad. I felt mad indeed, just then. I found myself doubting my own mind. Had all this been a dream?

"I stood without speaking, feeling absurd, my eyes fixed on the floor. Then I thought of the man in the dark entry leaning against the door with the dagger in his heart, and at that recollection, as though a hand had been placed on each of my shoulders turning me, I turned, rushed to the door of the room, and left the house.

"I had entered that house to kill Giovanna, I left it half crazed, balked of my purpose, not knowing what to do.

"Then I found myself at my own door.

"The house was still in darkness, as before. But as I turned the key in the lock and entered, I heard my father's voice calling to know if it was me. He was lying in bed in his own room at the right of the passage, and as I entered I saw him there on his pillows propped up, a shaded lamp beside him and a book on his knees.

"'Ah, it is you,' said he. 'Where is Arturo?'

"You will remember that I said I had a twin brother, a sailor, as like to myself as one pea is like another.

"'What do you mean?' I asked. 'Arturo is at sea.' Even as I said the words a fear like the hand of death seized my heart.

"'Arturo returned today,' said my father, 'seeking you. I told him he would find you at the Fonte Maggiore at six o'clock where you were due to meet Giovanna.'

"Then I sat down beside the bed and, leaning an elbow on it, I said to my father:

"'I was late in reaching the Fonte Maggiore. Arturo got there before me. Giovanna mistaking him for me spoke to him and he, knowing that she must be my fiancée, and, for a jest, did not undeceive her. He was wearing a false nose and spending his money like a sailor. He saw her to her house, still keeping the jest up, and then when he had left her he made for home, reckoning to meet me and have the laugh on me. He did not know that I was following him, thinking him a stranger, with rage devouring me —'

"My father suddenly, as though a bullet had struck him, gave a leap on the bed and cast the book to the floor.

"'What are you saying?' he cried. 'Where is Arturo?'

"'Dead!' I replied, 'with my dagger in his heart.'

"I said the words as though I were repeating them from some other person's lips. I was quite calm. I could not seize what had happened at all with my real mind.

"Yes — that is the whole affair. They did scarcely anything to me, the pity of it was so great. I told the whole story just as I have told it to you.

"Then I married Giovanna. We went to Pisa to live; that was many years ago. So we have gone through the world never prospering greatly, coming at last to this.

"Well, at the end of the road what does it matter?"

We finished the wine and he showed me to my bedroom, and then lying awake and watching the white bars of moonlight on the bare wall of the room and listening to the wind in the olive trees, I could hear Giovanna's grumbling voice — "Well, you have come to bed at last. A nice thing, truly, keeping me awake like this."

THE LONG REACH

THIS STORY was partly smelled and seen, and it is impossible quite to convey it to you without the faint fragrance of sawdust and stale tobacco smoke, the picture of the bar whose window shows Chinese shrimp boats and freighters pounding up the blue bay, and the figure of Billy Meersam — and his face, like an old figurehead for fixity of expression.

Billy had been acting partner with the sea in many a job benefiting many an owner, with rivers, too, from the Cañon River to the Fly; a hard-bitten and earnest man with no book learning, but a huge lore of knowledge and fixed opinions about many things from a Zanzibari dance to the problem of native races. He had known Bully Hayes and Louis Becke, and he had seen R. L. Stevenson down in the Low Islands; when Krakatoa blew out he had heard the report of it, being in a ship only a hundred miles away; he was off Martinique when Pelée erupted, and he had a nephew quartermaster on the *Titanic*. Big sea occurrences seemed to have acted on him or his relatives like magnets, for there was scarcely anything in this way you could mention that he had not seen or heard, either personally or through the ears and eyes of relatives.

He had a curious lapse of memory once when someone baited a conversation trap for him with the great earthquake of Lisbon. However, when he swore that he had put out of Lisbon port only the day after that event, the thing fell flat on the joker owing to the ignorance of the bar audience and the fact that Meersam was standing drinks. Some people called him a liar, but I am inclined to think that his complaint, when it showed itself, was more in the nature of a functional derangement of memory.

However, this is the story he told me, and pretty much how he told it:

"The time I'm speaking of, Narbutt wasn't more than a youngster of twenty-five, maybe. He was a red Welshman out of Pembroke docks and used to playing on the accordion when the devil left hold of him for a minute, which mostly occurred when other folk was wanting to get asleep. He was one of those uneasy chaps that drinks standing instead of sittin' down like Christians, and when he was on the batter, he was on his legs right from the time he left his ship till he was landed in the cell. He didn't trouble no lodging houses nor breakfasts, he was busy taking cargo most the time, and the balance he was being bailed out. Often and again that chap ought to've been jugged for good. But he never was, the devil always managed to get him bailed, fearin', maybe, he'd forget how to play on his accordion.

"Those days there were a lot of hard ships about. I've seen myself the *Three Brothers* come into Frisco Bay with half the chaps in irons and the rest crazy and jumping overboard for the police boats to pick them up, but the hardest ship sailing out of Frisco in those days was the *Hawk*."

"I've seen her," put in one of the audience.

"She was scuttled before you was born," said Meersam, turning a cold eye on the interrupter. "Scuttled by Prowse, though they never brought it home to him, the same chap that shot himself a matter of seven years ago over that San Lorenzo business — well, this chap Narbutt was on his beam ends one day, out of a berth and sittin' in a bar when who should come in but Sam Packard. Heard of Sam Packard? Well, he was almost before my time. He was one of the old lot in the sandalwood trade, wore long white whiskers and a plug hat, looked like a missionary and talked like one ashore. He was master of the *Hawk*, and owner, married to a colored woman that run an opium joint and carried a reputation to match. He was on the lookout for a mate, and seein' Narbutt, stood drinks.

"Narbutt didn't have no luggage to collect, his accordion was under the seat, and his bundle he concluded to leave at his lodgings to pay what was owing. He signed on, got ten dollars advance, spent it on booze and joined his ship when old man Packard bailed him out and stuck him on the quarterdeck. The crew was chinkies and a chink stood for second mate.

"Y'see, not a white would as much as sniff at the *Hawk*, and the crimps had a down on Packard owin' to his having given evidence against Black Sam, a chap that used to run a shanghai shop down on the wharves. He give the evidence so as to suck up to the authorities, and then he found himself froze out, and much the authorities did for him. But there were two whites aboard the *Hawk* along with the chinks, two pore orphans by name of Blake and Dowie; 'prentices, Packard called them. They berthed with the Chows in the fo'c's'le, and on deck they spent their time bein' booted round by Packard and Narbutt.

"I've took notice that the afterguard never lays their hands much on chinks, they've got a kind of fear of chinks, maybe because of their slit eyes and unknown ways and the habits they have of easing off grievances by putting a light to the cargo or using knives on dark nights. Anyhow, Dowie and Blake got all the shoe leather on that ship and mostly from Narbutt. He treated them cruel, till one night they lays their heads together and goes for him, catching him aft of the galley, one before and one behind. He hadn't no real fighting pluck, and they wiped the main deck with him a treat before they were hauled off by old man Packard and the chinks. After that, Narbutt let them alone, and the old man didn't boot them so often, nuther. Once a cat gets the name for scratching it's left alone pretty well, and if old man Packard had left the gin alone it would have been all well enough for them two guys, but the old man drank hard and secret. You know them sorts of gin abolishers that's never drunk, citizens that goes from cradle to coroner's jury walkin' straight and always gettin' there? That was the sort Packard was, only he missed the jury.

"One night down south near the Solomons, Packard took it into his head that the devil had come for him at last, and, to give him the slip, went overboard so quiet that the chink at the wheel didn't notice.

"Narbutt did. Narbutt had just turned from a look into the binnacle, and he saw Old Whiskers lettin' himself down quiet. He run to the rail and saw the old man a fathom under blazin' with phosphorous and two sharks lashin' round him, blazin' likewise.

"The sharks was pullin' him to pieces same as a terrier pulls an old shoe, and Narbutt didn't wait to see no more. He made one bolt for the cabin and the gin bottle and there he sat till he'd drunk the sharks out of his head.

"Then when next morning came he found himself master of the *Hawk* and boss of Blake and Dowie. The chinks didn't care what had become of the old man, they was ready to take the orders of Narbutt, and this is what that scamp did. He had them two 'prentices up on deck and 'cused them of murdering Packard. They swore themselves blue they hadn't. That didn't matter to Narbutt. He swore he'd seen them do it. The chinks was standing by not caring a dump who'd murdered who, and when Narbutt give the order for a boat to be got ready and them two murderers to be sent adrift the chinks didn't grumble.

"They'd raised a big low island that morning, one of the Solomons most like, and it was still hanging on the starboard quarter some fifteen mile away and Narbutt, he says: 'That's your port and dest'nation, reach it if you can,' says he, 'and save your necks from the gallus.' There was a sea on, that didn't matter to Narbutt; he bundled them two 'prentices into a boat, the chinks lowered away and Blake and Dowie managed to cast off the falls and push out before they was stove. Not a biscuit nor a drop of water, not a blessed thing but the oars — and it would have been better for Narbutt if he'd left them oars out of the boat; he most likely forgot them, being in a hurry and his mind full of gin.

"The last thing he saw of them two 'prentices, they was standin' up by turns to curse him, then he went below to talk to the gin bottle, and when he come up again they was gone.

"You've heard chaps talk of their conscience as if they'd bought it at a jeweler's and paid a long price. Well, it's my experience, the lowest down shyster in Frisco has one of them things hid away somewhere, not that he uses it in business or takes it out for pleasure to look at same as a hundred-dollar Waltham — it's just there. Narbutt had one, and that night as he was walking the deck he had to go time and again to the after rail to see if them two chaps wasn't following him. He needn't have bothered, they was following him right enough. He woke up that night in his bunk and felt them in the cabin, and next morning as he was drinking his coffee they were sittin' in the bottom of the coffee cup. On deck it was the same, rattling him, and he quieting himself with gin. But you can't drown a Welshman in gin, and after a bit the bother let up on him and he began to sniff at his grub and get a purchase on his nerve. They reached port — Valdivia it was if I remember right — and discharged cargo, and Narbutt slung a yarn that was good enough for Valdivia, then he took up a cargo and run the old *Hawk* ashore at Point Blanco, where she was salved after a three months' job and taken to Sydney by the chap who'd bought her as a wreck.

"That saved Narbutt from going back to Frisco and facing the nigger woman in her weeds and the kind inquiries of all and sundry. Besides, he'd managed to bone the ship's money to say nothing of Packard's gold watch, which he'd left in the cabin before doing his dive; and he skipped at Sydney, changing his name to Jones, and started life again as one of them 'longshore dudes that don't seem worth nothin' but all the time with his eyes and claws open and Packard's money hid away careful. He got in with a scamp be name of Coolman, a German Jew, and the two of them colluded together and started a marine store hole of a place, by the docks, with a whisky joint in the back premises, and between cards and drink they was doin' pretty well till Coolman came a smash over opium smuggling and blew out, leaving Narbutt master of the show which he shut down prompt and started a pub.

"One day into the pub comes a chap by name of Wiserman, and he and Narbutt gets pretty thick, scenting each other for rogues and this Wiserman calls the next day and they gets thicker, till one day this chap lays a proposal before Narbutt. A friend of his had got the location of a guano island, the friend's name was Jaggers, and he looked it when Wiserman went out and called him in. Looked as if he'd swapped duds with a scarecrow and got left over the deal, but his goods were all right.

"Narbutt examined the credentials, got the chap to tell his yarn back'ard and forward, filled him with whisky, lent him a dollar, and sent him out kickin' and blind with stuff that made him wallop a p'leeceman and get jailed for a month.

"Narbutt had took a wife with the pub and he left her in charge whiles he and Wiserman and a chap called Hunt, one of them round-the-town boys with more money in his pocket than brains in his head, fitted out an old schooner to sample the guano.

"Hunt did the paying — trust Narbutt for that. It was a fifty-tonner, an old pearler by name of the *Wear-Jack*, and the smell of her would have lifted the lid off an oyster can to say nothing of the cockroaches and the rats as big as rabbits; for she'd been layin' up a matter of two years and been used as a store for all sorts, and one chap who'd hired her made a floatin' pub of her till the water police jugged him, but not before her fixin's had been kicked to pieces by drunks and the bedding laid on by them till it wasn't no more use for bedding. She was a holy show, but Hunt, he didn't mind, he said it was all in the game, seemed to like it. There's asses made like that, who thinks nothing's a picnic unless the rain's coming through the roof. Hunt was like that, and the old *Wear-Jack* played up to him. She give him no cause for complaint.

"In those days the Pacific wasn't charted same as it is now. What between the Germans and the British and the Americans and Japs, there's nothing now bigger than a footstool that's not on the charts and bein' used as a coaling station or a target for gun practice, same as Ten Stick Island, or a home for consumptives or drunks.

"In those days missionaries were being boiled and eaten on beaches where you see girls bathing now in Paris hats, and black-birding schooners cleaning themselves where the excursion steamers put in now to show the passengers the view. There was money to be come by in those days without a German trader in pajamas to head you off, and this island these chaps was after was as good as Klondike if it lay where it was located by Jaggers and answered to the manifest.

"East of the Solomons isn't a place for pleasure cruising, and east of the Solomons one bright morning they found themselves on the spot, and there sure enough toward noon the island showed up. What they sighted first was a hundred and twenty thousand million gulls like a bank of cloud in a whirlwind, and miles away and coming against the wind they could hear them catcalling and mewing, and then came the noise of the sea breakin' and that was the island. The most onholy place, not a tree nor a lift of the land, and a thundering big surf running on the reef, till they nosed round to the eastward and run in through a break that give them ten fathoms still water where they dropped their mud hook and lit ashore.

"It was a gull island. Lord only knows what makes gulls pick out an island and start a town same as you see them doing at Molekua and Midway, for they'll pick an' choose between two rocks stickin' out of the sea and choose the unlikeliest looking. But this place wasn't a rock, it was just a slab of guano, maybe with rock farther down but none showing. And it was half a mile wide and more than half a mile long. It was covered with gulls' nests and it was the hatching season, and Narbutt and the two other chaps, having prospected round, came back to the beach where the boat was, and put off.

"On board they had drinks. Then Narbutt spoke up and, says he, 'Boys, we're made, we sure are. There's enough guano there to fertilize Europe.'

"'What's it worth the ton?' asks Hunt.

"Narbutt gives him the figures. There's nothing this chap couldn't give you the figures about, and when they'd done calculating the weight of the find and present prices, and come to the conclusion that Rockefeller couldn't touch them, they fell to talking of how to make the grab.

"The place didn't belong to no one, but it was in British waters so to speak, lying between Malaita in the Solomons and the Ellice Islands. What I mean to say by British water, is that no German or American or French government could say: 'That's closer to us and part of our 'group,' for as I said, the Ellices lay to the west, and the Solomons to the east. South, the Santa Cruz Islands hedged it in off from the New Hebrides, and north the Gilberts lay between it and the Marshalls, and the German part of the Solomons was too far off to make trouble. No, sir, that bit of the sea is a British lake, same as the bit farther west that lies between Washington Island and Suwarrow, and Starbuck and St. Augustine.

"Narbutt points this out, and they agrees to claim it for the British government and run up the flag, say nothing about the guano, take a sample back to Sydney and having got a lease of the place get a syndicate together for the working.

"They concluded to start working next morning, and having finished business they started to drinking and playing cards.

"Narbutt always carried cards with him, cards and his accordion. I reckon the customs when he landed the other side of the Sticks found them on him same as Hunt did to his sorrer, for them two guys, Narbutt and Wiserman got Hunt between them that night and skinned him to the tune of ten thousand dollars and a third of his share in the guano business.

"They kept it up till five in the morning and then went to their bunks to be woke up before noon by the noise of the gulls and the snores of the three chaps they'd brought by way of crew, who'd managed to get on the drink and was layin' about on deck promiscuous.

"As soon as they'd got on deck Narbutt, who'd been drinking less than the others, having his eyes on the fleecin' of Hunt, saw there was something or another wrong with the island, either that or his mind was going.

"It was low tide on the reef but it was high tide on the beach.

"He was the only man who ever came up from a night's jamboree to find low tide to starboard and high tide to port and he felt like it.

"'Hunt,' says he, 'take a squint at that reef.'

"'What's the matter with the reef?' says Hunt.

"'How's the water on it?' asks Narbutt.

"'Dead low tide,' says Hunt.

"'Now take a squint at the beach,' says Narbutt.

"'What's the matter with the beach?' says Hunt.

"'How's the water on it?' asked Narbutt.

"'High tide,' says Hunt. Then his mouth fell open like a trap and his head turned from beach to reef and reef to beach, then he let one yell out of him and dived below for gin. Narbutt wasn't long after him, nor Wiserman, and they had a fight for the bottle. When they'd steadied themselves up they came on deck again. There was the flat level of the lagoon with a low-tide reef on one side of it and a high-tide beach on the other, and the gin having picked up their courage them swabs began to laugh at the business.

"Hunt said it was plain as day. He said the water had got tilted in the lagoon sideways be some reason or other, just as a chap might tilt a table. He reckoned an earthquake must have tilted the floor. He said that as a nacheral curiosity it would bring them in more money than the guano and wouldn't want no syndicate to exploit it.

"Then they kicked the chaps on deck awake and opened some tins and sits down to breakfast.

"Well, all that day they watched the tide rising on the reef and rising on the beach of the island till high tide showed the beach clear under and the water threatenin' to flood the land.

"Do you think them gin-addled gumpers twigged the truth that the island had been sinking since the night before and the reef standing fast? Not they. But they twigged it next morning when they woke up to find the land a foot under water and still sinking and the reef carrying on just as before. Lucky for them it did, for if it had done a dive, same as the island, the big swell would have been in on them and turned the *Wear-Jack* truck over keelson onto a liquid manure heap.

"By noon that day the whole contraption had turned into an atoll — one of them pond islands where there's nothing but a ring of reef, and nothing to show but a big harbor with the gulls yelping over it and their lost nests. The thing had sunk steady and silent as a piston in a cylinder, havin' stood there since the time of Noah, for the purpose of guying Narbutt — which wasn't a bad purpose neither — for the chap that went for him now was Hunt. Went for him he did and blacked both his eyes, the remembrance having risen in his head how he had lost a third share in the guano through cards — dealt by Narbutt.

"Folks is curious. I've seen a woman, whose child was near drowned by fallin' into a canal, cuffin' it over the head and then kissin' it and cryin' over it, and then cuffin' it again — like a jam sandwich, and here was Hunt blacking this chap's eyes, who'd no more to do with the sinking of the guano than the equator — and the stuff being gone it didn't matter if he'd lost his full share in it. But Narbutt got his black eye, anyhow, which was a blessing, and they clawed up the mud-hook and cleared out.

"And they didn't clear out none too soon, for the lagoon fish was coming to the surface poisoned by the guano, and the whiff of them would have blown the *Wear-Jack* from her moorings if they'd held on another few hours."

Mr. Meersam paused for liquid refreshment, and then went on:

"There was nothing left for them but Sydney and they put south, and it wasn't a happy ship. Hunt and Wiserman had both taken a down on Narbutt. He hadn't done nothing and the fault wasn't his, all the same they joined up against him. Maybe it was his red head, maybe it was his accordion or just the man himself it doesn't matter, there the fact stood. He couldn't do no right, and if he as much as opened his mouth they jumped down his throat.

"It held like that till one morning after sunup when they raised a big island away on the port bow. It was one of the outlying Solomons somewhere between the Santa Cruz Islands and Cristoval, and not ten minutes after they caught sight of a boat with two chaps in it and one of them waving an oar.

"Hunt and Wiserman were on deck and Narbutt was down below in his bunk. They didn't bother to call him up, but altered the course, and in less than ten minutes the chaps in the boat were clawing on to the *Wear-Jack* and Hunt was helping them aboard.

"They were natives, and they'd been out fishing in the boat which was an ordinary ship's quarter boat salved from some wreck, maybe, and they'd been caught in a squall which had taken their sail and they had lost an oar. They'd tried to work back against the current, paddling with one oar — they hadn't the knowledge to scull her from the stern — but the current was too strong for them. Well, Wiserman and Hunt give these chaps some water and grub and had the boat brought aboard. There was nothing on her but the bottom boards and some oysters, half open and empty shells, and Wiserman, handling one of them oysters suddenly let a shout, for a big pearl had popped from it into his fist.

"'Pearl oysters!' cries Hunt.

"The two Kanakas was seated squattin' on the deck munching their grub like a pair of graven imiges with clockwork paws, but they had enough savvy to know what was asked them, part by signs and part by the few words of the native that Wiserman had, and they signified the oysters had come from the same place they'd come from which was the island, now on the starboard quarter and maybe ten miles off.

"Five minutes after when Narbutt came on deck, he found the *Wear-Jack* off her course and heading west, a ship's quarter boat on the deck, two Kanakas squattin' in the sun, and Wiserman and Hunt playing with oyster shells and talking of fortunes.

"But all that was nothing to Narbutt, for he'd caught a glimpse of the name on the boat half rubbed out with sun and sea battering and that name was *Hawk*.

"He went to the boat and laid his hand on the gunnel. It was the quarter boat of the Hawk, the same he'd cast them 'prentices loose in, and there right before him was the island he sighted that day near ten years ago.

"He was no sluggard at thinking was Narbutt, and when he'd got a word from Wiserman about the Kanakas he saw what had happened same as if he'd been watching it in the movies.

"Them two 'prentices had got ashore and been eaten, maybe, and the boat had been kept by the natives for fishing.

"'What have you put her off her course for?' says he.

"'Pearls,' says Wiserman, showing the pearl and the shells, 'there's dead loads where these came from and that's over there — have you any objections?'

"Narbutt looked at the stuff same as a rat might look at the bait that'd taken him into the trap. He was a supistitious chap, as Welshmen mostly are, and he saw clear that things was laying for him. The two 'prentices had followed him a good bit during the last ten years, he'd dropped them a bit of late but now he knew they'd overhauled him and got the cinch on him sure.

"He begins to argue the matter with Wiserman and then he begins to shout and carry on, same as a chap when the police has got hold of him and he's being taken to the lockup. He wasn't far wrong, for you take my word for it, son, there's police going about that don't wear no uniform, that nabs chaps in the end such as Narbutt. I've lived fifty-five years and seen it. Well, Narbutt he makes a jump for the wheel to put the helm down, but Hunt stops him and gives him another pair of black eyes, and down he goes to the cabin and dives into the gin, the *Wear-Jack* holds on her course and in a while they come up to the reef and one of the Kanakas pilots them through a break into a lagoon, a pearl lagoon as rich as Tiffany's, and with no owners visible. No sooner had they brought the old *Jack* to her moorings than the two Kanakas took headers one to port, one to starboard, and swam off like rats for the beach and made a dive for the trees.

"Then Narbutt came up rocking and singing with gin, and wanting to go ashore for more booze, thinking they'd arrived at Sidney. Not a native showed up on the beach though there were canoes there enough for a hundred, but Hunt and Wiserman were so set on the pearling prospects that they didn't bother about that nor about Narbutt.

"They got the *Hawk*'s boat over and began right away to prospect the lagoon for shell. Hunt knew something about pearling and Wiserman knew a bit and could dive, so they spent the whole length of that afternoon paddling round here and there, picking up pairs of shells and marking the lay of the beds, for a pearl lagoon isn't all shell, no more than a pie is all plums. When they'd got through they reckoned they was rich for life, and they came aboard at sundown with twenty or thirty pairs of shells and the lay of the place in their minds.

"Narbutt had sung himself to sleep, and when they had finished supper they sat on deck by the light of the moon and opened the shells. One pearl they got out of them and some seeds, enough to show the bank they was floating over. It was better than the guano, so Wiserman said, and Hunt didn't make no objections.

Then they sat and talked, reckoning what they'd do with the money, and the carriages and horses they'd have, and the big layout at the Paris House they'd start off with. They talked of brands of champagne and race horses and all such, and then they went off to their bunks and went to sleep dreaming of the good times that was coming, and they hadn't been dreaming an hour when the savages came on them like a tornado across the lagoon.

"They'd hid up careful at sight of the *Wear-Jack* steering for the island — it was their way with ships coming in. They'd hide to count the number of guns and men, and if the number was over the tally they'd come down dressed in flowers and singing hymns to trade for sin. They'd et enough missionaries, them chaps, to have the doxology in their systems, so to speak. If the number was under the tally, they'd wait till night — and then they didn't come dressed in no flowers.

"The anchor watch of the *Wear-Jack* was asleep and never woke no more. Then these Solomanders come down below and met Hunt coming up in pajamas to know what was the matter.

"They trussed him like a fowl, and then they went down and fetched up Narbutt and Wiserman which they treated likewise.

"Finding nothing more in the way of live stock, they dumped the prisoners into a canoe and brought them ashore and stuck them in a hut.

"Next morning there was a big powwow, and the three chaps were inspected by a deputation that felt their ribs same as the cattlemen do steers, and Narbutt was picked out, being the fattest, and taken off and given a big breakfast. The whole lot of them was set free, seeing that they couldn't run away, and Wiserman and Hunt was given poi and taro-root, but Narbutt had the delicacies, and two girls waited on him — and he knew.

"Narbutt in the next week tried a bolt for the woods, but he was caught before he'd made a hundred yards and brought back and set down to a big dinner — and next morning, reckoning him fat enough, them savages cooked him.

"But before he was stewed, seeing that the Long Reach had got him, he made a confession of his sins to Wiserman and Hunt, and he got out of one of the Solomanders, who could talk a little English, havin' learnt it at a missionary school — the last one that had gone bust on that island — all about the 'prentices.

"They'd come ashore in the boat and had been treated kind and eaten, same as Narbutt was going to be. Narbutt turned pious before the end of him and reckoned his sins had found him out, and he was held up by the thought that Wiserman and Hunt would be served as a chaser, and he had the impudence to tell them to repent of their sins.

"Well, he wouldn't have died so happy if he'd known what was coming, for just as he was done to a turn and the Solomanders were sitting down to table, a siren let off outside the reef and a British cruiser come into the lagoon with her guns nosing the sky and a chap in the chains swinging the lead.

"They hanged a dozen of the Solomanders right there and then and buried the dinner, and then Hunt and Wiserman, having borrowed some firearms from the Britishers, collected a dozen of the Solomanders and made them fish for pearl. Swore to the cruiser's captain they were there for copra and didn't begin the fishing till she was out of sight.

"They skinned that lagoon to the tune of fifty thousand dollars, pearl and shell, and then lit for Sydney with six of the Solomanders to help them work the schooner.

"Wiserman told me this yarn and showed me Narbutt's accordion to back it. It looked like the sort of thing that'd belong to a chap like Narbutt — and that's all I have to say by way of confi'mation."

THE MYSTERY OF CAPTAIN KNOTT

IN OLD CHILE they used to have revolutions between earthquakes. Sometimes they coincided as in the great earthquake revolution year when Don Carlos Aranzas Alonzo Bolivar made his scoop. His real name was Smith, and he came from Hoboken and he scooped five million dollars in gold coin and bars, the property of the acting Chilean government just before it died.

"Bolivar" Smith could talk Spanish like a native, and he dropped into Valparaiso from somewhere in Peru with plenty of money at his command, stolen no doubt. At the end of two months a revolution was well under way with Bolivar as chief designer and engineer. On the eve of the burst-up the acting president under the suasion of Bolivar had all the gold coin and bullion bars removed from the bank for safety and placed on board the *Leonora*, a four-hundred-ton brig.

The shipment was done by night with secrecy and dispatch, and at dawn the *Leonora* put out under a forged order to the port authorities done by Bolivar, who was on board as supercargo. The earthquake and the revolution came along a few hours later when the *Leonora* was far at sea. Nothing more was heard of her till years later, somewhere in the eighties, when an old salt dying on board the *Kermadec* made confession to Captain Jim Lubbock owning to the fact that he had been bos'n of the *Leonora* and stating that she had been lost at sea after caching the treasure on Farragut Island.

Farragut or South Island lies south of Naumoo in the quadrilateral bounded by 10 and no degrees south latitude and longitudes 120 and 130°. North of Naumoo lies Farallon or North Island, the three islands equally spaced and in a line as straight as the line that holds the belt stars of Orion. Dowsett was the name of the old salt, and he gave explicit directions to Captain Lubbock as to the exact position of the cache, then he died, and the hunt began.

It broke Lubbock, who put all his savings into an expedition. Jarvis was the next man on the job and it broke him. Then in the passing years came others. They turned Farragut Island upside down and shook it, but not a coin dropped. Then the thing died down for ten years or so and woke to tragic life again with the Knott expedition in 1902. The story of that expedition has never been told till now. It was given to me by Chandler, master of the *Brunhilde*, a steam yacht owned by Burton Williams of San Francisco.

"Burt was the name he went by," said Chandler. "He'd made his money in phosphates, a big red-faced man with an open manner and a breeze about him better'n an electric fan in hot weather. I've never seen that chap down in the mouth. He didn't look to have brains, much, nor to be a noticing chap, but I reckon what Burt didn't see wasn't worth seeing.

"I was out of a job. I'd been ten years on the Emperor line and was working up to be commodore when the *Emperor of Japan*, my boat, got rammed coming into Frisco Bay by a lousy Shireman freighter that smashed her bow plates and flooded her fore-hold and left her off the Presidio with her nose down like a diving duck and her propellers beating the air, twenty thousand dollars' worth of damage done in fifteen seconds, and all through a tomfool of a first officer who'd made a misjudgment of speed and distance.

"I took the blame and, having a temper of my own, managed to get fired instead of suspended. Then I met in with Burton Williams. He knew all about the business, but being a man who knew men, it didn't worry him. I was engaged after fifteen minutes' talk, and a week later I was sailing his boat out of Frisco. It was a business and pleasure cruise. Burt didn't want money, but he wanted to make it. Work was Burt's idea of fun.

"We touched at Honolulu and then came along down to the Gilberts, then right across to the Marquesas, taking St. Augustine and Penrhyn on the way, After that we struck Farallon Island which is north of Naumoo which is north of Farragut. Those three islands are spaced about equal distance from each other. Farallon is the biggest. We raised it one morning about an hour after sunup. It's clean surrounded by a reef with a break to the west, and when we got into the lagoon, a white chap came out in a boat manned by Kanakas to give us the best anchorage. He was the trader of the place, Carstairs by name, an Englishman from Devonshire, and back of the beach he had his house with a big garden. The native village lay beyond — along a road where the palm trees stood like soldiers.

"We sat on Carstairs' veranda and had drinks and he gave us news of trade, which wasn't flourishing any too much just then, and after we'd had a bit of dinner we put back to the ship and let out for Naumoo. Burt, who was standing by me on the bridge, asked me what I thought of Farallon. I said what was in my mind, that it was as pretty as a picture, but a week of it alone like Carstairs would drive me clean bughouse, and he agreed. Then he hung silent a bit till he begins talking of copra and allowing there was little trade to be done nowadays since the best pitches were collared by the soap companies. That brought him up to the subject of the treasure that was supposed to be hidden on Farragut, the next island beyond Naumoo.

"I'd heard something about it and the expeditions that had started after it years ago, and I suggested to Burt that we should go and have a try. I was joking, of course, and then we forgot the thing, watching Naumoo rising out of the sea with its two lumpy hills cut on the sky and the sea gulls banked like a cloud rising and falling over the western reef spurs.

"In all the seas, I've never struck an island so lonesome looking as Naumo. Black rocks and cliffs, broken reef and gulls and something, I don't know what, that seemed to shout, 'Get away!' The nearer we got, the worse it looked, and it's the living truth that Burt was going to put the ship about and run for Valparaiso, our next port of call, when Providence came on deck in the shape of McCall, our chief engineer.

II.

"He didn't look like Providence. Looked more like a Scotch terrier in slacks, and he came along up to the bridge to tell us that the engines had developed a defect that would lay us up for a day or two; there was nothing for it but to keep on for Naumoo, which we did, reaching there before sundown and dropping our anchor in six-fathom water inside the easternmost line of reef.

"Next morning we went ashore, and once we were on the beach the place didn't seem so bad. The trees were few compared to Farallon and the rocks were black where they showed through the growth; but the groves went inland up two valleys where the tree ferns stood twice the height of a man and where there was wild pig to be found; also the finest fruit we'd struck yet in the Pacific. There was a tribe of Kanakas living in the place, but no whites, not enough coconut trees and nothing doing in the way of shell or turtle.

"It was a poor island, but the Kanakas were about the decentest lot I've ever met. There were only thirty or so of them, and they told us the population had been pretty much the same for years.

"We found a queer thing about them. They kept up a sort of post with their friends and relations on the other two islands by means of using frigate birds as carrier pigeons. It's done in several island groups, but it was new to us and when we came to poke into the thing it turned out as intricate as the New York telephone system, for there were birds that went between North and South Island without touching at Naumoo and birds that went from North and South Island to Naumoo and back and never farther.

"Sru put us wise on it. He was the chief of the Naumooites and nearly a hundred, and postmaster general as well.

III.

"Day before we were due out, Sru came on board with something in his hand. Seems he had gone to the tree where the messenger frigates came to roost — sort of post office — and found a South Island bird, one that wasn't due to stop at Naumoo but to go right over to North Island. It had a folded paper with a message tied to its leg, and Sru took the message off but could make nothing of it as it was written in English. Before he could restore it, the bird flew off and there was Sru left with the paper in his hand.

"Now the bird had come from South Island. It was flying, evidently, for North Island when for some reason it dropped on Naumoo. Sru put these facts together in his woolly head and then he added another one. The message was evidently intended for the trader on North Island, since it was written in the language of the white man. But there were no white men on South Island. That got him so bad that he came right down to the beach with the paper in his hand and pushed off for the yacht. Burt and I were on deck under a double awning when Sru came over the side. Burt took the paper Sru handed to him and read what was on it, then he handed it to me. It was a piece of paper ruled with red lines and torn out of a notebook and the message on it done with ink and evidently with a fountain pen was just five words:

> "Struck it today,
>   OLD CHUM.

"Nothing very exciting in that, was there?

"Then Sru begins his talk in *Beche de Mer*, explaining how he'd taken the thing off the bird and so on, and Burt leads him out to the end and then tells him that the message is evidently meant for Carstairs on North Island, but that it's not important and sends him off the ship with a glass of gin inside him.

"I was sitting there in the deck chair under the awning smoking and watching Burt while Sru was paddling ashore. Burt held the paper, looking at it back and front and reading it again, then he stuck it in his pocketbook.

"He goes to the rail and looks over and then he comes to where I was sitting and asks me what I make out of that paper. Then without waiting for an answer he says:

"'There are no whites living on South Island, and South Island is the only place that message can have come from. Get me? Well, since that's so, some ship must have put in there and the chap on board must have struck something worth making a song about — what? Turtle — copra? No, sir; treasure. Some expedition has started to hunt for that cache where the Spanish gold was supposed to be hid and found it.'

"The thing was plain enough and only for the hot weather making my intellects work slow, I'd have seen it as quick as him. It hit me now like a belt on the head, and I jumped off the chair like as if I'd been kicked. Gold's a powerful thing, beats strychnine as a tonic, and as I stood there with my back to the rail looking at Burt, I had all my starch back in me and was ready for anything.

"'The bother is,' Burt goes on, 'what in tarnation did they send that message for? There's only one man it could have reached and that's Carstairs. It's a thing they'd want to keep secret and if Carstairs was in the know about the expedition, they'd easy have told him by word of mouth, for it wouldn't have taken them any time to put in to North Island on their way back.'

"'That's so,' said I, 'but there's no accounting for how men may act. Anyhow, the fact's pretty plain, they've struck the stuff. What do you propose to do?'

"'Nothing,' says Burt. 'That's to say if they've collared the stuff and got it on board their hooker. I'm not the man to cut in and claim shares, which would be blackmail. But if they've only located the stuff without moving it and if by any manner of chance I come on the location by my own instincts — well, there's no saying.'

"With that he sent a quartermaster for McCall, who comes along and gives news that the repairs were all but finished and we could put out at sunup next morning.

IV.

"I didn't sleep much that night. I'd got the gold fever and got it bad. When I did get off to sleep I was shoveling gold by the barrelful into baskets without any bottoms to them and frigate birds were coming all the time with messages to hurry up as the Spaniards were in sight. When I got up on deck I found Burt there before me. It wanted half an hour to sunup and McCall had nearly got steam on her.

"Half an hour after sunup we were beyond the reef and making for South Island, taking it easy at ten knots, the current being against us, and reckoning to reach there under five hours.

"We had breakfast, and coming up after, there she was fifteen miles off and showing well, though not near so high as Naumoo.

"As we closed up Burt handed me the glasses he'd been using, and I picked out beyond the north reef the spars of a schooner against the trees. The reefs here are pretty tricky, the only safe break being a bit to the east. We made that and coming round found a big stretch of water running west where you might have anchored the Atlantic fleet. Along there and close to the shore lay the schooner, swinging to the tide as innocent looking as pie and with nothing to show of treasure hunting or bustle about her more than a chap who was fishing over the after rail. He was a chink. There were several more chinks about and, as we dropped our hook, a cable length away from them, a white man came on deck and had a look at us.

"'Well,' says Burt, 'what do you think of that, cap? Looks as if I were wrong, don't it? Chaps don't go treasure hunting with a chow crew unless they've got a big after guard and there's no sign of that unless they're ashore. Well, we'll see — look, the chap's coming off.'

"The white man got into a boat that was lying alongside the schooner, and two of the chinks rowed him off to us. He was a big red-bearded chap, and as he came aboard, light as a cat for all his size, I took a liking to him right away; he'd got the pleasantest face on him I'd seen in years, and when he spoke his voice didn't hit his face any.

"'Captain Knott, of the *Tennessee*,' says he, introducing himself. And I gave our names and pretty soon we were all under the awning with iced drinks in our fists talking U. S. politics and the price of stock, Knott said he'd put in for water, and it flamed up in my intelligence that he'd had plenty of time to water his ship, seeing her size, if he was the man that sent that message by the frigate bird. Then he went on to say that he was owner of the *Tennessee* and that she was in ballast making somewhere for a cargo of copra.

"Then Burt, fresh from his clack with Carstairs and pretending ignorance, asked him how copra prices were ranging and without the wink of an eye he gives the prices all wrong — dollars out. That gave me a turn — the way he told that lie as ready as if he were quoting from a price list. Then I remembered the treasure business and the fact that he naturally would lie to strangers over it.

"Burt asked him plump out if it was true that the natives of South Island had trained frigate birds same as the natives of Naumoo, and he said yes, that was so — that only last week he'd seen several birds arrive and put off and that the natives there were always sending messages to their friends and relations over at North. I was thinking of asking him whether he was watering his ship last week as well, but didn't. Then giving us a good day, off he put, and Burt said to me that if he had twenty-one guns on board he'd have given that chap a salute as the king of all damn liars.

"'Well,' I said to him, 'what are you going to do?'

"'Nothing,' he says. 'If he's collared the stuff and got it on board the *Tennessee*, it's no business of mine. But I'm going ashore to have a look. There'll be evidence of digging maybe. Anyhow, I feel interested enough to get ashore and poke round.'

"Half an hour after, he ordered a boat out and we went on shore. We weren't afraid of Knott suspecting us, for our *Brunhilde* wasn't the sort of craft Knott would bother about.

"There were half a dozen Kanakas on the beach, pretty much like the chaps at Naumoo; but we didn't bother about them, just struck in among the trees past the village and went wandering, taking the rise of ground as a direction till we'd reached the hump of ground that stood for a hilltop.

"We saw nothing of any digging marks on the way and from the hilltop we took notice of the trees, few palms, but plenty of others such as screw pine and breadfruit and an undergrowth thicker than ordinary. Then we sat down in a shady place to cool ourselves and Burton Williams opened his mind.

"'I've got it in my head,' he says, 'that I was right. Knott's got the stuff, but I'm thinking he hasn't shipped it, for the very good reason that that message was sent off, ten to one, as soon as he'd located the cache. He wouldn't have had time to ship it. That message must have been sent off yesterday morning. Of course it may be that he sent it off after he'd got the stuff on board, but it's unlikely. Carstairs is a friend of his, most likely partner, and in the flush of the strike he sent him news of it right off. That's my reading of it.

"'It's most likely he's been here months on the business and keeping up correspondence with the chap. Well, now, what we've got to do is plain enough. If Knott had treated me fair and told the truth, I'd do nothing; but now I'm just going to develop engine trouble and lay here till the *Brunhilde* rots or that chap gets out; and meanwhile I'm going to hunt the woods on my own, day after day, with you and the first officer to help me. There's sure to be some sign somewhere of digging having been done.'

"'Right,' I said. Then we came down and put off for the *Brunhilde*.

"No sooner had we got on the beach than the clank of windlass pawls began to come over the water, and we saw that the *Tennessee* had got her canvas on her. She was going to put out, taking advantage of a wind that had sprung up, and Burt, as we shoved off, gave a laugh, as much as to say, 'That's one for me.' Then he hung silent while we got on board and by then the *Tennessee*'s anchor was up and she was passing us for the break, with Knott by the steersman waving his hand to us.

"Burt waved back and we dipped our flag to her. I felt pretty much flattened out and I didn't like to think of what Burt must be feeling with all his deductions gone wrong, but I didn't know Burt. He stood there watching till the *Tennessee* was beyond the reef, then he gave orders for all hands to be piped aft.

V.

"He lit a cigar while they were crowding up. Then, when they were all in a bunch, Burt takes the cigar from his mouth.

"'Men,' says he, 'I've reason to believe there's money hid on that island. Maybe I'm wrong or maybe I'm right, anyhow I'm going to have a try to get it, and it's half shares for me and half shares for the crew to be divided equal if we hit it; and if we don't it will be a week's extra pay for the trouble you'll take. I'm going to comb those woods for signs of digging having been done in them, and every man jack of you's got to join in the hunt except Mr. McCall and two of the crew who'll keep ship. Mr. Jameson, pipe the boats away, we'll start right off.'

"The chaps let a cheer out of them and five minutes after they were crowding into the boats wild as schoolboys to get at the business.

"They spread through the woods under direction of the first officer and they hunted till dark. Next day was the same and by noon we'd scoured that island without finding a dropped toothpick for evidence of treasure lifting. I came off to the *Brunhilde* with the news and found Burt under the awning reading a novel. He dropped the book on the deck and nursed his knee while I told him. Then he says: 'The stuff's there all the same; but I'm thinking of something else more important than gold, cap. We've been fools. We shouldn't have let Knott clear out.'

"I couldn't take his meaning and said nothing. The lads were coming back to the ship, and he stood up and watched them come on board. Then he gave orders for steam to be got up and two hours after we were clearing the break; outside he gave orders to put back to North Island.

"I watched him as he stood there on the bridge, and I couldn't make him out at all, he was a different man from the Burton Williams I'd left that morning when we started for the treasure hunting — manner quite different, brooding and quiet, and scarce a word out of him, whereas he'd always been full of chat as a magpie.

"It was pretty much the same at dinner that night, so much so that I opened right out and asked him what was wrong and whether I'd done anything to displease him.

"'Not a bit,' says he, 'but I've got something on my mind, that's all, and I'm not going to speak about it if it's all the same to you. It's one of the stiffest propositions I've ever struck and I've always worked better with a shut head.'

"We raised North Island next morning and put right in while Burt went ashore. I saw Carstairs meet him on the beach and then the two went off to the house, leaving the boat's crew chattering with the Kanakas. Then the time went by, hour after hour, while I kicked my heels wondering what in the nation those two could find to clack about all that while and wishing the chaps that buried that treasure had been forced to help in the hunting for it and made to dig with their noses.

"Presently, about four o'clock in the afternoon, off Burt comes, leaving Carstairs on the beach, and as soon as he was on board he goes down to his cabin after giving orders to put out and lay a course for Frisco.

"At dinner he didn't say one word about Carstairs and what they'd been talking about or the message or the treasure; you'd have thought, by the way of him, that nothing had happened out of the ordinary and I said so blame right out, as we were sitting over our coffee. Burt, he cocks his eye at me.

"'Lots of things have happened,' he says, 'but if you can't guess it's not for me to talk. I work best with a shut head, as I've told you before, and so we'll leave it at that. Someday maybe you'll find out all about Knott and his doings.'

VI.

"We'd bunkered at Penrhyn and done a lot of distance under sail, so we weren't bad off for coal, but we had to take it slow all the same, using the canvas as much as we could, and it was a pretty slow run to Frisco, giving me plenty of time to turn the business over in my mind. But turn it over as much as I could, there was nothing in it to clutch hold of or to account for the way Burt was carrying on.

"St Frisco I looked for my discharge, but Burt, as soon as we'd docked, told me he was going to keep me on, full pay and nothing to do except to keep myself at his house on Pacific Avenue every evening at six.

"I began to have suspicions that a bug had got in old man Burt's bonnet, but it was a gold bug for me, and every evening I had a cigar and glass of wine served by the butler with the news that there was no message yet for me, till one day Burt himself popped into the room and shut the door and took his seat.

"'Well, cap," he says, 'there's something doing at last. Knott has sold his ship at Valparaiso, and he's coming to Frisco by mail boat.'

"Then it came out that he'd been warming the wires all down the coast and his agents had been on the lookout at likely ports. He'd dragged the Havens detective people in, and between the lot of them old man Knott had been like a fly under a microscope. He'd not only sold his ship, but changed his name and was coming to Frisco under the alias of Kellerman.

"'But look here,' I says, 'what's he coming for and why in tarnation has he changed his name?'

"'I'll tell you,' says Burt. "First of all we've frightened him, putting in as we did. The stuff's on the island right enough. Second, he wanted to diddle his partners out of their share. And third — but I won't tell you that, not till I get the guy face to face with me.'

"'Was Carstairs a partner?' I asks.

"'He was,' says Burt.

"'And who was the other partner?' I asks.

"'James Bowie,' he replies. 'The same Bowie that struck it rich on the Aranzas Claim — and I'll tell you what Knott's going to do soon as he gets back here. He's going to pick up a small boat of some sort and post back for Farragut with a couple of hands, and do Bowie and Carstairs out of their share.'

"'But see here,' I says, 'if he's so busy about hiding things up, what in tarnation did he send that message for?'

"'You'll know that,' says Burt, 'when I confront him with Bowie.'

"As he was showing me out, a big man was knocking at the door.

"'Hullo, Bowie,' says Burt, 'glad to see you! This is Captain Chandler I was telling you of — the chap who was down at Farragut with me.'

"Bowie holds out his hand for a shake and I go off, scratching my head all down Pacific Avenue. Couldn't sleep that night, thinking over the tangle. The thing was clear enough up to a point, and there it broke down. There were only three men in the know over that business, Knott, Carstairs, and Bowie. You think it out for yourself, and you'll maybe lie awake as I did; I'll make the proposition clearer for you by stating right now that that message we took off the frigate bird was sent to Carstairs and it could only have been written by a white man and there were no white men in the know about the treasure only those three, Knott, Bowie, and Carstairs.

"I knew Bowie hadn't been on the island, I knew Carstairs was away up on North Island, so it could have only been written by Knott. Knott, the chap who was wanting to keep things dark. It bothered me for days till I gave it up and bought a jigsaw puzzle to amuse myself evenings and keep those three Hooligans and their doings out of my head. But it was pleasant enough to think of Knott coming to Frisco under the name of Kellerman, unknowing that Burt was waiting to receive him; and it was pleasant enough to think of what he'd say when Burt brought him face to face with Bowie.

"One evening a bright idea took me and I said to Burt:

"'See here, we're wasting time. Bowie and Carstairs must know where Knott expected to hit the cache. Let's start out after it right away, you and I, and leave Bowie to face Knott.'

"'No use,' says he, 'Knott was the only man who knew the likely locality; the other ginks only put money into it, trusting him on his face; you remember the blighter's face, all smiles and affability. Lord, cap, when nature puts a face piece like that on a man, she's just fitting him out for crime and he generally helps her in her intentions and don't you forget it.'

"I haven't, and whenever I see a bluff and smiling mug nowadays I generally feel for my bank roll to make sure it don't jump out of my pocket.

"Next day after that talk with Burt, the *Alphonso the First* put in from Valparaiso. I was on the wharf to meet her with one of Havens' best detectives.

"I watched the passengers as they came ashore, and as they stood crowding the deck I was half hid so that Knott wouldn't see me and had a big, broad-brimmed hat on to help, and as I stood there I couldn't see a single bearded mug on all that crowd, and said so.

"'Gosh,' says the tec, 'where's your intellects? The chap will be clean shaved,' and as he said the words Knott jumped into my eye, I spotted him by his size. Clean shaved he was, but it was Knott. Same old walk like a cat in a larder as he came down the plank.

"'That's him,' I says.

"'Sure?' asks the tec.

"'Sure,' I says.

"'Right,' he says; 'you needn't bother any more; it's my job now.'

"Then I went off to get some luncheon and left things to work themselves.

VII.

"I called at Pacific Avenue that evening at six as per usual and found Burt in his library. He told me that things were going fine and that Knott had been located at the hotel he was staying at and notified that if he'd call at Pacific Avenue, quarter after six, he'd find an old friend waiting for him.

"Will he come?' I asked.

"'Sure,' says Burton, 'and if he doesn't he'll be fetched — trust Havens' men for liming the twig properly.

"And sure enough, just before the clock struck six, there was a knock at the door. Burt shoved me behind a big screen and told me to sit there and count my fingers till I was wanted. Then I heard the door open and Knott come in.

"'Good evening, Mr. Kellerman,' says Burt.

"'Good evening — why, what the devil are you —' says Knott.

"'Remember me down at Farragut, Captain Knott?' says Burt. 'I see you shaved your beard. Hot weather, I suppose. Captain Chandler, will you step forward.'

"I stepped. Knott had taken his seat on a chair. He sat for a moment looking from one to the other of us. Then he laughed.

"'Well, I'm damned,' says he.

"'You sure are,' says Burt. 'You've robbed your two partners, or tried to, and now you're in front of Justice. Do you recognize that, Captain Knott?'

"Knott laughed.

"'Well,' he said, 'it's true enough. I haven't run straight as a mail train with them ginks, but the whole thing was illegal anyway, seeing that the Chilean government owns the stuff we were after, and I reckon Justice has no more to do with the business than the King of Siam. How's the law to touch me?'

"'Now, you listen,' says Burt. 'Carstairs and Bowie were traders on North Island. You blew in as mate of a copra schooner. You had the knowledge of that cache in your head, picked up from a rogue that had been on Jarvis' expedition. You told your story and Carstairs and Bowie put up the money for an expedition. Bowie went with you to Frisco and you bought the *Tennessee*.'

"'Yes,' says Knott, 'but she was bought in my name, and how's the law to touch me for selling her?'

"'One moment,' says Burt. 'You bought her and you and Bowie sailed straight for Farragut to lift the treasure. What became of Bowie? He wasn't with you on Farragut.'

"'Bowie went overboard in a squall somewhere in the latitude of Nukahiva,' said Knott; 'lost at sea.'

"'Quite so,' says Burt, and rings a bell on the table. The butler opens the door.

"'Show in Mr. Bowie,' says Burt.

"Knott tried to get up but sat down again, and in came the big man I'd seen on the doorstep. Knott, when he saw him, gave a great sigh as if the Rocky Mountains had been taken off his chest and sits quiet.

"Bowie came and stood before him.

"'Now, you damned villain,' says Bowie, "what have you done

with my brother Jim, the man who sailed with you for Farragut, the man you betrayed?'

"Knott, quite himself again, fired up.

"'I've told these gentlemen,' said he. 'Ask them.'

"'He says your brother was lost at sea in a squall before reaching Farragut,' said Burt.

"'That's so,' said Knott.

"'Well, then,' says Burt, 'if he was lost before reaching Farragut, how did he send this message by frigate bird — unknown to you and guessing you to be a villain — to his partner Carstairs?' And he took a photograph of the frigate bird message from his desk and handed it to Knott. 'It's his writing,' finishes Burt, 'as his bankers will prove.'

"Knott reads out loud in a voice that seemed to come over sand-paper:

>"'Struck it today,
>
>OLD CHUM'

"'You murderer!' said Bowie, 'You killed him after you'd struck the cache, that same evening.'

"Knott didn't seem to hear him. His face was going blue as a mulberry. Then he stood up and fell as if he was pole-axed, as dead as the man he'd done in on Farragut. Worst was, he died with the knowledge of where the cache was in his head.

"I've said Burt was a noticing chap though he didn't look it, and what roused his suspicions first, as he was reading a book on deck that day while we were hunting the island, was the fact that Knott was alone there with a chow crew and had given no explanation, for it's the law that every chow-manned ship must carry a white mate. I never thought of that, but then I'm not Burt. If I was I'd be worth a million dollars made out of phosphates."

UNDER THE
FLAME TREES

I WAS sitting in front of Thibaud's Café one evening when I saw Lewishon, whom I had not met for years.

Thibaud's Café, I must tell you first, is situated on Coconut Square, Noumea. Noumea has a bad name, but it is not at all a bad place if you are not a convict. Neither is New Caledonia, take it all together, and that evening, sitting and smoking and listening to the band and watching the crowd, and the dusk taking the flame trees, it seemed to me for a moment that Tragedy had withdrawn, that there was no such place as the Isle Nou out there in the harbor and that the musicians making the echoes ring to the *Sambre-et-Meuse* were primarily musicians, not convicts.

Then I saw Lewishon crossing the square by the Liberty Statue and attracted his attention. He came and sat by me, and we smoked and talked while I tried to realize that it was fifteen years since I had seen him last and that he hadn't altered in the least — in the dusk.

"I've been living here for years," said he. "When I saw you last in Frisco I was about to take up a proposition in Oregon. I didn't, owing to a telegram going wrong. That little fact changed my whole life. I came to the islands instead and started trading, then I came to live in New Caledonia. I'm married."

"Oh," I said, "is that so?"

Something in the tone of those two words "I'm married" struck me as strange.

We talked on indifferent subjects, and before we parted I promised to come over and see him next day at his place a few miles from the town. I did and I was astonished at what I saw.

New Caledonia, pleasant as the climate may be, is not the place one would live in by choice. In those days, the convicts were still coming there from France. The gangs of prisoners shepherded by wardens armed to the teeth, the great barges filled with prisoners that ply every evening when work is over between the harbor quay and the Isle Nou, the military air of the place and the fretting regulations, all these things and more robbed it of its appeal as a residential neighborhood. Yet the Lewishons lived there and what astonished me was the evidence of their wealth and the fact that they had no apparent interests at all to bind them to the place.

Mrs. Lewishon was a woman of forty-five or so, yet her beauty had scarce begun to fade. I was introduced to her by Lewishon on the broad veranda of their house, which stood in the midst of gardens more wonderful than the gardens of La Mortola.

A week or so later, after dining with me in the town he told me the story of his marriage, one of the strangest stories I ever heard and this is it, just as he told it.

"The Pacific is the finest place in the world to drop money in. You see it's so big and full of holes that look like safe investments. I started, after I parted with you, growing coconut trees in the Fijis. It takes five years for a coconut palm to grow, but when it's grown it will bring you in an income of eighteen pence or so a year according as the copra prices range. I planted forty thousand young trees and at the end of the fourth year a hurricane took the lot. That's the Pacific. I was down and out, and then I struck luck. That's the Pacific again. I got to be agent for a big English firm here in Noumea and in a short time I was friends with everyone from Chardin, the governor, right down.

"Chardin was a good sort but very severe. The former governor had been lax, so the people said, letting rules fall into abeyance like the rule about cropping the convicts' hair and beards to the same pattern. However that may have been, Chardin had just come as governor and I had not been here more than a few months when one day a big, white yacht from France came and dropped anchor in the harbor. A day or two after, a lady appeared at my office and asked for an interview.

"She had heard of me through a friend, she said, and she sought my assistance in a most difficult matter. In plain English, she wanted me to help in the escape of a convict.

"I was aghast. I was about to order her out of the office, when something — something — something, I don't know what, held my tongue while, with the cunning of a desperate woman in love, she managed to still my anger. 'I understand,' she said, 'and I should have been surprised if you had taken the matter calmly, but will you listen to me and when you have heard me out, tell me if you would not have done what I have done today?'

"I could not stop her, and this is what she told me.

"Her name was Madame Armand Duplessis. Her maiden name had been Alexandre. She was the only child of Alexandre the big sugar refiner, and at his death she found herself a handsome young girl with a fortune of about twenty million francs — and nothing between her and the rogues of the world but an old maiden aunt given to piety and guileless as a rabbit. However, she managed to escape the sharks and married an excellent man, a captain in the cavalry and attached to St. Cyr. He died shortly after the marriage and the young widow, left desolate and without a child to console her, took up living again with her aunt, or rather the aunt came to live with her in the big house she occupied on the Avenue de la Grande Armée.

"About six months after, she met Duplessis. I don't know how she met him, she didn't say, but anyhow he wasn't quite in the same circle as herself. He was a clerk in La Fontaine's Bank and only drawing a few thousand francs a year, but he was handsome and attractive and young, and the upshot of it was they got married.

"She did not know anything of his past history and he had no family in evidence, nothing to stand on at all but his position at the bank, but she did not mind — she was in love and she took him on trust and they got married. A few months after marriage a change came over Duplessis. He had always been given rather to melancholy, but now an acute depression of spirits came on him for no reason apparently. He could not sleep, his appetite failed, and the doctors, fearing consumption, ordered him away on a sea voyage. When he heard this prescription he laughed in such a strange way that Madame Duplessis, who had been full of anxiety as to his bodily condition, became for a moment apprehensive as to his mental state. However she said nothing, keeping her fears hidden and busying herself in preparations for the voyage.

"It chanced that just at that moment a friend had a yacht to dispose of, an eight-hundred-ton auxiliary-engined schooner, *La Gaudriole*. It was going cheap and Madame Duplessis, who was a good business woman, bought it, reckoning to sell it again when the voyage was over.

"A month later they left Marseilles.

"They visited Greece and the islands, then, having touched at Alexandria, they passed through the canal, came down the Red Sea and crossed the Indian Ocean. They touched at Ceylon and while there Madame Duplessis suggested that, instead of going to Madras as they had intended, they should go into the Pacific by way of the Straits of Malacca. Duplessis opposed this suggestion at first, then fell in with it. More than that, he became enthusiastic about it. A weight seemed suddenly to have been lifted from his mind, his eyes grew bright, and the melancholy that all the breezes of the Indian Ocean had not blown away suddenly vanished.

"Two days later they left Ceylon, came through the Straits of Malacca and, by way of the Arofura Sea and Torras Straits, into the Pacific. The captain of the yacht had suggested the Santa Cruz islands as their first stopping place, but one night Duplessis took his wife aside and asked her would she mind their making for New Caledonia instead. Then he gave his reason.

"He said to her, 'When you married me I told you I had no family. That was not quite the truth. I have a brother. He is a convict serving sentence in Noumea. I did not tell you because the thing was painful to me as death.'

"You can fancy her feelings, struck by a bombshell like that, but she says nothing and he goes on telling her the yarn he ought to have told her before they were married.

"This brother, Charles Duplessis, had been rather a wild young scamp. He lived in the Rue du Mont Thabor, a little street behind the Rue St. Honoré in Paris, and he made his money on the Stock Exchange. Then he got into terrible trouble. He was accused of a forgery committed by another man but could not prove his innocence. Armand was certain of his innocence but could do nothing, and Charles was convicted and sent to New Caledonia.

"Well, Madame Duplessis sat swallowing that fact, and when he'd done speaking she sat swallowing some more as if her throat was dry. Then she says to Armand:

"'Your brother is innocent, then,' she says.

"'As innocent as yourself,' he answers her, 'and it is the knowledge of all this that has caused my illness and depression. Before I was married, I managed to forget it all, but married to the woman I love, rich and happy, with enviable surroundings, thoughts of Charles came and knocked at my door, saying, 'Remember me in your happiness.'"

"'But can we do nothing for him?' asked Madame Duplessis.

"'Nothing' replied Armand, 'unless we can help him to escape.'

"Then he went on to tell her how he had not wanted to come on this long voyage at first, feeling that there was some fate in the business, and that it would surely bring him somehow or another to Noumea; then how the idea had come to him at Ceylon that he might be able to help Charles to escape.

"She asked him if had he any plan, and he replied that he had not — that it was impossible to make any plan till he reached Noumea and studied the place and its possibilities.

"Well, there was the position the woman found herself in, and a nice position it was. Think of it, married only a short time and now condemned to help a prisoner to escape from New Caledonia, for, though she could easily have refused, she felt compelled to the business both for the sake of her husband and the sake of his brother, an innocent man wrongfully convicted.

"She agreed to help in the attempt, like the high-spirited woman she was, and a few days later they raised the New Caledonia reef and the Noumea lighthouse that marks the entrance to the harbor.

"Madame Duplessis had a big acquaintance in Paris, especially among the political and military people, and, no sooner had the yacht berthed than the governor and chief people who knew her name began to show their attentions, tumbling over themselves with invitations to dinners and parties.

"That, again, was a nice position for her, having to accept the hospitality of the people she had come to betray, so to speak. But she had to do it. It was the only way to help her husband along in his scheme and, leaving the yacht, she took up her residence in a house she rented on the sea road; you may have seen it, a big white place with green verandas, and there she and her husband spent their time while the yacht was being overhauled.

"They gave dinners and parties and went on picnics; they regularly laid themselves out to please. Then one night Armand came to his wife and said he had been studying all means of escape from Noumea and had found only one. He would not say what it was, and she was content not to poke into the business, leaving him to do the plotting and planning till the time came when she could help.

"Armand said that before he could do anything in the affair he must first have an interview with Charles. They were hand in glove with the governor and it was easy enough to ask to see a prisoner, but the bother was the name of Duplessis, for Charles had been convicted and deported under that name. The governor had never noticed Charles and the name of Duplessis was in the prison books and forgotten. It would mean raking the whole business up and claiming connection with a convict. Still, it had to be done.

"'Next day Armand called at the governor house and had an interview. He told the governor that a relation named Charles Duplessis was among the convicts and that he very much wanted to have an interview with him.

"Now the laws at that time were very strict and the governor, though pretty lax in some things, as I've said, found himself up against a very stiff proposition and that proposition was how to tell Armand there was nothing doing.

"'I am sorry,' said the governor, 'but what you ask is impossible, Monsieur Duplessis. A year ago it would have been easy enough, but since the escape of Benonini and that Englishman Travels, the orders from Paris have forbidden visitors. Any message you would like me to send to your relation shall be sent, but an interview — no.'

"Then Armand played his ace of trumps. He confessed, swearing the governor to secrecy, that Charles was his brother. He said that Charles had in his possession a family secret that it was vital to obtain. He talked and talked and the upshot was that the governor gave in.

"Charles would be brought by two wardens to the house on the Sea Road after dark on the following day. The interview was to take place in a room with a single door and single window. One warden was to guard the door on the outside, the other would stand below the window. The whole interview was not to last longer than half an hour.

"Next evening after dark, steps sounded on the path to the house with the green veranda, Madame Duplessis had retired to her room, she had dismissed the servants for the evening and Armand himself opened the door. One of those little ten-cent, whale-oil lamps was the only light in the passage but it was enough for Amand to see the forms of the wardens and another form, that of his brother.

"The wardens, unlike the governor, weren't particular about trifles. They didn't bother about guarding doors and windows. Sure of being able to pot anyone who made an attempt to leave the house, they sat on the fence in the moonlight counting the money Armand had given them, ten napoleons apiece.

"Half an hour passed during which Madame Duplessis heard voices in argument from the room below, and then she heard the hall door open as Charles went out. Charles shaded his eyes against the moon, saw the wardens approaching him from the fence, and walked off with them back to the prison he had come from.

"Then Madame Duplessis came from her room and found her husband in the passage. He seemed overcome by the interview with his brother.

"She asked him had he made plans for Charles' escape, and he answered: 'No.' Then he went on to say that escape was impossible. They had talked the whole thing over and had come to that decision. She stood there in the hall likening to him, wondering dimly what had happened, for only a few hours before he had been full of plans and energy and now this interview seemed to have crushed all the life out of him.

"Then she said: 'If that is so there is no use in our remaining any longer at Noumea.' He agreed with her and went off to his room, leaving her there wondering more than ever what could have happened to throw everything out of gear in that way.

"She was a high-spirited woman and she had thought little of the danger of the business; pitying Charles, she did not mind risking her liberty to set him free, and the thought that her husband had funked the business came to her suddenly as she stood there, like a stab in the heart.

"She went off to her room and went to bed, but she could not sleep for thinking, and the more she thought the clearer it seemed to her that her husband, brought up to scratch, had got cold feet, as the Yankees say, and had backed out of the show, leaving Charles to his fate.

"She was more sure next morning for he kept away from her, had breakfast early and went off into the town shopping. But the shock of her life came at dinner time, for when he turned up for the meal it was plain to be seen he had been drinking more than was good for him — trying to drown the recollections of his own weakness, it seemed to her.

"She had never seen him under the influence before and she was shocked at the change it made in him. She left the table.

"Afterward she was sorry that she did that for it was like the blow of an ax between them. Next morning he would scarcely speak to her and the day after they were due to leave for France.

"They were due out at midday, and at eleven Duplessis — who had lingered in the town to make some purchases — had not come on board. He did not turn up till half an hour after the time they were due to sail, and when he did it was plain to be seen that all his purchases had been made in cafés.

"'He was flushed and laughing and joking with the boatman who brought him off, and his wife, seeing his condition, went below and left the deck to him — a nice position for a woman on board a yacht like that with all the sailors looking on, to say nothing of the captain and officers.

However there was nothing to be done and she had to make the best of it, which she did by avoiding her husband as much as she could from that point on. The chap had gone clean off the handle. It was as if his failure to be man enough to rescue his brother had broken him, and the drink which he flew to for consolation finished the business.

They stopped at Colombo and he went ashore. They were three days getting him back and when he came he looked like a sack of meal in the stern sheet of the pinnace. They stopped at Port Said and he got ashore again without any money, but that was nothing, for a chap coming off a yacht like that gets all the tick he wants for anything in Port Said. He was a week there and was only got away by the captain of the yacht knocking seven bells out of him with his fists and then handing the carcass to two quartermasters to take on board ship.

"They stopped nowhere else till they reached Marseilles, and there they found Madame Duplessis' lawyer waiting for them, having been notified by cable from Port Said.

"A doctor was had in and he straightened Armand up with strychnine and bromide, and they brushed his hair and shaved him and stuck him in a chair for a family conference, consisting of Madame Duplessis, the old maiden aunt, Armand, and the lawyer.

"Armand had no fight in him. He looked mighty sorry for himself but offered no explanations or excuses, beyond saying that the drink had got into his head. Madame Duplessis, on the other hand, was out for scalps — do you wonder! Fancy that voyage all the way back with a husband worse than drunk! When I say worse than drunk I mean that this chap wasn't content to take his booze and carry on as a decent man would have done. No, sir. He embroidered on the business without the slightest thought of his wife. An ordinary man full up with liquor and with a wife touring round would have tried to have hidden his condition as far as he could, but this blighter carried on regardless, and, when the whisky was in, wasn't to hold or bind.

"Of course she recognized that something in his brain had given way and she took into account that he was plainly trying to drown the recollection of his cowardice in not helping Charles to escape. All the same she was out for scalps and said so.

"She said she would live with him no more, that she had been a fool to marry a man whom she had only known for a few months and of whose family she knew nothing. She said she would give him an allowance of a thousand francs a month if he would sheer off and get out of her sight and never let her see him again.

"He sat listening to all this without a sign of shame and when she'd finished he flattened her out by calmly asking for fifteen hundred a month instead of a thousand. Never said he was sorry, just asked for a bigger allowance as if he was talking to a business man he was doing a deal with instead of a wife he had injured and outraged. Even the old lawyer was sick, and it takes a lot to sicken a French lawyer, I can tell you that.

"What does she do? She says: 'I'll allow you two thousand a month on the condition I never see your face or hear from you again. If you show yourself before me,' she says, 'or write to me, I'll stop the allowance. If you try to move the law to make us live together, I'll turn all my money into gold coin and throw it in the sea and myself after it, you beast,' she says.

"And he says, 'All right, all right, don't fly away with things,' he says. 'Give me my allowance and you'll never see me again.'

"One day an old woman turned up at her house asking her to come at once to where he was living as he was mortally ill and couldn't hold out more than a few hours.

"She didn't think twice, but came, taking a cab and being landed in a little old back street at the door of a house that stood between a thieves' café and a rag shop.

"Up the stairs she went, following the old woman, and into a room where his royal highness was lying with a jug of whisky on the floor beside him and a hectic blush on his cheeks.

"'I'm dying,' he says, 'and I want to tell you something you ought to know. I was sent to New Caledonia,' he says, 'for a robbery committed by another man.'

"She thought he was raving, but she says, 'Go on.'

"'Armand and I were twins,' he says, 'as like as two peas. Armand could do nothing. He stayed in Paris while poor Charles — that's me — went making roads on Noumea. Then you married him.'

"'But you are Armand,' she cries, 'you are my husband or am I mad?'

"'Not a bit,' says he. 'I'm Charles, his twin brother.

"'A year ago you and him came in a big yacht to Noumea and the governor sent me one night to have a talk with him. When we were alone he told me how his heart had been burning a hole in him for years, how he had married a rich woman — that's you — and how when he was happy and rich his heart had burned him worse so that the doctors not knowing what was wrong with him had ordered him a sea voyage.' Then Charles goes on to tell how Armand had come to the conclusion that even if he helped Charles to escape this likeness between them would lead surely to the giving away of the whole show, make trouble among the crew of the yacht and so on — besides the fact that it was next to impossible for a man to escape from Noumea in the ordinary way. But said Armand, 'We can change places and no one will know. Strip and change here and now,' he says, 'the guards are outside, I'll take your place and go to prison and you'll be free. I've got a scissors here and two snips will make our hair the same, and by good luck we are both clean shaven. You've done half your sentence of ten years and I'll do the other half,' he says. 'The only bargain I'll make is that you'll respect my wife and live apart from her and, after a while, you'll break the news to her and, maybe, when I'm free in five years she'll forgive me.'

"Charles finishes up by excusing himself for the drink, saying if she'd served five years without the chance of a decent wet all that time she'd maybe have done as he'd done.

"He died an hour after and there was that woman left with lots to thank about — first of all her husband wasn't the drunkard that had disgraced her, but he was a convict serving his time and serving it wrongfully.

"The thundering great fact stood up like a shot tower before her that Armand wasn't the drunkard that had disgraced her in two ports and before a ship's company, wasn't the swine that took her allowance and asked for more. That he was a saint, if ever a man was a saint.

"She rushed home, telegraphed to Marseilles and recommissioned the *Gaudriole* that was still lying at the wharves. A week later she sailed again for Noumea.

"On the voyage she plotted and planned. She had determined to save him from the four years or so of the remains of his sentence at all costs and hazards, and when the yacht put in here she had a plan fixed on, but it was kiboshed by the fact that the governor, as I have said, was changed. However she took up residence for a while in the town. People she had known before called on her and she gave out that her husband was dead.

"You can fancy how a rich widow was run after by all and sundry, myself included — not that I had any idea about her money. I only cared for herself. She knew this as women know such things, by instinct. She had asked for my help. I'm a strange chap in some ways. I had liked her enough to ruin myself for her by risking everything to give her husband back to her, and between us we had worked out a plan that was a pippin.

"It would have freed Armand only that we found on inquiring about him that he had already escaped — he was dead. Died of fever two months before she came.

"I heard once of a Japanese child that said her doll was alive because she loved it so much, adding that if you loved anything enough it lived. Well, in my experience, if you love anything enough you can make it love you.

"That woman stayed on in Noumea and I made her love me. At last I married her. You know her — she is my wife. She loves Armand still, as a memory, and for the sake of his memory we live here. It's as good a place to live as anywhere else, especially now that they have settled to send no more convicts from France."

THE SLAYER

SUNRISE SHOWED Maneta, gigantic on the starboard bow, with the level light full upon it, from the reef foam to the peaks cut against the western sky. It was after the rains, a few light scarves of cloud were passing from the shoulders of the hills, and a permanent white plume of mist showed the track of a racing torrent bursting from the foliage of the cliffs.

Savage handed the glass to the captain.

"The place looks all right," said he.

"Oh, there's nothing wrong with Maneta," said Captain Dolbrush, after a momentary peep through the glass as if to make sure. "The Kanakas are a pretty decent crowd, and so are the whites; then you've got the mountains. I can't make out how men live for choice where the land's flat; one of those atoll islands, for instance — flat lagoon and flat sea, with a few palms sticking out of it."

"No, I couldn't fancy an atoll," said Savage; "not that one has much room for fancy where trade is concerned. What did you say was the name of the other trader here?"

"Well, if the same chap is here as the one I left, his name's Theodosius."

"Foreigner?"

"He don't look a foreigner somehow, nor speak like one. I expect he's Greek originally, but he's a straight man, and well liked."

They went below for coffee, and an hour later, like a being surrounded by a wizard's spell, the schooner had on all sides of her the fume and song of Maneta — the fume of the high woods, of moist earth and fragrant plants, of flowers; the song of the sea on the reef, the winds in the trees, and the rainbowed torrent.

She passed the reef opening, and as the anchor fell two boats put off from the lime-white beach which fronted the town.

The bigger boat belonged to the club, over whose palm-thatched roof a bit of bunting was flicking in the tepid wind and saluting the new arrivals. Pilsbury, the Yankee who ran the club, was coming out for drinks and mails. The lesser boat showed in her stern a man dressed in white drill and wearing a sun hat. His black, pointed beard showed like jet against the white of his garments.

"That's Theodosius," said the captain, "come out to make your acquaintance. He's a very polite chap — more polite than most English. I reckon that's the main thing foreign about him."

Savage was a hard man, a big, strong, clean-shaven Englishman, Yorkshire born, and ungiven to promiscuous friendships. He had pushed his way in the world. He had come here to trade on his own, and felt quite capable of standing on his own feet. Still, in a place like Maneta there are numerous little things that an inhabitant can do for a stranger. Little things that make for comfort in a place where comfort is made up of little things.

"I had news from Wyman by the last mail that you were coming," said Theodosius, as they stood together on the deck, "and I've taken the liberty of putting a couple of hands on to tidy up your house and garden. Leave a garden ten minutes here and it's overrun with oap and Heaven knows what."

"'nk you," said the undemonstrative Briton. "Good of you, I'm sure; we're opposition traders here, aren't we?"

"Oh, no; just traders," replied the other. "There's copra enough for us both to deal in without crowding one another. Shall we go ashore, and you can look around?"

They went ashore in Theodosius' boat, leaving the red-faced Pilsbury down below, yarning and drinking with the captain. On the beach, Savage stood for a moment, as if sniffing the place and finding the smell of it good.

The groves came down from the mountains, tossing their green plumes to the wind, and above the little white town, all showered with shadow and broken by gardens and trees, two gigantic birds wheeling in the sparkling blue clanged a greeting to the new arrival. Canoes casting jet shadows lay on the blinding beach, and a few natives, come down to see the strange ship, stood, dark-eyed and silent, in the sun blaze, while the inevitable loafer, Jimmy Finn by name, came from the trees to inspect matters and assist, if necessary, with criticism and advice.

Jimmy Finn was a living testimony of the goodness of man to man; useless, a drunkard, a blot on the scenery, and a general pest, he just managed to live and get drunk on occasion. On a German island he would have been shot into the lagoon; at Maneta he enjoyed a certain popularity.

"Has either of you gentlemen a fill of tebbacca?" demanded Jimmy.

Savage, hard man though he was, produced his pouch and handed over a pipe-full without letting the pouch from his hands.

"You're new," said Jimmy, shooting a bloodshot eye at him over the match blaze and blue tobacco smoke. "Whacher name, may I ask?"

"Savage."

"Oh, you're the new trader. Well, see here, Mr. Whacher-name, you come to Jimmy Finn — hic — if you want to know the ropes of this here island, I been here longer than most — hic — I'm a Britisher," continued Mr. Finn, with a glance at Theodosius, "same as you, an' proud of the fac'; too many durned furriners in these parts — hic."

"Come along," said Theodosius.

They passed on, leaving the beachcomber in possession of the beach.

"He's no good," said Theodosius. "People think him funny. He's not; he's bad, and he has a down on me; not that I care. This is the one street of the village."

Savage saw before him a vista of white houses and gardens covered with foliage in parts, and here and there lit by the sun blaze; the patter of leaves and the dancing shadow showers were the only sounds and signs of life in this happy street along which they went, passing the club and the house of Theodosius and the house of Pilsbury and the little church, till they reached the house that belonged to Savage.

He had come here to take the place of a man named Wyman, who, coming in for money and seized with a desire for cities, had sold him the station and house for a song.

The house was coral built, white as a pigeon, and fairly spacious. The garden, thanks to Theodosius, was in good order. Wyman had sold the furniture and fixtures with the house, and in the front room, waiting to be approved of and hired, Savage found a native woman servant secured by Theodosius.

The godown for trade goods lay behind the house.

II.

Next day Savage had the trade brought along and stowed in the go-down, and when the last of the stuff was on shore the schooner put off, leaving the lagoon empty.

You can never understand what company a ship can be till she picks up her anchor and clears away, nor how she can fill a harbor with her presence, till she leaves you with nothing to look at but a sea-beaten reef, native canoes, and coconut trees.

Even Savage felt lonely and cut off from the world, but he had little time for retrospection. "Sufficient for the day is the evil thereof" might be the motto of Maneta, and Savage, what time he could spare from business, found himself caught in the island's microscopic but vivid social life. They played cards at Pilsbury's, and forgathered at the club. He gave a dinner party as a housewarming, and was entertained in turn by Pilsbury, Theodosius, Adams, the missionary, and old Captain Tricot, a Frenchman who had returned here to end his days, a valuable man who kept a cellar and the best cook in Polynesia. Then ships would drop in with thirsty captains and mates, bringing news and lies from all over the Pacific, and mails sometimes.

Savage fell into this life completely. He was a man of simple tastes, and he lived untroubled by regret or desire or unattainable wish, till one day, an ever-memorable day in his life and in the life of another man as well.

He had bought copra from some villages on the western side of the island, and he was receiving it from the natives who had brought it in when he found himself face to face with a girl, who had just put down her load.

She was beautiful, straight as a dart, liquid-eyed, and with an expression haunting and mysterious, as though she had just awakened to life and was gazing upon the world for the first time.

Savage looked at her.

"What is your name?" asked he.

"Kiniea," replied the girl.

That was all. She went off with the others, and Savage, receiving a new lot, went on with his work. But that evening, as he sat on his veranda drinking tepid beer and smoking, Kiniea came back to him as a vision. He had never bothered about girls; his heart was as sound as his lungs, and it is just this sort that the disease attacks with most virulence.

Kiniea came again next day with the copra bearers, and Savage talked to her for a few minutes, asking the name of her village and its direction.

Standing before him, with a flower of the scarlet hibiscus in her hair, she answered his questions, looking at him with level eyes, and speaking with the simplicity of a child. Then as she turned to go she glanced back and smiled at him.

Next day Savage met Kiniea in the woods. He held her hand while he talked to her; he said all the old, foolish things that men have said to women since speech was invented by women for the purpose of talking to man. They sat on a fallen tree under a great cable of blazing convolvulus, and Savage produced from his pocket a hammered silver bangle. He had found it among his trade goods and put it in his pocket on the chance of meeting her.

He slipped it over her little hand, and she held out her arm for the sunlight to catch it. After that day they met frequently, and at last one afternoon, Savage taking the mountain road, started off for the village of Kiniea to interview her parents.

It was a wonderful road, treed with soaring palms and screw pines and breadfruit trees, less a road than a cutting in the forest, and from the village of Kiniea through the trees he caught a glimpse of the Pacific to westward and a scent of the sea on the ever-blowing wind.

The village consisted of less than thirty houses, and most of the villagers were away at work, but the father and mother of Kiniea were at home, and Savage, at sight of his future father and mother-in-law, felt a check at his heart. Tama, the mother, was old, shrunk, and carried herself with a fawning air, always speaking with a side glance at the man, who, seated on the ground in front of their hut, was engaged in making a basket. That was his trade and he pursued it all the time they talked and bargained.

They were getting old, and Kiniea was their main support; baskets were of little account nowadays, as ships brought gunny sacks. If Savage married Kiniea, and she went to live with him over there at his house, what would they do? It was quite clear they would probably starve. Besides, a white man had already fallen in love with her, a very wealthy man.

"That does not matter," said Savage grimly. "The girl cares for me; she will marry me, and I will be good to her. All the white men in the world don't count, and I am rich enough to make up your loss over the business. I will pay you either in trade or American dollars for what you will lose by her marrying me, but, once I have paid you, there the thing ends. I will not pay more than once."

The father and mother of Kiniea consulted over the matter together, and the man named a sum, expecting half. But Savage did not cut him down; his pride would not allow him to bargain, and he agreed that the sum demanded should be paid on the day he made Kiniea his wife.

Then he departed, leaving the basket maker and his wife filled with wild regrets that they had not demanded double what they had asked.

When Savage got back that evening he opened a bottle of tonic water, and as he sat on his veranda drinking it and smoking, satisfied and content in heart, who should come up the garden path but Adams, the missionary.

Adams was a Bostonian, an earnest man, true to his faith and living up to his principles. Adams was the one black spot in the life of Pilsbury, just as Pilsbury was the chief black spot in the life of Adams.

"I'm glad to find you in," said Adams. "I've come for a moment's talk with you. I hate meddling in other peoples' affairs, but the natives here are literally my flock, and a shepherd, if he's worth his salt, must not let his feelings interfere with his work. I just came to ask you, Savage, are you a wolf? There, it's out!"

Savage for a moment thought that the sun had got to Adams' head.

"A wolf?" said he.

"I'm referring to the girl Kiniea," said Adams. "I baptized her. You meet her in the woods; I met her yesterday and she was wearing a bangle. How do you stand with her?"

Savage began to laugh, and Adams, mistaking his laughter, rose up in wrath.

"Sit down," said Savage. "I'm not laughing at you; only at your question. I have just come back from interviewing my future father-in-law. I'm going to marry Kiniea, and I'm going to ask you to marry us."

Adams sat down.

"I beg your pardon," said he. "I had her welfare at heart. Well, I'm glad — and still —"

"Yes?" said Savage.

"Oh, I don't want to cast cold water on your position. All the same, and you will excuse me for saying this, I have seen a good many marriages between us and the natives. As a rule they don't turn out well. I'm just talking bluntly as man to man. Marriage is all right if it inspires affection. Love is all very well, and I don't want to say anything against it, but it passes; affection holds. If you have that power in you, you will be happy; if not, and you have the power to reason with yourself, throw the thing down right now, for I tell you in a mixed marriage like this, when the glamour passes, then comes the time of stress, when the man comes to look down on the woman, and all her strange ways and ideas jar on him. Excuse me saying all this, won't you?"

"You need not trouble," said Savage. "It's well meant, but you need have no fear. She and I will never part once we're tied, and as far as affection — well, I feel all right on that point."

"I believe you," said Adams.

III.

The marriage was fixed to take place in a fortnight, and presently the fact began to leak out — how who can say, for Savage had laid strict injunctions of silence upon Adams, It was probably from the native side. People began to talk, and Jimmy Finn waxed quite eloquent over the matter.

Finn, when he was sober enough to wish for more drink, sometimes did a little work, and these bouts of work always left him more captious and critical.

"Here's another blessed piebald marriage," said Finn to Olsen, the bartender at the club, whom he met in the street, "*Heard* the news? That chap Savage has linked up with a Kanaka — disgracin' us. What's to become of the respect due to the white? — hic — that's what I want to know. What's the use of *bein'* white? That's what I want to know. Not a bit. Gimme a match."

But later in the day joy came to Jimmy Finn with the name of Savage's fiancée. "Kiniea?" said he. "Why, that's the piece of goods Theodosius is sweet on. Lord, this is lovely! Done him in the eye! Are you certain sure of what you are sayin'?"

The informant was, and Mr. Finn went off, slapping his thigh, to sit on the beach and contemplate the lagoon and gloat over the fate of Theodosius.

Jimmy Finn could hate; it was the only thing he could do well.

Next day Theodosius called on Savage. It was evening time, and Savage was seated on his veranda going over some accounts. He saw at once that something was wrong.

"Thanks," said Theodosius. "I won't sit down. I just came to ask you: Is it true?"

"Is what true?"

"That Kiniea has promised to marry you."

"It is true enough — but I didn't want a fuss made over it. Who told you?"

Theodosius did not answer the question.

"I have known that girl for a year," said he; "you have known her only a couple of weeks, if that. I cared for her, and she cared for me. I was going to have married her."

Kiniea had explained to Savage in a vague way that another white man had cared for her, that she had liked him, but now all that was as smoke blown away by the wind.

"I am sorry," said Savage.

"Your sorrow won't mend matters," replied the other. "The fact remains, and it is a terrible fact for me. You have nothing more to say on the subject?"

"No," said Savage.

"Then good morning," said the other.

He walked off, and Savage watched him going away beyond the palms.

"Rum beggar," thought he.

The something foreign in Theodosius had always gone slightly against the grain, and the smothered anger that he read in his face disturbed him. He would rather Theodosius had blazed out. However, when a man is busy with accounts and in love at the same moment he has little time to bother about a jealous rival.

He did not see Theodosius next day, and when they met one afternoon later in the week Theodosius did not avoid him. They passed each other in the street, it is true, but Theodosius gave him a nod of recognition and showed nothing at all of unfriendliness, either in his manner or his face.

Perhaps, of the two, it was Savage who felt the most awkward over the business. He began to avoid meeting Theodosius. If Theodosius had turned bitter over the affair and used threats, Savage would not have minded in the least, but this formal friendliness unnerved him. The silence of reproach made him feel his own position as the destroyer of Theodosius' happiness more than all the bitter words in the world. What time he was not engaged on business or with Kiniea he remained at home, looking after his garden or reading and smoking on the veranda. He began almost to hate Theodosius.

IV.

One morning, just as he was leaving his house to call on Pilsbury, he saw a crowd of natives coming down the street, and among them Tama. The old woman, seeing Savage, broke from the others and came running up to him.

"Kiniea gone," cried Tama. "What you done with Kiniea?"

"Gone!" cried Savage. "I have not seen her since yesterday noon. What you mean?"

Then the story came out. Kiniea had not returned yesterday — she had been absent all night — and this morning she was still away. Savage, for the first time in his life, felt the crazy and wild alarm that comes to a man when the object of his love is in danger and he is powerless to save.

He stood for a moment without speaking; then he made for the club, followed by the crowd. He sent runners for Pilsbury, Adams, and Theodosius. Every white man in the town responded to the call, and there in the open air before the club veranda a council of war was held, Savage explaining matters and Theodosius cross-questioning Tama.

"There's no sense in it," said Pilsbury. "There's nothing on the island to hurt her, no traps or things she can have fallen into, but search is the word. You leave it to me; I'll roust out every Kanaka, and if she's to be found she'll be found. I'll engineer this business for you, Savage."

He had a big gong hanging near the club veranda for the purpose of calling help in fire emergencies and so forth. He set it roaring, and the town gave up its contents even to Jimmy Finn, roused from sleep and dreams of Sydney-side bars on the beach.

Pilsbury divided the natives into four parties — one under himself, the others under Savage, Theodosius, and Adams, and then the business began.

They took provisions with them for twelve hours, Pilsbury, despite his red face and drinking habits, being a leader of foresight in his way, and then they spread through the woods and glens, across the valleys and hills, stopping every now and then to call and listen, and receiving no answer but the echoes, the murmur of waters, and the whispering of trees. Kiniea had vanished as though she had never been.

They continued the search next day, and for a week after Savage and Theodosius working alone hunted the woods, but they did not find Kiniea. Then Savage gave up and returned into himself, rarely leaving his house and never receiving visitors. If the girl had been killed before his eyes, his mind would have suffered less; it was the uncertainty as to her fate that nearly took his reason away.

As for Theodosius, he went about like a man who saw little and heard less, but he continued his business in a mechanical sort of way, though avoiding the club.

"Those two chaps are beginning to give me the hump," said Pilsbury to a newly arrived schooner captain. "This island has ceased to be a cheerful place to live in. What do you think, Adams doesn't play cards, the old Frenchman's deaf, and here am I with no one to talk to but the bartender and the Kanakas *and* Jimmy Finn. I declare to you I've had Jimmy up for company, deodorized him, and made him keep on the veranda. It's been a fine time for Jimmy, and he's had more free whisky in the last week than he's had in years."

It was the free whisky perhaps that moved Jimmy to call on Savage one day.

Savage was in the front room of his house when he heard a knock at the open door, and saw a shadow on the threshold.

"What do you want?" said Savage, coming to the door.

"A word with you," said Jimmy, holding onto the doorpost to steady himself. "It's about her. I didn't say nothin' at the time, but day before she went I saw Theodosius in the woods up beyond; he and a girl. Didn't think nothin' of it, my mind bein' upset from sittin' in the sun with an empty stomick — hic — but now, thinkin' things over, I'd swear it was her. He'd got a spade with him, and they were goin' up north. What's the meanin' of it? Well, I says the meanin' of it is he's killed and buried her. Thought I'd tell you. It's been on my mind."

Savage stood motionless as a frozen man.

"Say that all over again," said he.

Jimmy Finn, despite his condition, repeated his statement.

"It makes me dry," said he as he finished. "Haven't you a drink of whisky to offer a body now I've told you?"

Savage went into the house, and came back with a full bottle of gin.

"Say nothing about this to any one," said he.

"Right," said Jimmy.

He made off with the bottle, and lay about all day, waiting to hear of the shooting, for to his drink-fuddled mind nothing seemed more certain than that Savage would go for Theodosius, accuse him, and then —

But Savage went for no one. He remained at home in meditation. The fate of Kiniea was quite clear to him now. He knew it as though he had seen it. Theodosius had murdered her and buried her. There could be no other solution; there was no other solution. He remembered how Theodosius had taken the business about Kiniea. That was the sort of man he was.

His dislike for Theodosius had been growing ever since then.

Sitting in a basket chair and smoking cigarettes, he revolved the whole matter in his mind. There was no use in invoking the law, first of all because the law in Maneta was a very makeshift affair, secondly because Finn was not good evidence. He was certain that Finn had spoken the truth, but others might not be so certain. Failing the finding of the body and evidence directly touching Theodosius, everything would fall to the ground, and he was certain that the murderer would have covered up his traces.

Besides, this was a matter between himself and Theodosius. Kiniea had to be avenged.

He rose up, threw his cigarette away, and came out on the veranda. He breathed freely now, and the world had regained something of itself again; the haunting oppression had gone from his heart, and had been supplanted by a strange and ferocious feeling almost of gayety.

He came down to the club, and there he found Pilsbury and the schooner captain. They were tossing with picture dice for cocktails. He joined them, and that night he dined with Pilsbury, playing cards after dinner, and going off home after midnight cheerful, to all appearance, and with twenty dollars in his pocket won from the American.

Next morning he met Theodosius in the street, and had a friendly chat with him for a moment or two; some days later they met at Pilsbury's. Things began to run in the old groove again, and an outsider might have fancied that Kiniea was forgotten. Even Pilsbury came under this belief, and expressed it to old Captain Tricot.

"Can't make Savage out," said he. "First he looked like a man done for, wouldn't leave his house, wouldn't speak to a body, didn't seem to eat, didn't seem to drink, lived on a cigarette mostly; then the other day he turns up at my place cured, took to drink like a man, and won twenty dollars off me at cards.

"I've a good deal of belief that men bluff themselves with believing they care for women, and then when something calls the bluff — marriage, for instance — the cards aren't there."

"Who knows," said the captain. "Men are strange things. As for me, I do not care to see sudden changes in men. Once, I remember, I knew a man — he was a Ponantaise sailor belonging to our merchant marine; he lost his wife, and for a time he was the most desolate man in the world; then he became of a sudden the most cheerful — and hanged himself."

"Well, Savage didn't look like hanging himself," said Pilsbury, and then the conversation ended.

Now, at Maneta the fishing was good but for one drawback; at certain seasons the fish were poisonous. The natives put the fact down to the influence of the stars, the whites to the influence of the coral, which in some seasons was supposed to change in nature. However it may be, the natives could tell, almost to a day, when the bad season was over and the good season had begun. This change from bad to good happened now, and one morning Savage, meeting Theodosius, proposed a fishing excursion.

"Let's go out and have a try for a palu tonight," said Savage. "If you have nothing better to do, we can take your boat."

"I don't mind," said Theodosius.

"I'll be ready at sundown," said Savage.

At sunset they got the boat down and the fishing tackle and bait aboard. The palu is a big fish and a good fighter, and runs from fifty to a couple of hundred pounds. At Maneta palu never came into the lagoon; they had to be sought for in the deep water beyond the reef, and preferably to the north of the island.

They reached the fishing ground they had selected just as the moon, nearing the full, was pushing her brow above the eastern sea line.

The breeze that had carried them out had died away, and there on that glacial calm nothing was to be heard but the far-away roar and rumble of the surf on the reef.

They dropped the anchor in fifty fathoms, and Theodosius, baiting the line, cast it overboard. Savage, leaving Theodosius to do the fishing, lit a pipe and sat watching the moon steadily freeing herself from the sea. She seemed to have come to look on.

The sea seemed to cling to her lower limb as she broke from it, and now the boat was floating on a vast river of silver, and the foam on the reef showed white, and above the foam the island stood, peaked and ravined, cutting with its shoulders the paling stars.

"The woods show up well from here," said Savage.

Theodosius, holding the line, turned his head.

"Yes," said he. He said no more, and the two men sat without a word, till suddenly the fisherman hauled in his line. Some bait snatcher had taken the bait. He rebaited and cast again, and scarcely had the line run out when the real tug came. A palu this time, and a big one.

Savage, steadying the boat, watched the fight, watched the weakening of the fish, watched the line steadily hauled in.

Then he saw the water break to foam and soapsuds under the moon, and the great, dark, flapping fan of the tail.

"Quick!" cried Theodosius. "The maul."

Savage already had the maul in hand, a heavy mallet of ironwood that had given many a palu its quietus.

He half rose.

Theodosius had discarded his hat. His head showed glossy black in the moonlight; the target was unmissable. If ever man was dead, yet alive, that man was Theodosius.

Savage had reasoned the whole thing out with himself. To accuse the subtle one would be useless and waste of time. Of all things certain, the most certain thing was that fact that he was a murderer.

The maul swung up, and then, for one tremendous moment, it stood against the sky, as though the arm that held it had become paralyzed.

"Quick!" said Theodosius.

Savage shifted his position with a cry that rang out over the sea like the voice of a gull, and the maul fell on the head of the fish.

He was not a murderer.

Against reason, hatred, and the wild desire to avenge that fact had balked him at the last moment. It had lain in his soul, only to be revealed at the supreme instant.

The great fish, though dead, quivered and sprang as they hauled it into the boat. It was enough for one night, and, as they put back, Savage at the stern oar rowed like a broken man. He had betrayed Kiniea; he had failed, not in manhood, but in the ferocity of the male who avenges the blood of his mate. The every core of his being seemed sapped; the mainspring of his existence broken. The primitive in him had been overthrown. It had been strong enough to assert itself till the last moment — the vital moment — the striking moment that had passed forever.

As they entered the lagoon, the light of torches met him on the beach. Ratupa, one of the chiefs, had captured a thirty-foot shark, which the Kanakas had hauled up, and their knives were flashing over the cutting-tip.

Savage heeded nothing. He went up to his house, closed the door, and opened a bottle of brandy.

He did not bolt the door — just left it on the latch — and next morning as he woke, parched, heavy-headed, and dulled by the fumes of the brandy that still filled his brain, he heard a knock at the door. It opened, and Theodosius came in. Theodosius held something in his hand, something wrapped up in a leaf. He came right up to the couch on which Savage was lying, unwrapped the object in his hand, and showed the bracelet of Kiniea.

"We know now where she went," said Theodosius, speaking like a man who is repeating words that he scarcely understands. "They found it last night — the shark; she must have been bathing when it took her."

Savage took the thing in his hand, and held it without speaking for a minute — and a minute is a terrible time when measured against human agony. Then he asked several aimless questions, and then he said: "Last night — I thought it was you — last night in the boat I was going to have killed you."

"I wish you had," said Theodosius.

And Jimmy Finn? Jimmy Finn was taken by common consent and ducked in the lagoon and beaten with paddles between two canoes. Then he was deported from that island on the first whale ship that touched. Three years' penal servitude was his portion, and the port of deliverance, New Bedford.

www.ingramcontent.com/pod-product-compliance
Lightning Source LLC
Chambersburg PA
CBHW030502260626
47157CB00005B/1607